Sleep No More

By

Angelo Marcos

ISBN-13: 978-1492930433
ISBN-10: 1492930431

Copyright © 2013 Angelo Marcos
(see back of book for further copyright information)

About the Author

Angelo Marcos is a writer, comedian and actor, and a graduate of both law and psychology.

He has performed stand-up comedy all over the UK, and has acted in numerous short films and theatrical productions.

He co-wrote the musical 'Love and Marriage' which was performed at the Edinburgh Festival, and his articles and short stories have been published both online and in print.

His explosive first novel - crime thriller **'The Artist'** - is available both in paperback and as an eBook.

You can find his website at www.angelomarcos.com

Still it cried "Sleep no more!" to all the house:
"Glamis hath murder'd sleep, and therefore Cawdor
Shall sleep no more; Macbeth shall sleep no more."

Macbeth (Act 2, Scene 2), William Shakespeare

Prologue

The suit they buried him in was over twenty years old and, up until the funeral, unworn.

It was the first time in years the mourners had been in the man's presence outside a small room thick with the stench of disinfectant, the first time in years that the widow had been able to speak softly to her husband without the rhythmic hiss of the respirator in her ear. Each sentence timed to coincide with one of the brief pauses. The breath of the machine kept his body alive, the widow dared hope her own breath may have had the same effect on his soul.

He'd been dead for only a few days, but had been mourned much longer. It had been two decades since he was robbed of what the newspapers called his 'prime of life'. He had lost everything but his body - a shell of organs and skin, kept alive by machines. A car without an engine, being pushed along in the futile hope that it would one day start again.

The doctors performed tests every so often, the results always communicated with a shake of the head, a consoling look. They spoke about levels of consciousness, and the Glasgow Coma Scale. They tested for eye movement with flashing lights, and pain responses with pinpricks to the feet. They were able to ascertain the exact levels of his non-responsiveness, able to keep him alive with the aid of the best medical equipment available.

In short, they did everything. Except heal him.

His widow watched the coffin – a different type of vehicle now - being slowly lowered into the ground.

The slings and arrows had hit their target, she thought, and they had won.

There was only one remaining truth that gave her any comfort now.

This isn't over.

One

In the deepest recesses of her mind - like an undersea trench impenetrable by light - Ariadne knows she is dreaming. She knows, but it doesn't matter. He is hunting her, and he is going to find her and he is going to hurt her.

Just like he had done every night for the past two weeks.

She stands in the deserted lobby of a plush hotel, her threadbare tracksuit crudely juxtaposed against the lavish surroundings. As she waits for the lift that will take her up to her room, she nervously shifts her weight from one foot to the other. Her gym shoes squeak on the marble floor with every movement but she doesn't care. The cathedral-like interior of the hotel and its smooth, polished surfaces work as a security system to her – the click of footsteps would ricochet around the space, notifying her of the arrival of any other person.

As long as there are no other sounds, she knows she is alone.

The secure feeling is short lived as an uneasiness begins creeping up on her. The shadow form that has been following her is growing closer, she can sense it. The shiver racing through her soul tells her that now she is most definitely not alone. She freezes, unable to do anything but impotently wait for the lift. The vehicle that will take her to safety.

She realises that she heard no footsteps. But then, there are never any footsteps with him.

The being – *he* – is getting closer. She sees the shadow lengthening, his head and shoulders leeching slowly up the wall of the lift doors. She measures his proximity not only through sight but also through the intensity of her fear. As she feels the violation of his hot breath on her neck, the lift arrives and the doors slide open. Immediately, her muscles are freed and she bolts into the metal chamber, finding the strength to turn and face her attacker. A thick shadow form of a man hangs impossibly in the air, his face a blur - always a blur - and always the same. He makes no attempt to move towards her, and stands defiantly watching as the lift doors close.

She begins the ride to safety and notices that the lift is mirrored on all sides. The small spotlight in the ceiling illuminates the tiny space as though it were floodlit. She glimpses her reflection – her tracksuit is gone, replaced now by a long red dress. She begins smoothing her hair and reapplying her lipstick. She isn't going up to her room anymore, instead she is speeding towards the grand roof-top party which has been organised in her honour by the hotel manager. The fear is a distant memory – an old acquaintance not invited and not considered.

The lift opens and she glides into the room, her elegant gown flowing behind as she flits from one guest to another. Now she sees an old friend, now an ex-boyfriend who cannot stop looking at her. She registers his glances, knowing he still loves her in spite of the woman at his side wearing the wedding ring. A waiter offers her a glass of champagne, which she gratefully accepts, playfully curtseying the young man to the accepting laughter of the crowd. The graceful music of the band swells as she makes her way around the room, gracefully nodding at the other partygoers. The floor-to-ceiling windows give a stunning panorama of the city of London. She is the belle of the ball and this is her city tonight.

The moon illuminates the metropolis spectacularly, the light bouncing off the Houses of Parliament and, farther away, the mighty buildings at Canary Wharf. She saunters over to the glass and peruses the streets below, deserted except for a handful of cars speeding along the back streets. She thinks it must either be very late at night, or very early in the morning.

The hands that violently grab her neck are cold, as though belonging to the undead. She tries to scream, but the pressure on her crushed throat is too great. The champagne flute drops from her hand and she watches as it somehow shatters instead of gently bouncing off the lush carpet. She bangs on the window with her clenched fist, desperately trying to signal for help, and is forcefully whipped around, her attacker now with his - because she knows it is *him* again - back to the window. His form stands defiantly again, this time against the backdrop of the metropolis below. It is his city now.

She twists her neck around and stares pleadingly at the partygoers, who gleefully raise their glasses and toast the spectacle. Red clouds descend over her vision, creeping inwards from the rims of her irises towards her pupils, and her oxygen-starved brain begins the process of shutting down. Her body goes limp and the stranglehold is released. She falls to her knees, her hands on the deep white carpet, her bruised neck barely able to hold up her head.

The crowd smile at her, and she hears the faint noise of an engine from the back of the room. Her eyes are half-closed, but she forces herself to look up toward the direction of the sound. The door is ajar and she sees the edge of a bed. Her gaze fixed on the heavy door, she watches as time slows and a car splinters through, the wood easily shattering like her wineglass an eternity ago. The front of the car now crushes the partygoers, who laugh and smile and dance as they bleed and contort and die in front of her eyes. The entire scene is speeding backwards away from her now, as though the faster the car races toward her, the faster she is being pulled backwards out of harm's way.

He wants to prolong the agony.

She sees that the driver's face is obscured, and registers the inevitability of what is about to happen. Impotently, she raises a hand to stop the vehicle coming towards her. The car does not let up and in a second decimates her hand, arm and shoulder. She is thrown backwards through the window, the glass exploding into a million shards. The car – pulled by gravity now - hurtles with her as she rushes backwards towards the empty street and her inevitable death.

She sees the blackness where the shadow's face should be. There are no features, but she knows he is smiling.

Just before her slight body is burst open by the street and crushed by the car, Ariadne finally – mercifully - wakes up.

***

Ariadne Perasmenos lies motionless in her bed, the duvet on the floor having been kicked off during the night. Her dog lies snuggled amidst the duvet - at least someone made good use of it. She looks blearily at the clock on her bedside table, 5.30am - too early to go to work, too late to go back to sleep. With an almighty effort, she wrenches herself out of bed, the weight of the dream hanging heavy on her shoulders. She walks to the bathroom – quietly so as not to wake the dog - and steps into the shower. She strips quickly and throws her clothes out of the cubicle and onto the tiled floor, wanting to wash the dream away.

The hot water feels good pulsing over her skin. She closes her eyes and allows the pressure to massage her face and shoulders. She runs both hands through her hair, her nails slightly scratching her scalp but reminding her that she is alive. She blindly reaches for the soap, a slight niggling feeling tugging at her, and begins scrubbing at her face, trying to remove any vestige of the dream.

As the water cascades down her body, she suddenly realises that she can taste something rich and metallic. She lets the soap drop onto the shower tray and rinses her face directly under the shower head, trying to get rid of the taste in her throat and stench in her nostrils. The tugging of the negative feeling gets more pronounced, as though she knows she should register what is wrong, but it's escaping her. Just like the car in her dream, the closer she gets to this undiscovered feeling, the farther away she is pulled from it.

She wipes her eyes with the backs of her hands, trying to remove the soap suds before opening her lids. Her face feels slick, as though the soap won't rinse off.

As she opens her eyes, in the milliseconds before her mind registers that there is thick blood running down her naked body and into the drain, she realises what bothered her so much only moments ago.

She doesn't have a dog. She is still asleep.

The adrenalin rushes her body, coursing through metres of veins and arteries in an instant. She looks up at the shower to see the rich red spray shooting out, the viscous liquid slamming against her chest and bruising on impact. She screams and gropes for the dial, frantically trying to switch off the shower. Inexplicably this makes the flow stronger, pounding against her, bruising her chest, neck and face. She claws at the door, trying to slide it open, but it does not move. To her horror she realises that the blood is no longer draining away down the plughole, but is filling the cubicle. It bubbles as though being heated from below. She panics as the boiling soup reaches her ankles, then her shins, then her knees. Almost waist deep now in her prison, she slams herself against the unmoving glass, her mind flashing back to the dream of only minutes ago.

She screams for help, the sound ricocheting off the walls but drowning in the thick, waist-deep blood. The relentless flow begins to get hotter, scalding her face and upper body as her waist and legs are boiled. The stench of cooked flesh stings her nostrils, and the steam burns into her eyes. Her mind flashes to a fish in a fryer, hissing and bubbling into blisters as it cooks.

As the temperature reaches a level she can no longer bear, the revving of an engine begins to rise above the noise of the shower and her screams. The terror she feels, previously felt to be entire and at its peak, ratchets up unbearably and shudders through her body. The car smashes through the glass, momentarily reliving the pressure of the boiling water and providing a gust of cool air. As she spins toward the vehicle she knows the driver is smiling again. Above the noise of the shower, the engine, the glass smashing onto the floor, she hears his cackle. She opens her mouth to scream and wakes up again.

Two

For the second time that day, Ariadne awoke, this time in her own bed, her own house. She jerked herself up into a sitting position, studying the room for anything unusual, any tell-tale signs that might have indicated that she was still asleep.

There were none. She was awake and in the real world now.

Her duvet was half-covering her, and the only pet in her room was her cat, Harry - a fluffy black and white lump, happy only when he was sleeping or eating. True to form, he was curled up into himself on the floor, sleeping and purring contentedly. If Ariadne had made any noise while sleeping the cat clearly hadn't heard, or more likely hadn't cared.

She checked the time on her mobile phone. It was 6.20am. Her alarm was set for 6.30am so she lay back down and tried to spend ten minutes calming herself and collecting her thoughts.

After forty futile seconds of trying to erase the emotional residue of her nightmares through positive thinking - it didn't work, it never worked - she got out of bed. Opening her wardrobe, she half expected a car to race through the mirrored door, destroying the wood and shattering the glass, and then her. The furniture and trinkets in her room were no longer comforting to her, everything seemed to be tinged with the horrors of the dreams, as though the trauma of them had somehow seeped into reality, and attached themselves to the things she held dearest. Her bed was no longer a warm, inviting place. It was a harsh wasteland now, the rough blankets had been doused in acid, the once-soft pillows now carved from stone.

Every so often Harry glanced up and meowed at her, the look on his face fixed in a perpetual state of disinterest. As Ariadne left the room to go downstairs, he padded after her, purring and bouncing down the stairs alongside. They both knew who would be getting their breakfast first.

That was fine with her. Since the dreams had begun two weeks ago she never had much of an appetite.

***

The journey to work felt longer than usual. Ariadne had managed to get a seat on the train, although found herself struggling to read the newspaper through painfully tired eyes. She eventually gave up trying, and gazed out of the window at nothing for a while, not registering that she had reached her stop until the doors had closed and the train had slowly started pulling out of the platform.

She was too exhausted to react very much. She knew more than most that the best and worse things about insomnia were the dulled perceptions it afforded the recipient. Yes, it meant that silly mistakes were made – like missing a stop, or pouring juice instead of milk into a bowl of cereal – but it also meant not caring when things did go wrong. Life was experienced through a vague fog of lethargy, the myriad knocks and bumps along the way not as damaging as they could have been.

Or at least not perceived to be.

She got off at the next station and crossed the platform, managing to hop onto the next train going the opposite way. This time she didn't get a seat, and had to share what seemed to be a square inch of floor space with two business men and a woman holding a bunch of flowers. Ariadne didn't know the correct etiquette for holding flowers on a train, but she was pretty sure that it didn't involve flapping them into the faces of fellow commuters. Clearly, this wisdom hadn't been imparted to this woman, who seemed to think that the best way to make friends on a train was to pollinate everybody.

Ariadne held onto the last remaining millimetre of

space on the greasy handrail and closed her eyes. As had been the case since the nightmares had started, she kept sensing the shadow man with the missing face. She knew he was watching, and smiling. His grin could not be seen but could be sensed, causing a ripple of fear through her soul. There was a cruelty to him, as though he were not merely a fleeting shadow, or a cloud across the sun, but an eclipse. An obstacle blocking all that is light and warm and good. He did not simply occlude the light, he destroyed it, along with any evidence that it had ever existed. As the hairs on the back of Ariadne's neck began to stand up she sprung her eyes open, bringing her back to reality.

The walk from the train station to the office took around ten minutes, although when she arrived she wouldn't have been able to remember anything notable that happened on the way. She was awake in body only, her mind still in the dream, desperately pleading with the shadow man to leave her alone, even for just one night. Long periods of sleeplessness did strange things to time, sometimes moments would stretch out for hours, other times a full day would go by seemingly in minutes. The sleep-deprived person functioned mainly on autopilot, registering and noticing nothing, but going to work, or spending time with friends, or driving long distances. All without being fully conscious of what was happening. It gave Ariadne a new appreciation for those signs on the motorway which told drivers to pull over if they felt tired.

Drivers. Cars.

Ariadne shuddered and tried to switch her focus to the present.

She got to her building and pressed the button to summon the lift. Her mind involuntarily flashed to the dream, and as the glass lift arrived she automatically thought of it filling with warm blood, the liquid rising until it forced itself into her throat, the metallic taste of life-giving blood this time taking life instead.

She steeled herself as if preparing for battle and

stepped in.

When she reached her floor, she saw Anthony sitting at his desk. He was younger than her by around five years, a fact which he often liked to tease her about. They often playfully taunted each other, sometimes crossing the line into flirtation – although never anything more. He was the closest thing Ariadne had to a best friend, she was not about to complicate that with a relationship. She had other problems to sort out right now, she didn't want to add awkward fumblings and prolonged silences over the photocopier to the list.

Anthony looked up as Ariadne walked towards him. He was smiling, although the friendly grin quickly turned to concern as he saw her face.

"You dreamed about him again, didn't you?", he asked rhetorically.

Ariadne nodded.

"What was it this time, Ari? A car again, or did he find some other vehicle to run you over with?"

As Ariadne replied, she took off her coat and got settled at her desk, forcing herself to be as natural as possible.

"First he strangled me, then let go before I died. Then he drove a car into me, which pushed me out of a window at the top of a hotel. Then I woke up except I wasn't really awake, and he tried to drown me in a shower cubicle full of my own blood and then drove a car into me. It smashed the glass first and then hit me. Then I woke up properly, and here I am"

Anthony's focus sharpened as Ariadne spoke and he looked across from his monitor at her. She was typing and doing a poor job of being 'normal'.

"You had *two* dreams? That's… No wonder you look distressed. Are you alright? Maybe you should go home, Ari"

"And what would be the point in that? To fall asleep on the sofa and dream about him again? It's not occasional, it's every night. I'm being tortured and murdered *every* night"

She hadn't meant to speak so loudly but she didn't care. Tears pricked her eyes. She blinked them away and continued typing.

Anthony shook his head. He knew from personal experience how tormented a person could be by their own thoughts, and how sometimes the mind and body couldn't properly differentiate between fantasy and reality. The physiological response was the same. A panic attack is real even if the cause of it is not.

She was beginning to exhibit signs of depression, he thought. He'd spent a lot of the previous year learning about various psychological disorders and problems. He'd suffered from post-traumatic stress himself, and had found over the past few days that Ariadne seemed to be displaying some of the same symptoms.

"Ari, I'm gonna get a tea. Do you want anything?"

She nodded, understanding the shorthand they'd developed in their friendship. She got up and followed him to the small kitchen area, picking up a disposable cup from the counter and filling it with water as they spoke.

"Listen, why don't you go and see someone? I'm worried about you"

"You don't have to worry about me, Jackson, there's nothing anybody can do anyway"

She always called him by his surname – at first to tease him but now out of habit.

He took a china cup from the cupboard and flicked the switch on the kettle.

"How do you know that?", he asked, "There are probably thousands of people who have been cured with things like this"

"Cured? I'm not ill. They're just dreams"

"Yeah but they're not though are they? You said yourself you're being tortured and mur-"

"I know what I said", she snapped, "I just don't

think anybody can help. My doctor won't see me unless something's falling off, and I can't afford a psychiatrist. And I don't need one anyway. I'm not crazy, Jackson"

She registered the hurt in his eyes and immediately regretted her words.

He lightly rested his hand on her arm.

"I know you're not crazy Ari. Sometimes we can't do things on our own and need help. It doesn't make you weak. Look at me after last year. The company arranged counselling sessions for me, and these people don't usually care about anyone. Even *they* saw I needed help! I didn't want to go, but I realised I couldn't deal with things by myself. You know all this, you were there and saw it yourself, Ari! It worked for me because I tried it. All you have to do is try"

"Jackson, I appreciate what you're saying, but I can't afford a psychiatrist, and these idiots definitely aren't going to pay for a counsellor for me. Your thing happened at work, mine all happens at home"

He paused at that. She had a point.

"Tell you what, remember my friend Mina with the hypnosis and crystals and everything? She must know someone who knows about dream analysis or whatever it might be called. If she does, I'll see if you can talk to them. I was gonna ask her a few days ago actually but thought you'd get angry, but I don't think that really matters anymore Ari. This is killing you"

Ariadne flinched slightly.

"Sorry, not…killing. You know what I mean. Look, the worst that'll happen is you waste a half hour talking to someone who might be a nutcase. Although to be fair we do that on a daily basis in this place anyway"

Ariadne smiled, although her focus seemed to be somewhere else. Anthony suddenly realised that his hand was still on her arm. He whipped it away as if her skin was on fire.

Ariadne barely noticed. She absent-mindedly

brought her cup to her lips and sipped some water. It was so cold she could actually feel it sliding down her pharynx, then speeding down her oesophagus into her stomach. Her mind flashed back to the shower dream and the blood in her throat, the memory triggering a rush of adrenalin. In a second her eyes refocused and she looked up at Anthony again.

"Ok. You're right. I know you're right, Jackson"

Anthony left his cup on the counter top and took out his mobile phone.

"I'll call her now. Don't worry Ari. It'll be alright"

As Ariadne took another sip of water, she wished her friend had sounded just the slightest bit convincing.

Or convinced.

Three

It took a total of fourteen minutes for Anthony to come back and tell Ariadne that he'd made the appointment. Doctor Max Illari was a 'sleep specialist' who, according to his website, had successfully treated hundreds of patients suffering all types of ailments - from snoring to bed wetting. Ariadne had an appointment booked with him at noon. She felt both relieved to be seeing someone so quickly and anxious that someone so apparently esteemed was able to see her at such short notice.

Her manager wasn't around, which meant she could take an extended lunch if she wanted to. Anthony would cover for her if anyone asked, so she wasn't concerned. They always looked out for each other at work. It was a strange relationship in that they never actually saw each other outside of the office, but would text and call each other frequently. There was never any explicit suggestion of sexual attraction – at least not from either of them - but they both knew it was there. Their relationship was less boyfriend-girlfriend than it was potentially-incestuous-brother-and-sister, with neither of them wanting to ruin the strong relationship that they did have by doing anything stupid.

The morning dragged as Ariadne counted down the hours to her appointment. Doctor Illari was based in Knightsbridge, which was fortunate as she only worked a few stops away, in Holborn. She realised that just the act of arranging the appointment had helped. She was being proactive, taking control. The appointment wasn't happening to her, it was something that she'd arranged to combat something. She was the one who had the power now, not the elusive figure in her dreams. The man made of shadows with no face – it was almost laughable.

And yet she didn't laugh. She couldn't, not yet. The last few dreams had felt so real, as though she was not creating these things in her mind but having them planted there by some other entity. She felt less as though she'd had a nightmare and more as though she'd been being haunted. A ridiculous thought to her now, as she sat at her desk in the cold light of day surrounded by ringing phones and the smell of photocopier toner in the air. But she knew that when the curtains were drawn and she lay alone in her bed, semi-clothed and drifting into unconsciousness, that he was the one in control. She had no power over him there. It was as though the embodiment of an ancient evil was visiting with her. Not just a bad dream, a very real meeting with an horrific presence.

There was so much blood, and he would grin. So much pain, and still he grinned. He enjoyed the pain she suffered and, just when she felt she could take no more, he would decimate her weakened body with the full impact of a car crash. Her bones would shatter and her spine would twist into impossible positions, the tension building until the inevitable crack. Her body lifeless, her very soul leeching through the mass of shredded muscle and destroyed cartilage left in his wake.

And still he would grin.

At eleven-thirty she locked her computer and put on her coat, Anthony mouthing a 'good luck' and giving a reassuring smile. She smiled back, grateful for the support of her friend. As she took the lift down to the exit, the previous power she had felt gave way to a niggling fear. What if there was nothing this doctor could do and she was stuck with these dreams, with *him*? Then she wouldn't have any power left at all, he would be in control and be even more sadistic due to her attempts to rid herself of him.

She tried to dismiss the thoughts as foolish, reasoning that she may have *felt* haunted, but that certainly didn't make it true. As real as this all felt, it was her mind that created it all, and it was her mind that could stop it. There was no 'shadow man'. The mention of this title embarrassed her now as she walked down the street in broad daylight. The shadow man was as real as Santa Claus, and she'd stopped believing in him as a child.

As she stood on the pavement and waited for the traffic to stop, she heard the all too familiar sound of an engine being over-revved. The noise stung her, and elicited the now-familiar adrenal rush. She fought the urge to run in the opposite direction and not look back.

They're just dreams…

But, as Anthony had said, they weren't were they?

She crossed the road as soon as she was able, passing the students ambling to their classes and the tourists taking pictures of big red buses.

When she got to the sleep clinic twenty minutes later, she saw it spread over two floors above a small florist's shop a few roads away from Knightsbridge station. Ariadne had found pictures of it on the internet, but was still surprised by the vision that greeted her when she arrived. The shop was absolutely minute, but displayed a stunning array of exquisite floral arrangements. She imagined that a bouquet from there would cost more than the clothes she was wearing.

The only indication that a clinic existed above the shop was the small doorway situated at the right of the window. The letters 'ISC' were etched into a brushed chrome plaque on the door. Ariadne guessed the initials stood for Illari's Sleep Clinic, although the only explanation she could think of for the omission of 'Doctor' on the plaque was that he wasn't trained. He wouldn't want to put anything in writing about being a doctor if he wasn't one – too much chance of getting sued.

She pushed the small buzzer at the door and waited for the customary 'awkward conversation between two strangers through an intercom' to begin. She was momentarily surprised that the door was buzzed open instantly, until she glimpsed the small camera above the doorframe. She felt exposed all of a sudden, as though this doctor already knew too much about her. There was an imbalance here, he had watched her without her knowledge and had seen her first. Her first impression had been made and registered without her knowledge, and before he'd shown her anything.

She walked up the narrow, pristine staircase and was greeted at the top by a receptionist sitting at a desk. The letters 'ISC' were writ large behind the receptionist on what looked like a marble tablet. The space seemed much larger than it had appeared outside and this, coupled with the marble in the room, caused an image of the dream's hotel lobby to flash into her mind.

In contrast to the large area, the receptionist was small, looking like some delicate librarian working in a quiet country parish. She smiled warmly at Ariadne, as if they were old friends.

"You must be, let's see now…", she ran her finger down a list on her desk, "Ms. Pe….Peras…Perasm-"

"Perasmenos. It's Greek"

The receptionist blushed and smiled a sheepish apology, "I'm sorry dear, I'm not very good with names"

"Don't worry. I was fifteen before I could pronounce it"

The woman laughed, not so much at the joke but seemingly at the relief of not offending anybody. She handed Ariadne a form and asked her to fill out her information. Ariadne did so quickly – mindful of the time - and handed it back.

The receptionist's eyes lingered on Ariadne's face for just a moment too long. Ariadne read her thoughts.

"Nightmares", she said, "Two consecutive weeks' worth to be precise. At the end of each one I get slaughtered in some horrific way. Last night I got murdered twice actually. The first time I got pushed by a car through a pane of glass at the top of a hotel, the second I almost drowned in scalding hot blood but was then saved from that and killed by a car smashing into me instead. Cars don't like me very much…"

Her second attempt at humour wasn't as well received by the receptionist who, unlike Anthony, wasn't accustomed to Ariadne's detached tone. It was a defence mechanism – if she made something sound normal and boring, then maybe it would be.

The receptionist gasped.

"You poor thing", she said, shaking her head and giving Ariadne a pitiful look.

Ordinarily Ariadne would've baulked at this, but the petit woman with her kind eyes and librarian's temperament seemed to be genuinely troubled what she'd said.

"Sorry, I… I shouldn't have blurted all that out like that. I tend to get a bit… I'm sorry"

"It's fine, dear. It sounds really quite terrible for you. Just one moment, and I'll let the doctor know you're here"

As she did just that, Ariadne looked around the reception area. It was, in a word, immaculate. The colour scheme was inoffensive, and for the first time Ariadne realised that there was soft music playing. It reminded her of a spa she had visited years ago.

Her eyes scanned the numerous paintings dotted around the office. There were no windows up here, at least none she could see, so the pictures provided the only views from this small room. She stopped on a picture of what looked like large pebbles underwater. It was painted as though being seen from above the water line, so the pebbles below were distorted by the ripples. One of the pebbles looked slightly larger and closer than the others, as though it had just been plopped into the pool. Ariadne thought that this must have been the artist's intention as the ripples in the water radiated from this single source, as though the pebble had just been dropped from above. It was a nice picture. Relaxing. She wondered if it was supposed to mean something.

The whole place seemed designed to induce a sense of calm in the patients. A haven, Ariadne supposed, where people would feel comfortable enough to open up about all the horrible things they experience when the sun goes down. Ariadne knew, now more than ever, that there was a loneliness to sleep. It was almost a rehearsal for death. No matter what, it happens to you alone. Lovers may fall asleep intertwined with each other, just as embracing passengers on a doomed plane may slam into the ground together. But that moment of sliding into the abyss of sleep – or death – happens to each person as separately as if they were the only person in the world. Nobody comes with you. Whatever you face, you face alone.

"Ms. Perasmenos? Welcome"

She turned to see an older heavy-set gentleman, probably in his mid-fifties, standing with an outstretched hand. He had a thick beard which was not completely white but definitely getting there. The feature that outweighed all others was his smile. A genuinely warm, friendly beam. Ariadne wondered if he and the receptionist practised their kind faces for the benefit of the patients.

She walked the few steps toward him and shook his hand, matching his smile.

"Hello, you must be Dr. Illari?"

"Guilty as charged I'm afraid. Please, come this way Ms Perasmenos"

He had used her name twice, and correctly. This attention to detail put Ariadne's mind at rest slightly, although she still felt some trepidation as they walked along the short corridor.

Arriving at his office, she noticed there were no pictures on the walls here, just a large window with the slatted blinds half-open. Ariadne found it interesting that even in a room which had a window the patients weren't given a 'real' view of anything.

The midday light diffused nicely into the space with its cream walls and sandy-coloured carpet, making it a warm and inviting place to be.

There was a desk but the doctor chose not to sit

behind it, instead walking towards one of the two armchairs which sat next to the bookcase. He smiled and gestured for Ariadne to sit down in the other chair. He had sat her in the chair facing his numerous qualifications and certificates which hung on the wall. Ariadne felt there may have been a slight arrogance in this – maybe he *was* a real doctor after all.

He saw the look on her face.

"They're basically the same three certificates repeated for effect. And even then I purchased them from the internet"

"And here I was thinking you were a real doctor"

"Oh no, no, no. There are no real doctors. We all just fumble around pretending we know things. And don't even get me started on those so-called 'surgeons'…"

They shared a laugh at this, Ariadne feeling more relaxed now that the ice had been broken – and now that the doctor had made his own first impression. Their positions were slightly more balanced.

In the comfort of the chair and surprising quietness of the office, her lethargy returned and she felt as though she could sleep quite easily.

"So, I've been given some information, but I'd like to hear from you what particular problems you're facing"

He was all business now, she noticed.

"It all started around two weeks ago", she began, sitting up in the chair, "I started having dreams, nightmares really. There's someone after me, and I can't always see him but I know when he's there or not. He looks… like a shadow. But he doesn't have a face. I know this sounds stupid"

"Not at all. Please, continue"

His warm smile returned and he gestured for her to keep going. Ariadne wondered if he was in this job because he was so good at it, or whether he'd become good at it over time. Either way, he had a very comforting presence.

In spite of that she found it difficult for a moment to formulate her thoughts. She was trying to be matter of fact about things, but it wasn't easy given what she was talking about. She couldn't decide if it was the setting or the fact that this man might actually be able to help. She wanted him to know how affected she was by all of this. She didn't want to hide behind a detached or glib tone this time.

"He's a shadow, and I know I said he doesn't have a face, but he does. I just can't see it. And I don't know how I know that but I just do. And I know that he smiles when he chases me. Even if I'm facing the other way. For instance, last night he was in a car, revving the engine in another room and I knew it was him, and I knew he was smiling"

"Was this another room in your house?"

"No, in the hotel. The dream was set in a hotel. But he started choking me at the window first, and then let go, then drove the car into me and through the window. I woke up then – or thought I did – and he killed me in the shower"

"So you dreamt that you awoke from the first dream, and this man found you again?"

"I know, it's silly-"

"Not at all! None of it is silly Ms, Perasmenos. I've been analysing dreams for years, and nothing is ever silly. The average person has almost fifteen hundred dreams per year, that's around four dreams per night. Believe me, I have heard a lot of stories! Think about the human mind for a moment and you'll quickly realise how unrestricted the possibilities of dreams really are. There are no limits to what we can imagine Ms Perasmenos"

He let that hang in the air.

"I apologise for interrupting, please do continue. You were in the shower?"

The full horror of the dream flooded back into her senses now. She thought of the blood bubbling up around her, the smell of her own skin being boiled, the feel of her muscles separating from her bones like meat in a stew...

Then the revving of the engine again, the smash of

the unrelenting car as it destroyed her. The second dream had been so much worse than the first. It had been more malicious, more cruel.

"I... I woke up in what I thought was my house, and there was a dog there but it wasn't until later that I remembered I don't have a dog at all. I know that sounds stu- Anyway, I walked to the shower, and stepped in, and turned the knob to start the water"

She was talking slowly now, her eyes glazing slightly as she relived the memory. As painful as it was for her, she knew it was important that she give as much information as possible. When she spoke again, it was the voice of the victim of some unspeakable assault.

"My eyes were closed. So I thought it was water, but it wasn't water. It was blood. And then it was getting hotter and burning me but I couldn't switch it off. It was just getting stronger and... scalding me. The blood wasn't draining anymore and it began filling up my shower enclosure with this boiling hot blood. Then the engine again, and then..."

Her voice trailed off, and the doctor noticed that she was not actually crying, but that her eyes were more moist now. He recognised that she was one of those patients who could compose themselves, and so didn't offer a comforting hand or a tissue. He just gave her time, and waited.

Once Ariadne snapped back into the present, her eyes refocusing, he continued.

"Thank you Ms Perasmenos. I know that must have been very difficult. If you don't mind, I'd like to just ask you some questions about your house. Is that ok?"

He gave that comforting smile again. She nodded.

"So, your bedroom. I assume you have wardrobes, mirrors, that kind of thing?"

"Yes. I sleep facing the door and my wardrobes. Then on the other side there are two chests of drawers. Oh, and the wardrobe doors are mirrored."

He took a pad from his pocket and made a note.

"Thank you. And do you have windows?"

"Yes. Two. They're on the wall, well, in the wall I suppose, at the end of my bed"

"Do you have curtains or blinds?"

"Curtains"

"Light or dark?"

She frowned as she misunderstood the question.

"Dark. They're curtains, how could they be light?"

The doctor gave a slight chuckle.

"I'm sorry, maybe I didn't phrase that correctly. I meant the colour, not whether they let the light into your room"

"Oh, I see. They're dark, then. A kind of chocolate brown colour"

"Thank you"

He was scribbling in his notepad.

"And what is your routine at night? Talk me through it if you don't mind"

She knew her evening routine backwards. She lived alone, there were no variables around bedtime rituals.

"I feed Harry, my cat-"

"Ah, you have a cat?"

He made a note.

"Does that mean something?"

"Not necessarily. I just forgot to ask. You mentioned that you don't have a dog, but I didn't ask about other pets! Do you have any others?"

"No, just the cat"

"That's fine. Sorry to interrupt again. Please continue"

"I put food in Harry's bowl downstairs, then I make sure the front and back doors are locked and I go upstairs. I get undressed and hang my clothes in my wardrobe, then put on my nightclothes..."

She stopped as she realised that the nightclothes she wore varied depending on whether she was on her period, and how heavy it was that month. She was telling this stranger intimate details about what she does when nobody else is looking. Bedroom rituals were sacred, shared only with ourselves or our loved ones – and even then that's because they in turn share their own rituals with us.

He sensed her apprehension and stopped writing. He looked up at her and chewed his bottom lip, as if thinking of the right words. When he spoke, both the speed and the volume of his voice had decreased.

"I know that this probably feels quite strange, I genuinely do. Nobody likes talking about these things, but I honestly only need to know them so that I can help you. For instance, the reason I wanted to know about the curtains is because sometimes the last thing we see at night can, for lack of a better word, stay in our mind and influence our dreams. If you see a black shadowy mass immediately before you sleep, then it may go some way to explaining why you see this shadow man in your dreams. There is also a school of thought that dreams are our minds' way of making sense of external stimuli that are happening around us while we sleep. So if you sleep with the television on, and then have dreams about certain things, it may be that your mind is incorporating the things from the television into your dreams. Some patients even go back and check the television listing from the days when they've had strange dreams. Sometimes there are patterns there. It's incredible, really"

Ariadne thought about this.

"So, you mean, our dreams are our minds interpreting things that are happening in the real world? But dreams are so varied. Can that be right?"

The doctor sensed the scepticism in her tone and held his hands up playfully.

"It's one of many schools of thought, Miss Perasmenos. We don't know, but we're trying to find out! Most dreams aren't as simple as that, although elements of it may be true. If you're too hot in bed, you may dream you're basking in the sun, too cold and you're dreaming about Siberia. It's not impossible, but at the same time I don't imagine it's a full enough theory to account for every dream we have"

Ariadne nodded.

"Is it ok to continue?"

"Yes. Thanks"

"Thank you. So, have you always had these curtains, or did you only get them a few weeks ago?"

"No, I've had them since I moved in. I've always had them"

"Alright. Well that may rule that out then"

He made another note.

"Now, my next question is quite delicate and personal, but please do understand that I have to ask you. Studies suggest that hormone changes during pregnancy may affect dreams, specifically the frequency and vividness of them"

Ariadne was barely able to contain the laugh that rose up in her throat.

"I'm not pregnant, Doctor! I'm sure of it"

"Very well. I had to mention that, I'm sure you understand"

"Of course"

A slight awkwardness hung in the air between them at how incredulous the thought of Ariadne being pregnant had been to her.

"Do you smoke?"

"No"

"Have you recently stopped, or do you use nicotine patches at all? They don't actually cause nightmares you understand, but they can sometimes increase the intensity of them"

"No to both. In that regard, I'm pretty healthy"

"Glad to hear it Miss Perasmenos. So, what about television? Do you watch anything before you sleep?"

"Not really".

She thought for a second.

"I mean, I do watch television, but not in bed or anything. Do you think that could be a factor?"

"Possibly. We do know there are connections between television viewing and dreams, although it's not entirely clear how far any correlations go. For instance people who watched black and white television as children mainly have monochromatic dreams, whereas those lucky enough to have had colour televisions dream in quite vivid colours. So there is a link. We are just investigating everything though Miss Perasmenos, and I dare say that if there were a single, obvious cause of your nightmares then it's likely you would have found it by now"

He sat back in his chair, and scribbled something down.

"Miss Perasmenos, have you made any dietary changes recently?"

"What, like eating cheese before bedtime?", she asked with a smirk.

He laughed.

"Well, that wasn't quite what I was thinking, but it might be possible that any big changes to diet or vitamin intake could have an effect. Do you think that could be a cause?"

She thought for a moment.

"I don't think so. My diet might not be the healthiest to be honest, but I haven't made any recent changes or anything"

He made another note.

The interview continued as it had begun - question, response, scribble. Occasionally the doctor would ask her to describe other routines in her life. He also asked about any medication she was taking and any psychological stress she may be under. She answered everything as honestly - and thoroughly - as she could.

After half an hour, he asked a question which surprised Ariadne, as it seemed totally unrelated to anything she had said.

"Do you talk in your sleep?"

"Do I..? No, not that I'm aware of. Only my cat would be able to tell you about that for the last few years anyway…"

The embarrassing truth that she hadn't shared a bed with anyone for years filled the room like smoke, crawling around her legs, swirling in between her and the doctor. As she searched her mind for a way to change the subject, she remembered something about her childhood.

"Actually, I used to talk in my sleep, when I was little. I haven't in years, at least I wouldn't know if I…have…"

She blushed. The smoke again.

"And do you know what you used to say? Was it full sentences, or just words? Did they make sense at all?"

"It wasn't gibberish or anything, I don't think. My mum once said she'd walked into my room and had a whole conversation with me. We'd spoken about school apparently but when I woke up the next day I couldn't remember any of it. I haven't thought about that in years…I almost forgot that had even happened"

She remembered that day now. Her mum had known things about school that Ariadne hadn't actually told her. It soon became apparent to her mum that Ariadne had been asleep when she'd spoken to her, and so had no conscious recollection of any of it at all.

"The reason I ask is that sometimes when people talk in their sleep they give a clue as to what is bothering them. For instance, you may have some unresolved past issues that are on your mind, and feel as though they are catching up to you. Hence being chased. Maybe you feel that there are unresolved issues in your life, and feel subconsciously that you should confront them. Maybe this shadow man is something you need to confront. From what you said about school, this might well be a good course to pursue. Do you have any kind of recording device at all?"

"Not really. I have my mobile phone, which I suppose I could use"

He frowned and bit his lip again.

"Hmm, I think it would need to be something that is activated by sound, otherwise it would probably just record hours and hours of silence. I have a small recorder which I could give to you, but I would need it back tomorrow. Do you think you would be able to come back then?"

"Yes, definitely. I can come at the same time if your schedule allows it"

"That may be difficult. The only reason I could fit you in today is due to two cancellations in a row I'm afraid. Ordinarily I haven't got a minute to spare. In addition, I would also need the recorder back before noon. Would you be able to possibly drop it in on your way to work at all?"

She began to think of the inconvenience of doing this. Then, as the image of being smashed through a window screamed through her mind, she dismissed her reservations as ridiculous. The doctor's office was only a few stops away from her office, and even if it wasn't, she needed to stop these dreams. That was her priority.

"That's fine. Thank you so much Doctor. It's very kind of you"

He walked over to his desk and retrieved a small black device, no bigger than a pack of playing cards. It had a lead running from it, which Ariadne assumed was the microphone. He gave her a quick tutorial in how to use it and where to place it for maximum effectiveness. A burst of excitement flashed through her as he explained it all - she was taking control again and actively doing something to stop these dreams. She felt powerful again. She was the one in control now, not *him*.

She walked from the doctor's office with a spring in her step. As though the battle had already been won.

As she would find out soon enough, it had not even begun.

Four

The afternoon passed in typically disjointed 'office time' – the minutes dragged torturously slowly and the hours sped by as deadlines loomed.

Ariadne had told Anthony all about the doctor. He seemed genuinely pleased, although that pleasure was dampened slightly by an emergency that had sprung up with one of his cases. They worked for a healthcare regulator, which meant that at any given time something urgent was happening that they were expected to drop everything to fix.

As soon as the working day ended Ariadne rushed to the underground station. The journey was surprisingly stress-free, although her threshold for stress had changed dramatically in the past couple of weeks. That was the only benefit she could see to what was happening – the less important problems in her life all of a sudden didn't look like problems at all anymore.

Didn't get a seat on the train? Big deal, I get murdered every night.

Passed over for promotion? That's ok, at least your head wasn't smashed in with a rock.

She smiled, enjoying the morbid humour. She felt powerful again, the jokes denigrating the dreams, alleviating their sting.

Missed your favourite television show last night? Who cares! I got stabbed with a broken bottle, my flesh lacerated and sliced, the only relief coming when the warm blood from my higher injuries gushed down my body and slithered over the lower ones.

She stopped smiling.

Then spent the rest of the journey trying not to think about anything at all.

***

As she walked into her house Harry came padding along to greet her at the door. He gave a small meow, rubbed his soft head against her legs, and wound his way in between them. She wasn't any kind of expert on animal behaviour, but she knew a hungry cat when she saw one.

Unfortunately she also knew a full bladder when she felt one, so this time went straight past the cat's empty bowl and rushed upstairs. The cat gave an insistent meow as she swept past.

"Sorry Harry!", she shouted, knowing that even if he could understand what she was saying, he'd still make her pay for it later. Cats didn't seem the type to accept apologies.

She felt an odd sensation in the bathroom. It was as if, even though she knew that all of the things she had dreamt had not actually occurred, she still felt…something. Her focus was continually drawn to the shower cubicle, the scene of the sickening horror which had stayed with her throughout the day. The emotional residue of the attack existed, even if the attack itself had not. She guessed that's what people must mean when they say their house is haunted by somebody who died violently a hundred years ago. The walls seeming to hum with the memory of the murder. Although in Ariadne's case, it hadn't ever actually occurred.

As she stood at the sink, her focus shifted to the water that was coming out of the tap and flowing over her hands. It was as if she was waiting for the flow to turn red and sticky between her fingers. She imagined the clear water turning into thick blood, clotting on the way out and coughing out of the pipes in chunks. She remembered the feel of the blood in her hair and over her body. It had been so vivid, so real.

There are no limits to what we can imagine Ms Perasmenos.

She knew the doctor was right. Of course it seemed vivid and real, her mind knew both blood and water, it wasn't difficult to switch one for the other in a dream. It wasn't even that hard now, she'd just been doing it hadn't she?

Walking downstairs, she froze on the third step down. Something – a shadow? - had drifted across her vision. It hadn't happened quickly enough for her to dismiss it as a trick of the light. It had been slow. Purposeful. A wave of fear and adrenalin rippled through her body. Terror seemed to be playing with her, pawing with its claws but not quite striking. Not yet, at least.

She found herself feeling that now familiar heightened state of alertness that she seemed to be adopting every so often. Her hearing was better, her vision sharper. She would have sworn that she could feel the smallest change in temperature on her skin, the faintest odour that up until now had been too slight to notice.

At the same time she found that she could not move.

Her eyes studied the environment as she stood on the steps, desperately looking for a point of focus that would explain the shadow. Maybe light from outside had reflected off something she was wearing, or maybe her eyes were playing tricks on her because she hadn't slept properly for so long.

Or maybe there was a presence in the house and she wasn't alone.

She called out - "Hello?" – and immediately felt foolish. If somebody was in the house, then they surely wouldn't answer. But then what was she supposed to do? She remembered watching a programme about burglars, apparently if they know someone is in the house they are less likely to-

A stab of terror shot through her, interrupting her thoughts. The back of her neck burned and she felt light-headed. She knew. She knew what had just happened and she knew why she was feeling that black terror.

He was grinning.

Her heart raced as sweat pricked at her hands and

forehead. Intellectually she knew he did not exist, and could not possibly be in the house – or anywhere else for that matter. He lived in her dreams, he couldn't possibly be there now, unless…

A new terror gripped her.

Unless she was asleep. If she was, he could be there.

And he could do anything.

No, she had been at work, seen the doctor, it wasn't possible. The thought niggled at her – what if she had fallen asleep on the train? Or what if she had *actually* fallen asleep in the doctor's comfortable chair?

Using all the strength she could muster, she forced herself to work her muscles and walk down the steps. At the bottom, she looked around the living room. Everything was as it should be, she could not possibly be asleep. She would have pinched herself like they do in films, to prove to herself that she wasn't dreaming, but decided against it. If she didn't wake up through torture, she wouldn't wake up because of a pinch.

She felt the overwhelming urge to run, not just from the house but from her life. She wanted to just escape, to just go somewhere else. She walked cautiously around the room, checking that everything was in its place, trying to prove to herself that she was awake.

She stopped and scanned the room. The only movement from anywhere was Harry sitting patiently by his bowl, every so often making small noises seemingly to remind her that he was still hungry.

As suddenly as it had arrived, the fear passed. The world was righted again, tilted back onto its axis.

Ariadne gave a burst of nervous laughter at the absurdity of the situation. She spoke to herself as an adult speaks to a child.

You're not asleep. You haven't slept in days, that's all. There's no presence, your mind is just tired. Now feed Harry so he stops meowing!

The act of feeding the cat felt good, familiar. It was nice reaching for the cupboard door, taking out the colourful cardboard packet and filling up the bowl. Control had passed back to her now, the act of doing something so mundane and ordinary reasserted her sense of power. This was her house. Her domain.

Harry munched ferociously, not pausing for breath. Ariadne decided to give him some biscuits. The vet had told her to ration them or he'd get fat, but she liked giving him a treat. Deciding the cat's fate in this small way gave her another boost. There was nothing to be scared of. She was the one with the power in this house.

The shrill ring of the phone startled her, causing her to drop the box of cat biscuits into the bowl. Harry ran to the front door, as spooked by the box crashing down as Ariadne had been by the phone's screeching tone.

She felt anger surge up inside her - her reaction to the ringing phone had knocked down her whole theory of power and control. A sudden unexpected noise, and the house of cards had collapsed. She mentally chastised herself for being so weak as she picked up the receiver.

"Hello?"

"That was quick! Usually I have to wait six rings!"

"Hi mum. I was near the phone"

"Waiting for Mr Right to call, hey?"

Ariadne gave a half-hearted laugh.

"Something like that", she said.

"What's wrong sweetheart? You sound a bit off"

"I'm ok mum"

There was a pause on the other end of the line.

"Oh no. It didn't happen again did it?"

"It happened twice mum"

"Oh, sweetheart. How on earth did it happen twice?"

"It happened once, then I thought I woke up but I didn't really wake up, then it happened again. And then I woke up properly"

"Why don't you go and see someone? I keep telling you, the doctor knows about these things"

"I did see someone", she said, immediately regretting it.

"You didn't tell me that!"

"No, it was only today. A friend of mine told me about him and he deals with these things so I went and spoke to him"

She spent the next few minutes telling her mum the whole story, trying to make it sound as normal and fine as possible. The last thing her mum needed was more stress.

"But you haven't spoken in your sleep since you were little! Does this man know what he's doing?"

"Well, I hope so! And who knows if I've spoken in my sleep? It's at least worth a try"

"Yes, it is sweetheart. I hope he gets to the bottom of it, I really do. Once you stop all of this you can get on with things again"

'Things' being shorthand for 'finding a husband'.

"I hope so too, mum"

Her mum sighed down the phone.

"I know I always say this, but –"

"I know mum, but I don't want to. I've got a job, I can't just not go in"

"But you have holidays, don't you? Just book a week off and come and stay with us. Oh, we'd love to have you. And you know how much Dad loves Harry"

"I'll see mum. It's not that easy, I've got cases that I'm dealing with, it's not really possible to just book a week off"

"Well, the offer is there any time you want it sweetheart. We miss you"

"I miss you too mum"

Ariadne took a deep breath.

"How's Dad?"

There was another pause, there always was whenever anyone asked that question.

"He... he misses you sweetheart. In his own way. You know how it is"

"I know mum. Is he ok though?"

"Yes. He's ok"

"And you? How are you, mum?"

"I'm fine! I'm always fine! Don't worry about me, you just get yourself sorted out so you can find someone and I can start planning the big wedding!"

They spoke a while longer about the latest news in everybody's lives – and she's keeping it! At her age! - and their plans for the weekend. Ariadne had started viewing the future with a certain pessimism. A surprising number of plans relied on feeling refreshed after a good nights' sleep. At the moment, she genuinely believed that may never happen again.

After they finished speaking, Ariadne sat and watched Harry for a while. He'd gone back to his bowl and eaten not only the food she had put for him but also the biscuits which had spilled out of the box when she'd dropped it. So much for the diet.

She began to wonder how many other houses he went to, begging for food. His life seemed so easy. Eat, get stroked, walk around a bit, nap. Repeat as required. Cats might be jumpy and scared occasionally, but they never seemed *fearful*. She never got the feeling that Harry was worried or anxious, or pondering the future. Something happened, he'd jump, that was it.

She suddenly laughed out loud at herself as she realised she felt jealousy at not being a cat.

She thought about her parents and felt a pang in her heart. She missed them. Especially now that things were feeling so bad. Lack of sleep had made her not only more emotional, but lethargic all the time and unprepared for the world. Even though the dreams themselves had put smaller problems into perspective, she still found that she would sometimes shock herself, and others, by overreacting to certain things which ordinarily wouldn't bother her. It was an odd situation, not being bothered by some things but overreacting to others. Sleep deprivation did strange things.

She thought about her mum's offer. She'd always told Ariadne that she was welcome, and she knew that she always was, but this wouldn't be a holiday or a nice little break. It would be running away. Defeat. She knew she'd have to come back to the house anyway, and the feeling that she'd run away would make her feel even weaker in the face of… whatever she was facing now.

Or, she thought, maybe she would feel better after going away and not so troubled, which in turn would make the dreams stop? And it's not as though her mum didn't need the help with her dad. Her mum definitely needed a break too, if Ariadne went to stay it might be good for all of them.

The stubborn streak in Ariadne rose up and stopped the idea in its tracks. It was running away, defeat - that was it. Any arguments to the contrary were motivated by fear, not by genuine concerns. She had to stay and fight. It was the only way she could win.

Although at this point winning seemed a strange, elusive concept.

She yawned and realised she wasn't fully able to properly evaluate anything at the moment.

She also realised that she was ravenous.

She decided to eat and just go to bed, and in a second the now-familiar fear kicked in, twisting and gnarling her stomach. It was something the rest of the world seemed to take for granted. To them, their beds were a haven of peace, a place to escape the world and get some rest. To her, it was the battlefield. She envied people at work talking about how they were going to "get an early night" so they would feel better tomorrow. That was never an option for Ariadne. It used to be, but not anymore.

She tried to repress the nausea and force herself to eat something. She knew she was hungry, and that her body craved food even if her mind told her otherwise.

Hopefully the voice recorder would shed some light on things tomorrow. Although she wasn't holding out much hope for that.

Or anything else for that matter.

Five

The street is empty.

Ariadne looks around, taking in her surroundings - pristine lawns, huge driveways, wooden detached houses. America in the fifties. Or the closest approximation her mind can make to it. Her red dress clings to her body, and she feels the hot summer sun beating down on her exposed shoulders.

The street is *too* empty.

No children playing, no proud husband washing his car and playfully spraying the kids with water, no dutiful wife calling to ask what he wants for dinner.

A ghost town.

Ariadne does not walk in the road, even though it is empty. She knows better than that even – especially? – when she is dreaming.

As she strolls along she detects a slight burning smell. It's not unpleasant, in fact it makes her feel quite hungry. Maybe burgers or hot dogs. Fifties America again. Out of the corner of her eye she sees a man standing on the lawn in front of one of the houses across the road. He's wearing chef's whites and standing over a barbecue, every so often turning a fat slab of meat with huge metal tongs. The handle is cutting into his fat thumb and forefinger, giving the appearance of two raw sausages.

There is still no noise, as if the entire street exists in some kind of vacuum. She instinctively tries to yawn in order to un-pop her ears but it does nothing. The only sound she can hear now is the hiss of the meat cooking, and the tiny explosions as the fat drips onto the coals and sizzles.

The man gives her a smile and a raises a chubby hand to his forehead in a small salute. She smiles back and waves, sensing the warmth of this stranger's affection for her. Something about him is reminiscent of her father, even though there's no physical resemblance at all.

"Sorry about the dog", she hears herself calling to the man, even though she has no recollection of actually intending to talk.

The words echo across the road, ricocheting around the empty space and towards the man like a pinball. The noise is more akin to two people standing in a cave, rather than across a suburban street.

The Chef laughs now. The amusement mixed with something else. Ariadne can't quite place the emotion, but its somewhere between anger and spite. The affection no longer seems present.

"It's ok", he says in a thick Texan drawl, "I can get another dog"

A tragic sadness washes over her. The end of a marriage. The death of a child.

"But you can't", she shouts, "you can never replace it"

The Chef's smile dims and he looks up, his eyes burning into her. She sees his face clearly now, his fat rosy cheeks, his dark beard. He continues poking at the meat, his chubby sausage-fingers slick with sweat as he tries to keep his grip on the tongs. Something mischievous flashes across his eyes and he sings her name playfully, dancing a slight jig. An uncle at a family gathering who's had too much to drink.

"Ar-i-ad-neee. Ar-i-ad-neee Peee. That's your name, isn't it? I don't think I ever knew your name"

"Nobody told me the name of your dog either"

The man abruptly stops dancing, the smile dropping completely from his face now. He looks down, a petulant child unhappy with a scalding.

"It hurt when he died"

"I know. I'm sorry for your loss"

"It's too late for that"

Something strange begins to happen to the passage of time in the dream, as though somewhere a slow-motion button has been pressed. Ariadne notices the smoke lazily rising from the barbecue, as the sounds of the small explosions of fat hang in the air a few seconds longer now.

The sounds of summer begin to drift in and fill the road between Ariadne and the Chef - children shouting, a thump of a foot kicking a ball, a lawnmower starting, the splash of a hose spraying a car. The sounds seem to be travelling along the road, getting louder as they approach. At the same time the noises are distorted, as though stretched and elongated. Slow-motion again.

The cacophony continues along the road, reaching a peak and seeming to stop in the centre, creating a wall of noise in between Ariadne and the Chef. The sounds have taken on a tangible quality, the sound waves becoming visible as Ariadne stares in wonder. Each sound dances in front of her eyes, like multi-coloured smoke vapours, capering and swaying to the rhythm of the particular noise. The intermittent blue of the children shouting, the occasional red injection as a football is kicked, the constant yellow hum of a lawnmower.

Curiously, Ariadne finds her ability to see the Chef is not affected – he is as clear as he was in the silence, even though the multi-coloured smoke hangs and swirls in between them. She wonders how much she is actually seeing, and how much she is sensing.

The Chef looks down at the grill, apparently oblivious to the show. He speaks slowly and without emotion, as if a plug somewhere has been pulled on him. His voice – like his appearance - somehow travels across the wall of noise between them, piercing through it with startling clarity. His voice is a dark green, snaking across the expanse, and there's a delay between his mouth moving and the sound reaching Ariadne. She watches his mouth shape the words a full second before the sound travels toward her.

"He's coming for you, you know"

She nods.

"I know", she says in a resigned whisper.

Her own words travel across the noise in a trail of purple, sliding and slipping through the other sounds and wrapping themselves around the Chef.

He doesn't respond.

She knows that her voice can be heard and understood by him. He gives no outward sign of this but she knows. She *senses* it, and even if she couldn't, she sees the purple smoke swirling around his head and drifting into his ears. The words have reached him, he just doesn't want to hear them.

The Chef still refuses to look at Ariadne, his focus entirely on the barbecue. He lifts the juicy red meat, turns it over and drops in onto the grill again. The greasy liquid sluices through the metal, giving that pleasing hissing sound again, and this time releasing orange smoke.

The sounds in between them somehow seem to get louder, warping and dancing in the middle of the road. Still in slow motion, still stretching out in all directions. New sounds and colours have been added now. The vague sound of somebody's too-loud TV coming from the windows of one of the houses (turquoise), the sharp clip of pruning shears (orange).

"That sound you can hear. It's not a lawnmower engine", the Chef says, still not looking at Ariadne.

"I know"

Her posture had been fairly neutral, but her shoulders slump now, mirroring the Chef's own body language.

"Will you run?", he asks.

"What would be the point?", she counters, not rhetorically but as a genuine question. If there is any possibility that running will help, she will take it.

The man opens his mouth as if to speak, but then closes it again. He pokes at the grill, and Ariadne follows his sausage hands down the tongs and to the meat. She sees there is nothing but a blackened log where the plump meat sat only seconds before. A charred lump. The man still looks down, seemingly oblivious to the ruined meat. Ariadne does not see but again senses his unfocussed eyes staring in the vague direction of the grill. A thousand yard stare, seeing nothing but seeing everything. Still looking down.

His shout breaks her out of her thoughts.

"You killed my dog!"

The words this time do not slide elegantly through the cacophony, but are fired through it like bullets. Ariadne sees them cut through the ethereal wall and looks down as they painlessly stab her in the chest and evaporate.

"I'm sorry about your dog", she says again.

"You killed him!", he shouts, aggressively pointing his tongs at her. He is looking at her now, his eyes burning into hers, the unfettered rage piercing into her, like his words only moments ago.

The buzzing of the lawnmower engine becomes sharper now. Like the man's voice it begins to cut through the other sounds. Not louder necessarily, but clearer, somehow more defined than the rest of the cacophony. Somehow becoming the only sound she hears amidst the din, the way a person can recognise their own name spoken in a chattering crowd.

The yellow smoke of the lawnmower grows and expands, reminding Ariadne of a disease, multiplying and consuming the surrounding cells until there's nothing left but the mass of sickness. As the colours are extinguished so are the sounds, leaving nothing but a hum, then a growl, then a roar of the engine. The yellow smoke darkens, becoming black and thick and occluding her view of the Chef. The black mass advances toward her. She steps back and hits a solid object. A cold, immovable wall. She tries to turn but the smoke is on her now, pinning her arms to her sides, crawling down her throat and choking her. She coughs, and with every consequent inhalation takes in more of the toxic black fumes. She finds herself unable to move, paralysed by the near-solid substance.

The noise now is deafening, taking away her last remaining sense.

She feels his presence again. Not the man in the chef's whites now, but him.

She tries to scream but cannot catch her breath. She fights like she has done so many times before, in so many other dreams, in so many other scenarios. The horror of suffocation engulfs her, and the panic spurs her on to fight. Willing herself to carry on, to survive, a small squeak somehow forces itself from her throat and manages to cut through the engine roar. Then she forces a louder shriek, and then a scream.

She screams and screams and as she does the smoke is pushed back. Her throat is raw and the taste of blood bubbles up into her mouth, but still she screams and manages to somehow force back the smoke. Her voice suddenly breaks through, louder than the horrific roar of the engine.

A sense of relief pulses through her as she realises that she is pushing the toxic cloud away. This small victory is short lived as the smoke morphs from a black shapeless mass into the figure of a man. The smoke slowly implodes into itself, forming the familiar shadow. Ariadne thinks of documentaries she has watched featuring imploding stars and the unimaginable power being unleashed in a nanosecond.

Her terror complete, she forces herself to look at his faceless head where the eyes should be. As expected, there is nothing there, and yet she knows he is grinning again. The sound of the engine still emanates from his position, and there is an electric charge in the air. Almost a humidity.

As these elements assault Ariadne, the as yet unseen car roars behind and then through the shadow man, causing his form to disappear with a hiss. Ariadne instinctively tries to step back and feels the smooth cold surface of the immovable object again. She turns, somehow afforded the time to do so by a new distortion of the dream, and sees a glass window. Then she is suddenly standing on the other side of the window, staring at herself as the car mercilessly impacts her doppelganger.

With a powerlessness that feels somehow familiar, she witnesses the crumpling of her own body, the shattering of her bones, the squashing and bursting of her fragile body against the unbreakable window. A glint of metal appears through the devastation that was her spine and waist, and scratches the glass with a screech as the front of the car cuts her almost cleanly in two. She sees the blood oozing onto the glass just like it did in the shower cubicle. The shadow man is behind the wheel, the featureless head impossibly emitting a sadistic glee.

As she watches the death of her double, she is suddenly shunted forward into the glass from behind, a powerful force thrusting her into the window from the other side. In the split-second it takes her to realise there is a second car - but somehow the *same* car – she jerks awake.

***

Ariadne leapt up from the bed, her muscles tight, her senses sharp. The hypervigilance was back and she scanned the room, registering everything and missing nothing. Subliminally, she noted the duvet on the floor, the sunlight peeping through the curtains, Harry standing by the closed door.

Nothing looked amiss but she felt a dull sense that something was wrong. The horrors of the dream still raced through her mind, but she felt there was something else too. Something that wasn't quite right. Her sleep-addled brain tried to piece things together. The nightmare still hung heavy on her shoulders, and she could feel her T shirt sticking to her slick body, just like in the dream. Her throat also felt sore, which probably meant she was coming down with some kind of virus now as well.

Her eyes never stopped searching the room.

The only thing that seemed amiss was Harry. Why was he standing by the door? Why did he look so... did he actually look *guilty*?

It wasn't clear whether the sight or the smell hit her first, but she quickly became all too aware as to why Harry looked that way.

"Oh, Harry!", she shouted, as she spotted the 'accident' he'd had on the floor.

"You dirty cat! That's disgusting Harry! Bad! That's bad!"

She jabbed her finger at him as she shouted, the adrenalin built up by the dream being given free rein now.

She yanked open the door, barely missing the cat's head as he scurried out, and rushed to the bathroom to get some tissue. The air rushing past the sweat on her body gave her a slight chill. As she walked into the bathroom and stood on the cold tile, her anger dissipated. The shower cubicle loomed over her, dwarfing her and giving a reminder that she wasn't strong. She could be got to.

She had been.

A shiver went through her body, and she knew it had nothing to do with the tiles on her bare feet.

Exhaustion smothered her like a cloak of lead.

She'd just watched herself die, writhing in agony as her blood and pulped organs seeped from her rapidly emptying body. Thinking of the dream while awake didn't dissolve its impact at all, and she was becoming accustomed to dragging fear around with her during the day. Or maybe it was dragging *her* around, she couldn't be sure anymore.

Just thinking about her nightmares in daylight often served to drain her energy even further, somehow bringing the horrors into reality and weakening her.

By the time she got back to her bedroom – only a matter of steps – the fear had already worked on her energy until she felt as though she had none. She knelt down by the mess on the carpet and began cleaning it with the air of a woman resigned to her fate. She was viewing everything through a slight haze, she hadn't fully woken up yet but still felt a real relief at not being in the nightmare anymore. She knew she was awake now, there was no chance this was all a dream – although the thought had occurred to her when she saw the cat standing by the bedroom door.

And what was wrong with that cat anyway? He never did that indoors unless the litter tray was there. For a cat, he was pretty well trained.

She started thinking that maybe he was ill. She kept him in her room most nights and nothing like this had ever happened. Once, at the vet, he'd had an accident, but that was because he was scared. There was nothing to be scared of here.

A wave of guilt lapped at her feet playfully, ready to sweep over and engulf her.

She thought of how she'd leapt out of bed – probably knocking Harry off the end of it – and stood like a mad woman. She'd frantically looked around the room, most likely scaring Harry who obviously couldn't understand the concept of bad dreams.

The wave now roared up and crashed into her.

Of course the poor cat was scared, she didn't doubt that if she'd caught a glimpse of herself in the mirror she would've been scared too.

She finished cleaning the carpet – no mean feat and necessitating numerous trips to the bathroom for soap, water and, at the lowest point of the exercise, a nail brush.

She walked downstairs and found the cat pacing back and forth. His tail was bristled but down, and his eyes flitted nervously from one point in the room to the other. She thought of an ex-boyfriend and a nervous laugh burst from her lips, the noise scaring the cat even more. Her ex had always told her that animals can't show emotion.

"Cats don't have a 'cute' face or an 'angry' face, Ari. They don't have loads of different expressions. They have one, and do you know what it's called? 'Cat'"

Looking at Harry now, she knew that was the farthest thing from the truth. Animals could feel fear and anger and love and happiness just like humans, and the emotions were not only written all over their faces but all over their bodies too. They were probably *more* expressive and honest than humans, given that they had neither the reason nor the capacity to lie.

She walked over to Harry, calling his name and apologising over and over again. She knelt down and tried to scoop him up, but he recoiled as though she were dangerous.

I must have really freaked him out, she thought as she stood and unlocked the door. It'd be best for him to go out and let off steam and calm down or whatever cats did when nobody was watching. He'd probably be back later with a rat's tail in his teeth and the rest of it in his belly, ready to curl up and be a pet again.

Ariadne checked the time and realised she needed to have left the house five minutes ago in order to drop the voice recorder off with the doctor and not be late for work. She rushed to the kitchen and found she'd run out of not only cereal but also milk and bread. At the same time, she heard a neighbour's car engine revving outside and felt a bear trap snap tight around her stomach.

This was going to be a long day.

Six

Ariadne stopped at the doctor's office and left the voice recorder with the receptionist, pausing briefly to admire the pebble picture again, before remembering she was in a hurry and rushing off.

She thought about the picture while standing awkwardly on the train, trying to bring some serenity to the hot, crowded carriage. There was something unmistakably calming about the image. Maybe it was the dropped pebble, frozen in time, never to reach its ultimate destination. Hanging in stasis, unaffected by its environment. It may have just been the peaceful effect that water always seemed to have, or maybe there was no real explanation for why it was calming. It just was.

She was jerked out of her daydream by a little foot knocking against her leg. She turned to see a mischievous toddler hiding behind his apologetic mother. She smiled at the woman, and wondered who in their right mind would bring a child onto a train at rush hour. Most of the adults were barely tough enough to endure it themselves.

Twenty minutes later and she was in the glass lift again, ascending to her office. As she slowly came to a stop she wondered whether there'd been some kind of fire drill. Nobody was sitting at their desks, although coats and bags had been left behind. The monitors all had their screensavers displayed too, so it must have been a pretty well-planned emergency if there had been one. A quick glance at the glass-walled meeting area told her where everybody had gone.

"Oh, crap...", she said to the rows of empty chairs, her throat still feeling dry.

She dumped her coat at her desk and rushed toward the room, trying to ignore the slight panic she felt at being surrounded by huge sheets of glass. A flash of the dream came to her, but she managed to suppress the images assaulting her mind. The associated emotions weren't so easy to ignore.

She entered the room by the back doors, taking her place with the other latecomers. Their tardiness was obvious too, not only because they were standing, but because of the sense of relief on their faces when she'd walked in – somebody had walked in even later than them.

The chairs were set up school assembly style, all facing the front. Standing half-in and half-out of the bright projection on the front screen was the head of the division, Edward Ford. He looked about sixty years old, and had suffered two heart attacks since accepting the job. Everybody but him seemed to recognise the effect it was having on his health. Denial is an odd thing.

He insisted that everybody call him Eddie in a desperate attempt to look like an approachable boss. Ariadne refused, pronouncing his full name of Edward whenever she needed to speak with him. It seemed more proper to her, more formal. And, as she so often reminded other people in the office, he wasn't a four year old. She also didn't want to engage in the faux-friendly atmosphere he was trying to create, especially since the staff had been so miserable since he'd taken over.

He glanced at Ariadne as she walked in, gave a quick insincere smile to show that he cared about his staff – for the benefit of his own manager who was also at the meeting - and then returned to his presentation. He had colour slides and pie charts and everything, this was serious business.

Ariadne scanned the room, looking for Anthony. She soon saw him sitting in the front row and stifled a laugh. His position at the front meant he had been late enough to miss the good seats, but not late enough to get to stand at the back. This meant he had to sit there, making eye contact with Eddie 'the friend of the workers', and was expected to smile and nod with orgasmic glee every time a new slide came up. From what Ariadne could see, he was being pretty convincing.

As the meeting wore on, Ariadne felt the tiredness descending again. It had started arriving in waves recently. Ever since she'd started having the nightmares she'd be either rushing around as if energised from within, or slumped at her desk. She'd started having episodes of near-unconsciousness too, where she'd space out for a while and disengage from the world. People would be speaking to her or the phone would be ringing but she wouldn't be aware of it. Anthony had been the first to notice. He'd come to her desk to speak to her and she'd be staring at some point in space, her eyes wide open but not seeing anything. On that occasion he'd tapped her on the shoulder to 'wake' her and she'd nearly jumped a foot into the air. All the other times she'd come back to reality as her neck muscles snapped her head up as it was drooping.

She considered herself lucky that her episodes of what she found out was called *microsleep* only lasted a minute or so. She'd read about one man who had episodes that lasted up to ten minutes each time. He'd been an airline pilot too. The only reason he even knew he had a problem was due to a near-miss one flight when his co-pilot noticed a flashing light on the cockpit console and had to deal with it himself as he couldn't 'wake' his colleague. Needless to say, his employment with that particular airline didn't last very much longer.

Ariadne stifled a yawn just as Eddie looked away from the screen and did one of his make-eye-contact-with-the-troops manoeuvres. She nodded vigorously and brought her hand up to her mouth in a futile bid to hide the grimace that now replaced her usually pretty face. He quickly looked away, but she knew he'd seen and had stored it in his bank for later. She was on his list now. Not that he would confront her, he was strictly passive aggressive, but he wouldn't forget. In some exchange or another he'd mention it. The thought made her feel even more tired.

She realised he was speaking.

"-questions at all?"

He swept the room with his gaze, each person lowering their heads or looking away in an inverse Mexican wave. This was the usual ritual. He'd finish whatever nonsense he felt the need to say, ask if there were any questions, make eye contact with everyone until they felt uncomfortable, and then they'd all file out back to their jobs, leaving him to sit and congratulate himself thoroughly. Not that Ariadne wanted to even think about what that might consist of. She was having enough nightmares recently.

Ariadne felt her phone begin to vibrate just as Eddie's gaze met hers again. She smiled, hoping that nobody else could hear the nest of enraged hornets in her pocket.

He finished scanning the room and told them they could leave in his usual way, the phrase "Be safe out there" and a hearty chuckle that nobody ever shared with him. Except the people sitting at the front. Anthony nearly slapped his thigh.

Ariadne rushed to the door and grabbed her phone. The number was withheld. She felt that slight apprehension people get whenever a 'withheld number' comes up, but felt something more too. She lifted the phone up to her ear as if it might bite.

"Hello"

"See? Six rings. I told you!"

She exhaled deeply on hearing her mum's voice, and wondered why she had reacted so dramatically to a withheld telephone number. She attributed it to lack of sleep. That was becoming quite the explanation for everything recently.

"Yes…Sorry mum, I was in a meeting"

She shuffled away from the doorway of the glass room.

"So what happened last night? It didn't happen twice again, did it?"

In a second she was back in the dream again. She saw herself crushed against the glass, almost physically feeling the agony of the car slamming into her all over again.

"No mum. It was the same as usual. Just once"

"Oh Ari... You're not just saying that so I don't worry are you?"

"No mum. Really. It was the same"

Ariadne smiled greetings at colleagues as they filed out of the meeting room.

"Alright. Well I was just calling to see if you're ok, sweetheart"

"I'm fine, mum. Don't worry"

She suddenly remembered something from the dream.

"Actually, mum? Did we have a dog when I was little?"

There was a pause on the line.

"Mum?"

"Yes? No, I mean. No, we didn't have a dog. What makes you... Why do you ask?"

"It was just something in the dream. I was talking to a man and he said I killed his dog. He was cooking food on a grill and wearing a chef's outfit... Never mind, it's silly"

"It sounds silly"

Her mum's voice was curt now, as if slightly annoyed.

"Are you ok mum?"

"Of course. Yes"

"How about Dad? Has something happened to Dad?"

"He's fine, sweetheart. Look, there's someone at the door so I should go really. We can speak later though ok sweetheart?"

"Um...ok. Well thanks for calling me to see if I'm alri-"

"You too sweetheart. Bye"

Ariadne heard the click of the receiver. She stood for a moment, running the conversation through her mind again.

Her mum had sounded strange after she'd

mentioned the dog. Over the past two weeks, she'd told her mum about decapitations and stabbings, shootings and car crashes, and she'd never once reacted like that. But as soon as she mentioned a dog…

Or was it the grill she'd mentioned first? She couldn't remember, but her mum had definitely seemed stra-

She felt the vibrating buzz of the phone in her hand. She looked at the screen and saw 'withheld' again. She answered the call.

"What was that all about, mum?!"

"Sorry?"

It was a man's voice, although she couldn't quite place it. A sudden panic overtook her.

"Dad?"

She heard a throaty laugh from the other end.

"No, Mrs Perasmenos, although I'm glad you feel we're that close!"

She smiled in spite of herself.

"Doctor Illari?"

"Yes, although 'Dad' would be fine too if you prefer"

"Sorry, the number was withheld and I was just talking to my mum, so I thought it was her"

"No need to explain, it's perfectly fine. I'm just calling about the recording. I listened to some of it and have to say I am disappointed with myself"

"Disappointed? Why would you be disappointed?"

"Well, I pride myself on asking as many questions as possible of my patients and building up a picture of their circumstances, but I'm afraid I must not have asked you the obvious question as to whether or not you're married. It won't necessarily complicate things, in fact it may be helpful to come with your husband to the next session too"

"Sorry Doctor, my husband? "

There was a slight pause on the line.

"Oh… I may have been rather presumptuous there. Is 'partner' the accepted vernacular now? I can never tell!"

Eddie walked out of the meeting room, the projector squeezed under his arm. He looked at Ariadne to ensure that she knew he'd seen her on the phone in the office. She turned her back to him in order to focus. He could give her detention later.

"No, wait. Sorry Doctor, I don't have a husband. I don't live with anyone. It's just me and my cat, Harry. You did ask me if I was married the other day, I'm sure of it. But I'm not"

There was a longer pause this time. Ariadne was the one to break the silence.

"Doctor Illari?"

"Forgive me, Mrs – I mean, Ms - Perasmenos. I'm having some difficulty with this. I was listening to the recording and you were indeed talking in your sleep last night. But... well, if you live alone, and were alone last night, then who was the man answering you?"

The floor seemed to suck Ariadne downwards. She would later swear that not only had a trapdoor been opened, but that monstrous hands had gripped her feet and jerked her violently down toward the abyss.

She vaguely heard somebody call her name, and felt the vibrations of footsteps rushing across the hard carpet of the office. She didn't feel it when her limp body slammed against the floor, but somewhere in her soul she felt one thing.

He was grinning.

Seven

The disembodied voice crackled through the speaker in the small office.

"- told me the name of your dog either"

To Ariadne, it had felt like a week since she had fainted. The smell of decongestant ointment that somebody had used to try to wake her still stuck in her nostrils. She'd actually attracted quite a crowd. Anthony had been the first to rush over. The only action he could think of taking was to go and get her a cup of water. He ran back with it just in time to see one of the first aiders lifting Ariadne's legs to try and increase the flow of blood to her brain. He hadn't thought of doing that, although even if he had, he doubted he would have actually grabbed and lifted her legs. In some odd way, it would've been improper. As with most friendships, the boundaries may not have been particularly logical, but they were concrete.

Ariadne had come around as one colleague held her legs in the air, and another had apparently decided to try to ram a pot of decongestant up her nose. For a confused minute, she half expected to hear the roar of an engine as the shadow man raced towards her. The mix of adrenalin that this caused, as well as the memory of the conversation with the doctor, overwhelmed her. Fear shot through her, and then a slower but deeper feeling of exhaustion flooded her body. Her reserves empty, she had begun to weep.

Now she sat with Doctor Illari in his office, listening to the tape and trying desperately to explain away what she was hearing. Anthony sat in the corner of the room, having taken the afternoon off work to look after her. Up until the underground station, he'd still been holding the cup of water, which he then gave to a bemused – but, he hoped, grateful – homeless man.

"Maybe it's a recording of a conversation between other people that your machine picked up, Doctor. It might not be me speaking at all. It's a whisper, it could be anyone really"

Her sore eyes pleaded with him to agree. He leaned forward in his chair, lowering his voice.

"I have to say Ms Perasmenos that I don't think that is a possibility. The voice sounds very much like you and the words spoken are the same as what you told me about your conversation with that man, the Chef"

Her brow tightened even further at the mention of the Chef. She had listened to the recording once all the way through, controlling the urge to vomit as she heard the gravel-voice of a stranger in her bedroom. The voice was almost a whisper, but the Texan accent was unmistakable.

"But don't people hear things in their sleep and turn them into dreams? They do, don't they? You said it yourself. So maybe I heard something from outside my bedroom – maybe there are American people in my street and they were shouting outside and I was answering them"

"The device was on your bed", he said kindly, "the voice of the other person sounds like it is coming from your room. There's no echo and it doesn't appear to be a loud voice from afar. It's as if…"

The doctor squirmed uncomfortably in his chair, the first time Ariadne had seen him not appearing totally in control.

"As if what, Doctor?"

"Forgive me for saying this, but it's as if he's lying beside you"

Ariadne felt her stomach contract, the twisting and knotting becoming almost unbearable. At the same time a fierce burning sensation flashed across the back of her neck. The recording was playing on a loop in the doctor's office, and was now the only noise in the room. She heard herself talking, and a man answer. In between there were long periods of the sound of her breathing, sometimes shallow, sometimes in stuttered breaths.

At the end, her screams.

The doctor had tried switching it off a number of times, but she'd insisted he keep playing it.

She wanted to listen to it to pinpoint exactly why it couldn't be true. She wanted to be able to say it wasn't her voice at all and the doctor must have mixed up the recording device with another, or that she had left the television on, or there was a fight outside and people were shouting and the device picked up those things instead. She wanted to listen to it until she could find something that would prove it wasn't true.

She barely allowed herself to accept the possibility that it might be.

Yet here she was, hearing herself saying the words she spoke in her dream, and hearing another person – a man – seemingly in her bedroom and responding with the very words of the Chef. In his accent no less.

She began to feel the oxygen in the room being sucked out.

"What am I going to do? There was nobody in my room! It must be... could it be a ghost?"

The word felt ridiculous in her head, even more so when she said them aloud.

"I'm afraid that is beyond my area of expertise Ms Perasmenos. I believe that you were alone when you fell asleep last night and when you woke up this morning. But from what I've heard and am hearing at this precise moment, there was someone speaking to you last night"

As suddenly as it came upon her, the panic subsided. She was surprised to notice that somewhere in her mind she'd rather be haunted than have a strange man in her room. If it was a ghost then it was part of the world belonging to the dream – an unreal world full of smoke and mirrors but no actual substance. She'd died a thousand times in her dreams and then woken up. Whatever this was, it wasn't *real*. The Chef also wasn't the shadow man, he had warned her about him in fact, so in a way he was protecting her.

This was good, she was thinking more clearly. Given the situation, that is.

She continued analysing and scrutinising. Where did the voice come from? Even if it was some 'real' manifestation of what had so far only existed in her dreams, that didn't explain where it had come from. It certainly didn't come out of her head and just appear on the recording device.

It couldn't be the television. She hadn't listened to the radio or television that night – she never did - and her walls may have been thin but not enough to actually hear clear speech as she'd heard on the recording. Maybe it was an old recording device then, and her voice was mixing with the last person's.

Her thoughts raced now, hunting for an answer.

Why wouldn't the doctor recognise the voice if it was someone who had been previously recorded on that device? Also, she didn't actually play anything from the device, so how would the speech have got from it into her bedroom , then into her dream and then onto the recording? It would be possible only if there was a record and play function that worked simultaneously, but there wasn't. And even if there was, that would be some coincidence.

Although surely that was more realistic than dreams coming true or ghosts visiting her in the night?

She ran through what she did before going to bed last night and her routine this morning. She remembered being late for work, and –

"Harry!"

The doctor jumped slightly at this outburst, having been silently studying Ariadne for any sign of distress.

"The cat?", Anthony asked.

"Yes, Harry. When I woke up he looked guilty or something. He definitely wasn't himself. I saw that he'd gone to the toilet in the room, which he never does, and I thought he was scared because I was panicked. But maybe he was scared because of the voice"

Doctor Illari sat and listened. When he spoke, he seemed to be trying to make his voice as gentle as possible.

"But what does that prove Ms Perasmenos? We know there was a voice, we can hear it"

"Yes, but it means it must have been loud enough to scare him. If it was a whisper why would he be so scared? Why would he go to the toilet on the floor? He must have been terrified. So it must have been a loud voice"

"But, forgive me, I don't see what that would show"

"It means the voice could have come from outside or somewhere else. So it could've been my neighbour's television or someone's radio or people outside. It could be! You have to admit, it might be a possibility"

Almost on cue, the Chef's voice came through the speaker again. The thick accent whispered huskily, as though from one lover to another.

Doctor Illari slowly nodded.

"It could be, Ms Perasmenos. I must be honest, I'm no expert on this subject and am only giving my personal opinion on what I've heard. I may well be wrong. I do feel that this voice is a whisper, and it sounds as though it is at the same volume as your voice, which would imply to me that...the person was as close to the microphone as you. But I may be wrong"

He smiled kindly at her. Something about his smile reminded her of the pebble picture outside his office, as though both had been designed in some way, created to look reassuring.

His next words were not as well received as his smile.

"Have you considered the possibility Ms Perasmenos, that the other voice on the recording might be yours"

Ariadne's face hardened.

"I'm not crazy, Doctor", she spat, more harshly than she had intended, "My voice is completely different, I don't have the same accent, and I'm not a man!"

She stood and turned to Anthony for reassurance, but he only smiled weakly. She read something in his eyes.

"You think I'm crazy too?"

"No! Ari, of course not. But people talk in accents all the time. What about all those people on TV who do impressions? They change their voices completely"

The hurt in Ariadne's eyes pierced Anthony.

"So you think I'm mad as well? When was the last time you heard me talk in an accent? Yes, there are people on TV that do that but I'm not one of them!"

The doctor spoke again.

"Ms Perasmenos, I'm very sorry. My intent was not to offend you, but the human mind is capable of a number of things. Some people for instance have a stroke or a serious illness, and later find that their accents have changed considerably. I was not in any way implying you were 'mad' at all, but this is a very strange situation, so we must consider all possibilities"

Ariadne fixed the doctor with a glare.

"That voice, *that* voice", she pointed vaguely towards the ceiling, "is not mine. I don't know who it belongs to, but it is not mine."

The doctor nodded gently. "Alright, Ms Perasmenos, alright"

She sat down and nobody spoke for a while.

Ariadne felt guilty, and horrified. What if they were right? Of course it could've been her voice, with the right training anybody can sound like anybody else. Another thought burst through as if in reply – she hadn't *been* trained, that was the difference. It can't have been her.

She realised that she'd snapped at the doctor and her friend not out of actual offence but out of fear. If that was her voice on the tape…what was *happening* to her?

She looked from the doctor to Anthony, both men standing awkwardly as though scared to speak to her again.

"I'm sorry", she began, "this is just.. it's odd that's

all. I'm very tired and... I'm sorry"

Anthony visibly relaxed, and was unable to stop himself exhaling loudly.

Ariadne turned to face the doctor.

"Will you keep listening to the recording?"

"Yes, I will. If I get any clues as to why you are not sleeping or what the words might mean then I'll let you know as soon as I can. In the meantime, I have made you a copy. I think you should take it, even if you don't intend listening to it. You may decide later today that you want somebody else to give their opinion on it, and it would be a shame to have to come back all this way in order to do so"

He walked to his desk and picked up a compact disc in a clear plastic wallet.

Ariadne hesitated for a second before taking the disc, as though accepting it was in some way bringing it closer to reality. She fought hard against the instinct to push it away, and after taking it from the doctor quickly buried it in her bag.

"It will be alright, Ms Perasmenos. I promise you"

She smiled at him, and remembered how, what seemed like a lifetime ago, Anthony had said the very same thing.

They both sounded as unconvincing as each other.

Eight

London Underground trains are surprisingly peaceful when they're empty. Walking down from the bustling streets above and stepping into your own personal quiet place. For a few short minutes, you could be the only person in London.

There was nobody else in the carriage when Ariadne and Anthony stepped on. The only sounds were the rumble of the train itself, and the various beeps and hisses as the doors opened and closed.

As they sat in silence, Anthony suddenly realised that they hadn't said a word to each other since leaving the clinic. Ariadne sat with her eyes fixed on the window of the underground train. Anthony wondered what she was looking at in the blackness beyond, what horrors she was seeing projected onto that dark screen.

Whatever it was, he felt it couldn't be anything good.

"So", he began, "what did you think about Eddie's presentation this morning? Are we all doomed or what?"

Ariadne tried to smile, although her gaze did not move from the window.

"I liked his slides", she said laconically.

Anthony laughed too hard.

"Yeah! I do think some of the changes might be good, but we'll just have to see. They like doing things without thinking them through, don't they?"

"Mmm"

Ariadne's eyes were still fixed on some point, some horror, seemingly located in the wall of the tunnel on the other side of the window.

The silence returned like a third presence in the carriage.

"You know, I remember another placed I worked", Anthony continued, "I told you about it, the bank. We had this manager who was this real idiot and kept trying to be friends with the staff. Then he'd realise that he was getting too friendly so he'd be a right bastard to us. I reckon Eddie's like that"

Ariadne didn't respond.

"Ari"

Still no response. Anthony wondered whether she was shell-shocked. He remembered watching a television programme about soldiers and their thousand yard stares. He'd seen quite a few programmes like that on recommendation from a therapist last year. He thought maybe Ari was doing what the soldiers had been doing – replaying all the mutilations and trauma and death, seeing them all over again in their minds on an endless loop. The pain, the murders, the blood.

Now the intrusion into her real life with that voice.

Anthony found his muscles tensing at the thought of any man in Ariadne's bedroom, although couldn't work out if it was a protective feeling, or a jealous one.

He looked at Ariadne's reflection in the black window in front of them, and saw his friend's face. She did look shell-shocked, she looked like less like a soldier though and more like pictures he'd seen of civilians in war torn countries.

Surprising both of them, he put his hand on her shoulder.

"Are you ok, Ari?"

She seemed to stir from her reverie, her eyes refocusing. Tiredness seemed to actually make her eyes move slower than usual, as though they had decided it was too much effort. Or that they weren't in any rush to see what might be next.

She nodded and smiled appreciatively.

"I'm ok, Jackson. Thanks for coming with me"

"It's fine. You'd do the same for me. You pretty much have done!"

She shifted and leaned her head against his shoulder,

her gaze returning to the window.

In that moment he felt more than protective, he wanted to hold and look after her, no matter who – or what – was approaching. The emotions made him uneasy – he'd already been feeling awkward about going to her house because it might look like he was taking advantage. Now he'd be walking in there knowing that he did want to be more than friends.

Amidst the uncertainty, he knew one thing – he wasn't going to let anybody hurt Ariadne while he was around.

***

Anthony insisted on going into the house first. It was an odd scene, him unlocking the door and rushing into the living space as Ariadne had to quickly step behind him and enter the number into the alarm panel on the wall.

A hero with no alarm code. Just like in the fairytales.

The first thing he noticed was the cat, curled up on the sofa like a fluffy pillow.

"Hey! So this is the famous Harry! I've seen photos of you, my friend"

Harry looked up from his nap, blinking and looking at Ariadne as though wondering who the idiot making all the noise was. Which happened to be *exactly* what he was wondering.

Anthony walked over and stroked him from the top of his head to the end of his tail. Harry gave a contented purr and immediately rubbed his face on Anthony's fingers. Apparently Anthony was no longer an idiot.

"He likes you", Ariadne said, dropping her jacket over the back of one of the dining room chairs. The downstairs area of her house consisted of a small through lounge – living room and dining room - which led to the kitchen at the back. There was also a door off the dining room which led to the stairs. She normally kept that shut on account of Harry. She realised she could hear the cat purring in the living room now, even though she was essentially at the other end of the room.

She felt much more relaxed now that she was home. For a moment she thought it was because she felt safe here, but soon realised it was something else.

This is where the fight would be.

All the other challenges were the preparation to fight, and feeling exhausted from the adrenalin, and anticipating nightmares, and suffering the effects of them. Here, she was in the arena. It was the only place where the adrenalin might actually help and some resolution might be found.

Anthony stood abruptly, and she looked over at him.

"I better check upstairs, Ari"

"I'm sure it's ok, Jackson"

"I'm sure it's all fine as well, but I'd prefer to take a peek just to make sure"

He inwardly cringed at his words, not wanting it to appear as though he was trying to snoop around or, even worse, that he would get some kind of thrill from seeing her bedroom.

"I suppose it's not a bad idea, although you might want to reconsider your use of the word 'peek' in public"

She smiled, and Anthony felt his cheeks get hot.

"I'll come upstairs too", she continued, "and we can look together. I wouldn't want anything to happen to my bodyguard"

He forced a laugh, which sounded fake to both of them. He hoped she didn't feel that he was being pushy, although she wasn't really giving any indication of that. But then, maybe she was feeling like that and just hiding her emotions from him, she'd done that before hadn't she? Like that time when she was having problems at work and didn't tell him and he didn't know until much later when she decided to tell him but he hadn't realised at the time and he felt bad about it for ages?

His whole face felt hot all of a sudden. He thought it might not be such a good idea to go upstairs after all.

"I'm sure it's fine Ari, like you said. Maybe I shouldn't come upstairs. It feels a bit…"

Ariadne looked at him, trying to read his face.

"Are you ok, Jackson? I was only joking about the 'peeking' thing"

"Yeah, I just… We're in your house, and it's your *bedroom* and everything…"

Ariadne laughed.

"It's fine Jackson! Come on, I'll keep my hands to myself, honestly"

She opened the door leading to the stairs and gestured for him to follow. He walked up the narrow stairs, craning his neck to see if there was anybody standing on the landing, or a face at the window. Anything abnormal. Halfway up the stairs he felt a chill race down his spine. It was as if ice water had been dropped from a great height, freezing into daggers on the way down. The sensation was so potent that he reached around and felt himself to check whether something had actually leaked onto him from somewhere.

Ariadne got to the top and burst into the bathroom, then checked the two bedrooms. Anthony followed closely behind her, feeling as though he should really take the lead as the man, but then thinking it wouldn't be right to barge into her bedroom. He also wondered where the line was between checking everything was ok, and plain old looking like a pervert.

He thought about how much more relaxed being in this house made Ariadne, and how much more awkward it made him.

"See?" she said as they stood on the landing, "Nothing. Shall I make tea?"

Something in her face was more than relieved, and

in an instant Anthony could tell that she was affected much more deeply than she'd been acting. She was less scared than she had been earlier, but he knew that she still probably felt much worse than she was appearing. She was craving normality, as if by acting fine then everything would indeed be ok.

In the absence of knowing how else to proceed, he decided to go along with the pretence that this was just another day.

"Tea would be nice actually. I've been waiting for you to ask. To be honest I've been quite offended that you haven't yet. Even the cat offered me its face"

"Just be glad that's all the cat offered you…", she said as she led him back downstairs.

They passed the same point on the stairs where Anthony had felt something cold slither down his back. There was no ice water this time, but he did feel a slight breathlessness, as if something had knocked him lightly on the back. Not too hard, but just enough for him to notice it. A gentle pat on the back from a friend.

Or, he thought, a gentle warning from an enemy.

He ignored the thought and started thinking maybe he needed to get some more sleep too.

"Sorry it's a bit of a mess", Ariadne said as they got back to the lounge, "You sit down and I'll make tea. I don't need to ask how you like it, do I?"

Anthony laughed and shook his head, stopping himself from referencing the innuendo in her question. As a friend, it would be harmless. But… what was he now exactly? Nothing had changed for Ariadne, he thought, but for him things felt different. Whatever role he now held, he knew that innuendo would somehow be inappropriate.

He sat on the sofa and looked across at the photos on the mantelpiece.

"You've got a lot of baby pictures here, Ari! They're not yours are they?!"

She walked back into the lounge as the kettle began

boiling, stifling a yawn as she answered.

"Yeah, I've just been keeping it under wraps. Of course they're not mine! They're all the nieces and nephews I've told you about. The one on the end is Dora. I've definitely told you about her!"

"No!", he sprang up and took a closer look at the photograph, "she looks so innocent"

"She wasn't innocent that day"

"This is the one who snatches, yeah?"

"The one who snatches and then bites, yes", Ariadne said as she walked back towards the kitchen.

Anthony laughed. In the picture was possibly the cutest toddler he'd ever seen. She wore a yellow summer dress with a big yellow bow in her hair. She beamed in the way that only naïve children can, the dimples in her cheeks and her huge blue eyes adding to the 'perfect child' effect. She certainly didn't look the type to dig her nails into her little sister and rip downwards, then bite a chunk out of her arm.

Anthony put the picture back down and returned to the sofa.

Harry stirred and gave a stretch, looking curiously at Anthony then padding over to him and snuggling into his lap. Anthony stroked him, and soon realised the cat had fallen asleep. Apparently he'd gone from idiot to friend to big human pillow in under thirty minutes. Impressive, in a way.

In the kitchen, Ariadne opened the fridge door and remembered she didn't have any milk. This fact wouldn't have bothered her on an ordinary day, but this wasn't an ordinary day. She felt overwhelmingly helpless, and as though she'd failed in some fundamental way. She couldn't even buy enough food and drink for herself, how was she supposed to deal with everything else that was happening?

She began to weep, and quickly opened one of the cupboard doors to shield her face.

This wasn't fair, she thought. She was a good

person, why was this happening to her?

She swiped at her eyes with the backs of her hands, trying to get herself under control. She thought of her mum's offer to go and stay. Maybe she should, just for a short while. At the very least it'd give her a break from Eddie and his bloody slides.

She allowed herself a slight chuckle at that, and tried to will herself to be happier. She focused on slowing her breathing and fought to stop her hands shaking. She felt like a mess, and thought she probably looked like one too.

She needed to get back in control. There was no milk, so what?

"Jackson", she called out from behind the cupboard door, "there's no milk. Is that ok?"

No response.

"Jackson?"

Still no reply.

Adrenalin flooded her body, and she froze. It wasn't possible that *he* was here, was it? Was she going to peek her head out from behind the door and see Jackson, crushed by a car against the fireplace, the shadow man sitting in the drivers' seat and grinning that horrific smile? If a voice from a dream could appear in reality, maybe *he* could too.

Her breathing began to get shallow again and the fear threatened to take hold completely. Forcing herself to confront whatever evil was in her house, in one movement she turned to the living room, slammed the cupboard door and shouted "Jackson!"

Anthony jumped, the cat giving a pitiful meow as he was jolted awake.

Anthony moved the cat as quickly but as gently as he could — although not carefully enough for Harry, who gave an angry hiss - and rushed over to Ariadne.

"What is it? Are you ok?"

Ariadne looked at him quizzically, her face a heart-breaking mask of fear.

"I called you about the milk, and you... I thought..."

"What?"

He looked into her eyes and could only imagine what she must have seen in her mind when he didn't answer.

"Ari, its fine. I was keeping my voice low because the cat was asleep on me. I didn't want to wake him. I answered you both times, it's fine about the milk"

Ariadne's shoulders slumped.

"Sorry", he continued, "I didn't mean to scare you"

"No", she said, defeated, "don't apologise. It's me, Jackson. I think I might be more spooked than I realised. I just feel like if I act ok, then maybe..."

The tears pricked her eyes. Anthony pulled her to him and hugged her tight, willing her to feel better, to not be so scared.

She gave her tears free reign now, crying on her friend's shoulder and holding on for dear life.

"Shhh", he comforted, "Ari, it's all going to be ok. Alright? I'm not going to let anything happen to you"

"It's all just a mess. What am I going to do?"

"We'll work it all out Ari. It's ok. This time last year I would've said there was no light at the end of the tunnel for me, but there was. I'm better now. And a lot of that is because of you. We'll get through this together Ari"

For a moment he questioned his motives for hugging her. He continued in the embrace though, she was his friend and she needed comfort, it wasn't her fault he had some kind of schoolboy crush.

She looked up at him.

"Stay. Please"

He looked at her tear-streaked face, her cheeks wet and red.

"I will", he said softly, restraining any thoughts that he was taking advantage or that he should go home. What if something *did* happen and he wasn't here? Even if stayed because he wanted to spend more time with her, what difference did that make, really? It's not like he was going to take the opportunity to try and seduce her. She needed him, and he needed her. That's all that mattered.

"I will", he repeated.

"Thank you Jackson", she said, her voice muffled by his shirt.

Anthony allowed himself to wonder whether this might be the point where their lives change, where he becomes the hero and Ariadne starts to see him as he now saw her. After she starts feeling better about things, maybe they could be together as a couple. He pushed the thoughts out of his mind. She needed a friend, that's all. He was being immature. Ariadne feeling better was the most important thing.

He looked over her shoulder, Harry was either staring at him jealously or hungrily, he couldn't tell which.

He squeezed harder, willing her to feel better. He allowed that rogue thought to return – this might be the decision that changes both our lives.

And that's exactly what it was going to do.

Nine

Mum would be furious if she could see me now, thought Ariadne as she sat on the sofa, Harry on her lap and a cup of tea in her hand. She could almost hear her mum's protests now. The nice young gentleman she'd brought home – with the stable job and the nice hair – stood in her kitchen and cooked dinner, while she sat around like Lady Muck.

In her defence, she had offered to help, although she'd stopped feeling guilty after the fifth "Are you sure?". At that point, Anthony had brought her a cup of tea and told her to rest while he cooked dinner.

He was a good man, she thought, as she heard the clattering of pans from the kitchen. It felt strange to think of him as a man. Not that she'd normally thought of him as a woman or anything, but considering him as a man had certain connotations. She wasn't sure what had changed, but he was definitely no longer just a colleague. Now, she supposed, he was the protector. That or, at the very least, the cook.

The dream-chef with the sausage fingers burst into her mind, ruining the moment of peace she'd been enjoying.

She froze for a second as the Chef's words intruded into her home – into her.

You killed my dog... You killed him...

The cat looked up at Ariadne, apparently wondering why the stroking machine had stopped. The movement of his head jerked Ariadne out of her troubling thoughts. She smiled at him and continued gently smoothing his fur with her palm. He lay his head back down, purring contentedly now that the world was right again.

Anthony walked into the room, carrying two plates and the face of a man who has seen terrible things in the line of duty.

"I hope its ok. It should be, I make it enough for

myself"

She gently moved Harry and began to stand.

"No, don't get up. Here", he said, handing the plate to Ariadne.

He'd made pasta with some kind of sauce. Ariadne knew she'd had a tin of chopped tomatoes and some garlic somewhere. There was also some grated cheese in the fridge and it looked like he'd put that on top too.

"It looks amazing, Jackson. I'm impressed"

"I bet you say that to all the guys…" He sat next to her on the sofa and balanced his plate on his lap.

"Only the ones that manage to make a meal out of an empty kitchen. Do you mind if I put the television on while we eat?"

"Of course not, it's your house Ari. Eat naked if you like!"

'Awkward' wasn't the word for the silence that followed.

After what felt to Anthony like a year of nobody talking. Ariadne eventually broke the silence with a burst of laughter.

"Sorry Ari, it was a –"

"No, no! Don't explain! Don't worry, Jackson I'm not offended or anything. It was funny!"

Anthony looked mortified.

"Really, it's ok Jackson. Honestly! It was a joke, I'm not worried, you shouldn't be either"

He smiled sheepishly.

"Ok", he said, wondering what on earth was wrong with him. He was acting like a twelve year old who'd just discovered girls. He needed to get a grip, otherwise this was going to be a long, awkward night for both of them.

They continued eating.

He contemplated asking her if she was sure she wanted him to stay, but decided against it. It'd just make things more awkward, if that was even possible.

He ran through funny lines in his mind – he could

tell her he didn't want to see her naked anyway, or go the other way and say it was a shame she *wouldn't* be eating naked.

Mercifully, Ariadne switched on the television, immediately changing the focus from his faux pas to the melodrama of some soap opera or another.

As far as Anthony could make out, the blonde woman had just found out her husband was having an affair with another blonde woman, who may have been her twin. She was dressed the same but still looked a bit different. Anthony wondered whether they were supposed to be twins in the programme and the producers just couldn't find two actual twins to use.

At the same time, Ariadne wondered about her friend. The naked comment was odd, but wasn't everything today? She tried to think of something else, but quickly realised that she'd rather think about the possibility that her friend may want more than just friendship, rather than the possibility a man was in her house last night.

Deep down, she didn't truly believe anybody had been in her home, and still clung to the hope that the voice recorder had just picked up the noise of a TV or radio or something. After her performance in the doctor's office, she was also ashamed to admit that she'd begun hoping it had been her voice on the tape answering her own questions. Yes it was unlikely, but was it really more unlikely than a man standing in her room and having a conversation with her as she slept, and then disappearing without harming her, or taking anything, or *leaving* anything?

Her focus shifted from the television to Anthony, eating silently next to her, his attention apparently rapt on the ensuing drama onscreen. She felt a deep gratitude that he was here, and that she didn't have to face this evening alone.

He noticed her staring and turned to her.

"Are you ok?", he asked.

"Yes", she said, "it's really nice Jackson, the food I

mean. Thanks"

He smiled and turned back to the television.

Ariadne hoped she'd feel this comforted by his presence later on if the dreams returned.

When they returned.

***

They'd had a nice evening, much to Ariadne's surprise. Not that she had thought that Anthony would be bad company, she knew she enjoyed spending time with him, but she did think that there might have been a cloud hanging over the evening. There was some awkwardness at the start – quite a lot in fact - but they'd ended up relaxing and having a pretty good time. The two glasses of wine probably contributed, she thought, but the company definitely helped. Even when they weren't actually talking to each other, she appreciated him just being there.

Anthony didn't have any nightwear, but said it didn't matter. He'd insisted it was fine as long as the temperature didn't plummet suddenly overnight. As he spoke, Ariadne heard her mum's voice booming inside her head, scolding her for not being more prepared for houseguests. Although she knew that if she did keep men's nightclothes at her house, her mum would've been the first to begin a lecture on not appearing too 'available'.

After all that, when the time came to say goodnight, it wasn't too bad at all. She'd been obsessing about what to say, and whether to hug him or kiss him on the cheek, or whether none of it would be appropriate. At one low point she even contemplated a handshake.

He'd helped her lock up the house and sort out Harry, then they'd both walked upstairs. She had thanked him for everything on the landing, he leaned in and gave a quick hug, told her it would be ok and to call if she needed anything. Then he disappeared into the spare room, and closed the door behind him. That was it.

Ariadne realised that she'd spent around four hours of the evening worrying about what amounted to roughly three minutes. Although obsessively worrying was something she'd been doing a lot recently.

As she put on her nightclothes, she thought of Doctor Illari and his questions about her routine. She suddenly felt exposed again, but quickly shook it off.

She got the feeling that she had more to worry about than the doctor knowing what she wore to bed.

Her stomach in knots – and any thoughts of relaxation now a distant memory - she got into bed and switched off the light.

She stepped into the arena.

Ten

She feels a weight on her chest. Not uncomfortable, but pressure where it shouldn't be.

It's just Harry, she tells herself.

But she knows it's not.

The weight increases slightly, causing her to stir and moan. Then something slowly slides over and around her neck. A small snake lightly coiling itself around her throat.

She keeps her eyes closed, telling herself that it's just Harry on her chest, that she has just got tangled in the covers. Then he – because it must be him – tenses with the strength of a vice, mercilessly squeezing her throat.

Her eyes open, wide and panicked, and he is sitting on top of her. His knees are pinning her arms down at her sides, his muscular hands still gripping her throat.

As if a dam has been broken in her glands, adrenalin powerfully floods her body. The fight or flight response is useless now. She can do neither.

She tries to kick out from under him but finds her legs will not move either. She swivels her eyes down to her feet, looking through the shadow creature on top of her and into a pair of cold, unfeeling eyes.

An old hag stands at the foot of her bed. Her face gaunt, her stare filled with malice. Not a shadow person but a real being, staring at her and grinning a horrific smile.

His horrific smile.

The woman's hands are pinning down Ariadne's legs, the grip tighter and stronger than that of the shadow man, whose own grip threatens to crush her throat.

His grip eases off slightly now, allowing the hag to have her turn.

The realisation that she is paralysed causes a claustrophobic panic to set in to Ariadne, her skin feeling swollen and tight, her mind not able to focus.

Drifting in and out of consciousness, a single

thought recurs through the haze - Anthony is here.

She tries to scream but her vocal chords are as useless as her legs. The only part of her that isn't paralysed is her eyes, as if he wants her to watch the torture and miss nothing. She wonders about her lungs, and whether he's paralysed them too. She can barely breathe. Is that because he is crushing her chest and throat, or because her lungs are slowly being paralysed?

She feels a strange sense of being drowned even though she is not in water.

The claustrophobia increases now too, although every time she feels as though she might pass out he eases off her and allows another shallow breath. Keeping her barely alive – a perverse life-support.

The shadow man slowly leans forward so that his face – or the approximation of it that he possesses – is millimetres from hers. His hands still wrapped around her throat like a hunter toying with his prey, deciding whether to snap its neck or let it live.

The form of his shadow warps and contracts and the haze begins to appear more tangible. Somehow more real, more dense.

In a horrific instant she sees the horror that should be his face. A decayed, horrific visage, seemingly constructed of molten tar. The sclera of the eyes are rotten, no longer white but instead a sick yellow-brown colour. The pupils are still sharp, and focused solely on Ariadne. A black liquid seeps from the back of his head, running down his cheeks and forehead and onto her skin. She feels the intense heat of the liquid, burning her flesh and emitting a sizzling sound instantly reminiscent of the Chef's grill.

The black eclipse of her fear now reaches totality. She tries to scream, the veins in her neck bulging as she strains to make a sound. A hoarse squeak comes out, nothing more.

Behind the sickening fluid and decomposed muscle that is his face, she knows he is grinning. At the same time she hears a cackle from behind him and knows it is from the old woman whose pincer-like grip is still locking her feet to the bed.

The shadow man rises up suddenly and roars with laughter, the booming noise ricocheting around and shaking the small room. Ariadne looks with horror at his dagger-like teeth, jagged and poised to rip flesh. Sensing her fear, he lurches forward violently, stopping short of her face, his breath hot on her cheeks. He holds himself above her with his mouth open and allows a purple-black saliva to drip from his mouth and onto her chin. She feels the thick hot liquid oozing down towards her neck, where his hands remain firmly in place.

A sudden surge of anger rises up inside her now, the panic giving way to a primal, determined instinct to survive. With nothing to lose she tries impotently to fight and kick as hard as she can. The shadow man and his hag laugh cruelly. In the same moment, they release their grips and the shadow man jumps back and stands at the foot of the bed next to the hag.

To her horror, Ariadne realises that she still can't move. The paralysis is total. Again, she tries to scream but her throat is blocked. She is barely breathing now and wonders how she can be so starved of oxygen and still be alive. Another surge of rage pulses through her, but does nothing.

She sees the two figures in the room clearly. The huge shadow form standing at the end of her bed, broad shouldered and muscled. Standing next to him, the short hag in torn, dirty clothes, wide-eyed and cackling. She wears a leather shawl around her neck, and Ariadne notices writing scrawled down the side of it on her left shoulder. The woman approaches slowly, creeping around the bed as if not wanting to wake anybody else. The room suddenly falls silent and Ariadne is in a vacuum again like in the last dream. The only sound is the shallow, sharp breaths of Ariadne herself.

As the woman gets closer Ariadne squints and tries to read the writing on the shawl. It looks like some kind of brand, and she wonders whether it is where the poor animal was marked before death. The hag reaches Ariadne and slowly runs her clawed hand across her neck and chest. Ariadne feels the slicing of her skin, and the warmth of the blood seeping from her wounds. She wants to scream from the searing pain but is unable to, in spite of how hard she tries.

Still, the only sound is Ariadne's breathing – even shallower now. The hag draws her hand along Ariadne's neck again, the sharp nails painfully catching and ripping her skin, drawing more blood. The shadow man grins, the black liquid dripping from his head and down his thick body.

The leather shawl hanging around the shoulders of the woman knocks into Ariadne's face. She instinctively tries to flinch and rear her head back but cannot move. The old woman looks down at the shawl and mockingly holds it in front of Ariadne's face. Her eyes focus on the leather and she reads the three short words – 'You killed him'. All at once she realises that the words are not branded on leather at all, but on a sheet of human skin.

This realisation, along with the pain, spurs Ariadne on to fight against the invisible bonds holding her down. She pushes against the force, whatever it is, and begins trying to scream again.

She feels a slight jerk in her hand and, as the control returns to her arm, realises she is winning. The shadow man and the hag simply stand at the foot of the bed, watching dispassionately. Not laughing now, not mocking, just observing. As though whatever the girl in front of them chooses to do is of no consequence.

Ariadne fights and struggles, trying to force a scream from her raw throat. She makes another hoarse noise, then a slightly louder one, then finally a scream breaks through. Totally and clearly.

"Jackson! Help! Jackson! Please!"

The figures slowly fade as she screams, and as they do the shadow man grins, as if satisfied with the work he and his partner have done.

***

Ariadne jerked awake and frantically kicked her legs in an attempt to push herself further up towards the headboard. She drew her knees up to her chest in a defensive gesture, grabbing at herself to check whether any part of her body was still paralysed. All the while, she continued screaming.

"Jackson, please! Help! No!"

Anthony burst into the room, awakened by Ariadne's horrific screaming.

He flicked on the light and looked frantically around the room, ready to protect his friend from whoever he might find. In any other context he would've looked comical wearing his boxer shorts, crumpled work shirt, and 'bed hair'. This wasn't funny in the least though, and the sight of a knife in his hand caused Ariadne to scream again.

"No!"

He saw where she was looking and dropped it.

"Ari! It's ok, it's ok"

He saw the blood on her chest and felt a new surge of adrenalin. Somebody had hurt her.

"Where is he?", he shouted, the panic manifesting itself as anger.

"I don't know"

The tears streamed down Ariadne's face.

He rushed over to her and took her in his arms. She had bled all over the bed

"You're ok, Ari", he said, "he's gone now. There's nobody here except me"

She flinched as his shoulder pressed against her wound. He gently let go, leaning back and looking at the cuts and blood.

"What happened?"

"She cut me"

"*She*? Who? I thought.."

"I don't know Jackson!"

He hugged her again, and felt an overwhelming sense of both duty and anger. He got up slowly so as not to bounce the bed too much and rushed to the other bedroom. He rifled through some things to find a box of tissues, or a cloth, or *something* to use but there was nothing there. He ran to the bathroom and wadded up some sheets of toilet roll, which he then ran under warm water.

He rushed back to the bedroom and began helping Ariadne to clean the cuts, all the time asking her what had happened, who had done this, was she ok.

Ariadne suddenly remembered something the doctor had said about her dressing gown, how dreams are the mind's way of making sense of things that are happening around us. His words returned to her, as clear as if he were in the room.

...a school of thought...our mind's way of making sense of external stimuli that are happening around us while we sleep...

At the time she'd thought it was interesting, but slightly ridiculous. Suddenly, it took on a new resonance, as her panicked mind tried to make sense of what was happening. How else could tonight be explained? The other night she hadn't actually been hurt, so maybe it was her imagination or things she'd thought about or watched before she slept. But tonight she had cuts and bruises. It was impossible that the people she dreamed about did this to her – how could they, they didn't even exist?! - which meant only one thing. She had been attacked *in reality*, her mind had just constructed it as an attack by the shadow man to make sense of it while she slept. She had been attacked, she had the cuts to prove it. Which meant...

She pushed Anthony away.

"Ari, what-"

"Get away!", she screamed, "No!"

She leapt back from the bed, grabbing the empty glass on her bedside table as an impromptu weapon. She held it in front of her as though ready at any point to smash it against the wall and plunge the shards into Anthony's chest.

"Ari, what do you- Surely you don't think that I had anything to—"

"No! Get away! There's nobody else here!"

Her mind flashed back to last year. Anthony had therapy for a while, didn't he? He'd been under stress and there'd been all that business with that man... How well did she know him *really*? He was a work acquaintance, and one who'd had a lot of psychological problems only a few months ago. He also knew she was vulnerable and that she'd probably blame anything that happened on the dreams.

His role in Ariadne's life changed yet again.

She rapidly looked around the room at anything else that could be used as a weapon. Her eyes settled on the knife that lay at Anthony's feet, and she realised she could never get to it first.

"No!", she screamed again, "please, Jackson!"

The tears ran down her face now, streams of fear and panic.

"I'm your friend Ari, it's me", he said desperately.

"Yes but who are you?!"

Anthony kicked the knife under the bed.

"Ari, I don't want the knife. See? I'd never hurt you Ari"

She was wailing now, grabbing her forehead with her free hand as though trying to keep the sanity in. The blood on her fingers smeared all over her brow.

"Ari, I swear... I was in the other room. I just came in to help you!"

"Why did you have the knife, Jackson? When did you sneak off and get that? You've got my blood all over you, when did that happen?!"

She was hysterical now, crying and shouting through

her raw throat.

That was when they heard the sirens.

Anthony stared at Ariadne. She looked like a scared, caged animal trying to escape. He felt an overwhelming sadness at what was happening to his friend.

Seconds later, they heard vehicles pulling up outside and loud banging from the front door. Anthony peeked out from behind the curtain.

"It's the police", he said to Ariadne, "Ari, please, you're not yourself. Please "

She held his gaze, and suddenly stood defiantly still, refusing to move. When she spoke there was steel in her voice, and an almost eerie calmness radiated from her as though something had been unplugged. She was a hornet's nest, unmoving on the outside, but humming with ferocious activity from within.

"Who did it Jackson? If not you, then who?"

His shoulders slumped as the bangs and shouts from the front door got louder.

"I'm going to go and let them in now Ari. I swear to you, I did not do anything. I just hope…"

He walked towards her but stopped when she visibly flinched.

"You know me, Ari. Please. I didn't do this"

"I don't know anything anymore!", she suddenly screamed, shocking both of them. "Go and get the police!"

He turned and walked downstairs to face whatever lay ahead. As he opened the door to the lounge the alarm gave a warning sound for three seconds and then erupted into a full, near-deafening blast. He panicked, and rushed over to the alarm panel by the front door, fumbling with the buttons as though the alarm code could be identified through guesswork and sheer determination.

It wasn't clear whether Ariadne reached the bottom of the stairs before the police knocked down the front door, but to Anthony it all seemed to happen at once.

The police burst in and saw the blood on his hands

and chest. They were on top of him in seconds. Ariadne, bleeding and bruised, stood silently at the bottom of the stairs, having staggered down them in a blur.

She wasn't angry anymore, she didn't feel anything. She stood in the centre of the hurricane, looking out dispassionately at what was unfolding. One of the officers rushed over to her and asked a question behind a haze of fog. She thought she felt herself shrug, or think about shrugging but never following through. She couldn't really. It didn't matter.

She thought she heard one of the strange men shouting about checking upstairs, which surprised her because she'd just come from there and she wondered why they would be checking there for her instead of downstairs where she was standing. She felt a strong but gentle grip on each arm as she was moved away from the doorway. Maybe she should tell them she's here so they wouldn't go upstairs. It was dangerous up there. That man had a knife.

One of the men was handcuffing someone, and placing what looked like a plastic bag over his hands. It seemed strange to her, but then, maybe she was dreaming again. She was doing that a lot recently, having bad dreams about bad people. She considered telling the men to check for the bad people, but realised that's probably what they meant when they said they were checking upstairs.

In a second the fog lifted and Ariadne was lucid again. Her body was flooded with adrenalin, the fear and panic overtaking any other emotion or feeling. She broke down at the horror she was witnessing and began to cry. The glass in her hand fell and smashed onto the floor, reminding her of the dream at the hotel.

Amidst the cacophony of the burglar alarm, the police, and her own heaving sobs, she realised she could hear only one thing.

He was laughing.

Eleven

Ethel sat in her chair. The television was on, but she wasn't watching. The volume was at zero.

Every so often she'd hear a car door shutting, or voices from people in the street outside. And she'd be terrified.

She was eighty-four years old, but on a good day knew she could give most sixty year olds a run for their money.

Today unfortunately wasn't a good day.

Up until eight years ago - when she'd stopped dyeing her hair - she probably could've passed for around sixty herself, albeit with a lot of make-up and in a room with very poor lighting. But the days when dyeing her hair could fool anybody were most definitely over. Not that she minded, it had always been a bit of a hassle and, as she often remarked to anybody within earshot "You're only as young as you feel".

Her hand trembling, she brought the delicate cup up to her lips and took a sip of the tea. It was cold, but she didn't notice.

She liked to keep active, taking a brisk walk around the block every morning without fail, even in bad weather. She'd pass neighbours and friends on the street and always gave a cheery greeting and a happy smile. She often stopped and chatted too. A person of the cynical persuasion might well have said that this was a good way for her to keep up with the neighbourhood gossip. Not that she went out and looked for things or people to gossip about, it was just a side effect of walking around every day, talking to the neighbours. A happy, satisfying side-effect.

She had nothing to say today.

She'd been woken by screams in the early hours of the morning, at first thinking it was a nightmare but then realising the sounds were coming from her neighbour's bedroom.

She always kept a phone by her bed with the police on speed dial, just in case of an emergency. The way that girl had been screaming over there – she could still hear it now – definitely made it qualify as one of those.

As she'd practiced a thousand times, she'd grabbed the phone and held down the '1' until the call connected, reciting the script she'd written for herself so that she wouldn't have to think about it in an emergency. She stumbled only when asked what the emergency was, wondering exactly what to report. She'd rehearsed "there's someone in my house" and "I'm having a heart attack" but this was different. After fumbling for the right words, she blurted "There's a murder next door. She's being *murdered*!". The poor operator probably still had her voice reverberating around her own head.

She'd put Ethel through to the Emergency Control Centre, where she continued to shout and scream about murder and rape, prompting a quick and severe response of the police. They'd gone into the house expecting to find a potential killer and his victim. As far as they were concerned they'd found both.

After the horrible episode of last night was over with – after that man had been taken away and her poor neighbour had been rushed off in an ambulance – Ethel found she couldn't sleep in her own bed. The screams had rang in her mind for hours. Every time her exhausted body had begun drifting into sleep, she'd hear the thumps and shouts all over again.

She'd eventually given up and come downstairs in the hope that something on television might be calming enough to allow her some rest.

Nothing helped.

The way she felt now, she didn't think she'd ever be able to sleep again.

Twelve

The smell was the first thing she noticed. That unmistakable, harsh smell of disinfectant and alcohol gel. Ariadne knew she was waking up in a hospital bed, but it took her a couple of minutes to remember why. Her mind was still hazy, confused.

She realised that for the first time in weeks, her sleep had been dreamless. She'd almost forgotten what it was like to wake up without the claws of fear embedded in her flesh, the tips intravenously pumping adrenalin into her veins with every squeeze.

The memories of the previous night began coming back to her, assaulting her in increasingly violent waves. The shadow man, the old woman, the shawl made of skin.

Jackson.

She closed her eyes.

Yes, she felt guilty for accusing him, but she wasn't in her right mind. And what exactly was the alternative anyway? Either he had tried to take advantage of her, or figments of her imagination had come to life and attacked her. She knew which option was more likely – and more comfortable - to believe. It was Occam's razor put into practice – the simplest explanation is probably the correct one.

A doctor rushed past her room, his white coat billowing behind, and she thought of the Chef. Specifically, his voice on the recording. That wasn't a figment of her imagination, Doctor Illari and Jackson had both heard it too. She could outwardly claim that it was the sounds of a fight outside or interference from a radio, but she knew that it wasn't. It had come from her bedroom.

Which presented her with another choice to make – was the voice hers, or did it belong to a stranger? The most likely explanation was that it was someone else. She could barely make her voice sound deeper, let alone adopt a completely different accent and a male timbre. No, it was the voice of a man, in her bedroom, speaking to her as she slept.

A chill ran down the length of her body at this and her hands felt like ice, even in the near-tropical climate of the hospital.

She could see only two possibilities now – either her nightmares were becoming real, or a huge amount of coincidences were being played out. Occam's razor suddenly didn't seem so simple.

She stared at the off-white ceiling of the hospital room, her thoughts drifting to Jackson and what might be happening to him. The sum of her knowledge about being arrested came from television shows and films. He'd probably be fingerprinted and interrogated. They'd want to collect evidence and statements in case there was a trial.

She shook her head at the thought of her friend being judged. At a *trial*.

Did she want that? Although, did she even have a choice in the matter anymore? If he was arrested for attempted murder then maybe it wasn't up to her to press charges, maybe the police would just go ahead with the prosecution anyway.

Jackson. An attempted murder trial. This was wrong.

He wouldn't have attacked her. He wouldn't attack anyone. They'd been friends for so long, and she'd barely seen him get angry let alone consider the possibility that he would physically attack someone.

But still, something niggled at her. He had suffered a lot of problems last year, and had been attacked himself. Who knew what that might do to him? She'd only been attacked in her *dreams* and she wasn't herself anymore.

Her mind continued going round in circles, analysing the same arguments, the same thoughts.

If Jackson hadn't attacked her, then who had?

Had her mind manifested these images so

powerfully that her body had thought they were real, so that a wound in the dream became a wound in reality? But then how would a recorded voice fit into that?

Or was she being haunted by some disgruntled spirit, who had grown tired of appearing in dreams and wanted to break through from the supernatural realm to do some real damage? So first he spoke, then he attacked.

Neither explanation sounded plausible to her, but the pain in her chest and the fact that she was lying in a hospital bed were testament to the fact that something had happened. However unbelievable it may be.

Ariadne's attention was suddenly drawn to an old lady standing in the doorway. Her breath momentarily caught in her throat and her heart gave a burst of palpitations as she began to consider the possibility that she wasn't awake at all, but trapped in another dream.

"Oh, I'm sorry, dear", the old lady began, "I didn't mean to scare you. I'm what you could call a resident here. I just wanted to come and say hello. I know how lonely these places can be"

Ariadne inwardly tried to compose herself and studied the old lady's face, looking for a trace of a lie or some malicious intent.

The old lady began backing out of the room.

"I'll leave you, dear. I'm sorry to disturb you, I just thought-"

"No, it's fine. I just didn't know anybody was standing there"

The old lady remained half in and half out of the room. Ariadne smiled and motioned for her to enter.

"Please, sit down. I'm Ariadne"

"What a nice name! My name's Margaret. It's a pleasure to meet you, Ariadne"

She said the name in the same way a person might read an exotic and hard-to-pronounce cocktail from a menu.

She sat down slowly, as though afraid her joints might crumble if she lowered herself incorrectly. She wore a nightgown and pink slippers, which looked almost as old as she was. Ariadne tried to place her age, and decided she was probably around eighty.

"I used to be able to sit down and stand up as much as I wanted and as quick as I wanted. Now… well, I might still be trying to stand up half an hour after our conversation ends"

Ariadne gave a smile. She wasn't sure whether it would be polite to join in the joke and she also didn't feel strong enough to expend any energy trying to alleviate someone else's discomfort.

"I'm in the ward opposite", the lady continued, "Victoria Ward. It's where they keep all of us old people whose bodies have nearly given up completely. I'm not going anywhere for a while yet though. I've been through two wars, it'll take more than age to keep me down. Why are you here, if you don't mind me asking?"

"No, I… I don't mind. I had a bit of an incident last night"

"Those scratches below your neck look a bit mean. Do they hurt?"

The old lady put her hand to her upper chest as she spoke.

"Not really. I think I'm a bit bruised too but nothing's broken. Well, as far as I know"

She glanced down at herself, looking for any more serious injuries. She noticed the dried brown blood on her hands and underneath her fingernails and quickly looked back up at her visitor.

"I hope so, dear. You do look a bit pale, although I think that's what this place does to people! But they've done a good job with your bandage. It looks very neat!"

Ariadne's brow furrowed. The old lady's expression changed to one of discomfort.

"You did…you did know your head was bandaged, dear?"

Ariadne shook her head slowly, trying to work out

how her head got injured. Nobody had hit her head, had they?

She searched her memory. She remembered the glass smashing onto the floor, but not much more after that.

Feeling exposed in front of a stranger yet again, she looked up at the old lady and forced a sheepish smile.

"I didn't know. But… it's ok. They'll tell me soon, I'm sure. Do you mind me asking why you're in here Margaret?"

"Not at all!", the lady said, as if an old friend had asked her to dinner, "I've had a few ops recently. The last one was on my right leg and it keeps giving way you see, so they've had to replace something old and broken with something new. Throw in something blue and you've got a wedding!"

Ariadne gave a genuine laugh. She was beginning to warm to this lady, and was quite relieved to escape her own thoughts for a while.

"How is it feeling now?"

"It's ok actually. They took the pins out a few days ago, but it's going to take a while for me to heal up completely, if at all. They like to keep us older ones in, just in case they let us out too early and we die at home and our families try to sue"

"I know what that's like. I work for a healthcare regulator"

"Well that's good to know. My daughter will know who to contact if I croak tonight"

"Oh, don't say that! I'm sure you'll be fine"

"That's sweet of you to say, dear, but you never know. When your time comes, that's it"

Ariadne wasn't sure how to respond to that. She decided to change the subject to something a bit more upbeat.

"So what's the food like in this place then?"

"Not bad, not bad at all. It won't win any awards but it's better than the mush they used to give out here. I've been in and out of this hospital for years, so I've seen the changes"

Ariadne wondered how many other times this lady had sat in this chair and had similar conversations with other patients.

"So I imagine you've seen a lot of people coming and going over the years then?"

"Oh yes. Some stay for longer than others though. And some stay for a while and never leave unfortunately"

The lady looked down at her lap. Ariadne watched as she reached into the sleeve of her nightgown and pulled out a tissue. She wiped at her eyes, then hurriedly put the tissue back, as though embarrassed by her gesture.

"Are you alright? Have I said something?"

The lady looked up and gave a smile.

"No, it's fine, dear, really. I lost a friend quite recently so I'm still trying to keep busy"

"Oh I'm sorry to hear that. Was she in this hospital?"

The lady nodded her head, her eyes glazing over slightly as she mentally relived her friend's passing.

"Yes", she said, "she was. Just down the hall. We'd been friends for a long time, dear. A very long time"

"I'm really sorry to hear that. What happened if you don't mind me asking?"

"Age, dear. It catches up with us all eventually, however much we all want to fight it. He was a dear friend though, we'd known each other for...let me see..."

She flicked her eyes up, as though the exact date had been painted onto the ceiling. Ariadne noticed her eyes slightly glazing over as the lady tried to retrieve the old memories and locate the information. An image came to her of the old lady standing on tiptoes in an empty library, stretching up to reach a dusty tome which hadn't been touched for decades but not quite managing to reach.

The old lady continued.

"Well, it'd be around forty-eight years. Most of my

life! But, anyway dear, I'm fine. Tell me more about you. And don't worry about the bandage, you're still very pretty!"

She retrieved her tissue and wiped at her eyes again, giving Ariadne a weak smile. In that second Ariadne saw this lady's life. She was the type of person accustomed to putting on a brave face, not out of pride, but out of the need to ensure that those around her weren't uncomfortable in any way. Ariadne admired her for that, it reminded her of her mum.

Ariadne wished she could reach over and take her hand, but it would've been too awkward to try to reach over. She realised that she hadn't thought about her own problems for quite a while now, and was especially surprised that sitting here talking to an old lady didn't remind her of the nightmare of the previous night. This lady wasn't physically similar to the one in the dream, she supposed, so there wasn't really any reason for her to have been scared.

"-then?"

Ariadne realised she'd missed the last thing Margaret had said.

"Sorry? What was that?"

"Oh nothing dear, I was just wondering if you wanted to talk about what happened last night then?"

Suddenly Ariadne *did* find herself thinking about her own problems again.

"I'm not...I'm not even sure myself. To be honest with you Margaret, I don't even know why my head's bandaged. I just pretended that I did"

In spite of herself, Ariadne felt tears prick her eyes. She not only felt exposed now, she felt foolish too for lying about the bandage. A child caught in a lie and forced to admit the truth.

"It's ok dear", Margaret said kindly, "Half the time I walk into rooms and don't remember what I'm doing there at all. At least you've got a reason for forgetting, I'm just getting old!"

Ariadne tried to smile but an image of Jackson

flashed across her mind, stopping any notion of humour.

"I blamed my friend for what happened", she continued, "But... it can't have been him. I mean, there wasn't anybody else there but he would never do something like that. Although, how could I get these injuries from a dream?"

Margaret looked puzzled.

"This happened in a *dream*?"

Ariadne nodded, the old lady probably already thought she was mad, why not go the whole way and tell her everything?

For the next few minutes she told the old lady about the dreams, the shadow man, the old woman, even the Chef and his dead dog. Margaret sat listening politely, every so often asking a question or nodding encouragement for Ariadne to continue.

When she'd finished, Ariadne looked into the eyes of the old lady, searching for scepticism or amusement. She found neither.

Margaret edged slightly closer and leaned toward Ariadne conspiratorially. She spoke almost in a whisper.

"I've never told anybody this, but when I was fourteen years old, I had a dream that I had a friend who died in a train crash. I didn't see her face in the dream but I knew she was someone really quite special. Ten years later, at my wedding in fact, I happened to be introduced to somebody and we became good friends. She was my husband's cousin. The feeling I had for her was exactly the same as what I'd felt for the stranger in the dream. As you might be able to guess dear, a few years after that, she died in a train crash in the exact way I had dreamed she would all those years ago. This was a person I hadn't even met yet, and I'd already seen her die in my dream a decade earlier. I couldn't explain it, I still can't – in fact I've given up trying - but it doesn't mean it didn't happen"

She leaned further forward in her seat, as though afraid somebody might be eavesdropping.

"I remember seeing the first pictures being beamed back from the moon and how exciting it all was. Think about all those years when we didn't know what the moon was or what the surface was like, or anything really. We can explain it now of course, but what about when we couldn't explain it? What about when we couldn't explain what that strange white ball in the sky was? It still affected the tide, didn't it dear? And it still does, and still will after me and you are both long gone. Not being able to explain something might be uncomfortable for us, but we can't know everything. Life's full of mysteries – believe me, I've been around long enough to witness some of them! Sometimes, we just have to accept that we don't know"

"But my dreams… How could they be actually attacking me? In *real life*?"

"I don't know, dear. Maybe they didn't. All I'm saying is, just because you can't explain how something happened, doesn't mean that it didn't"

Silence hung between the two women. Ariadne was seeing her visitor differently now, less as a doddery old lady, and more as a survivor. Someone who'd been through life and experienced all it had thrown at her, good and bad. And – cruel as it felt to consider – probably only a few steps away from coming out the other side.

"Do you want to know what I think, dear?"

Ariadne nodded, reluctantly.

"I think that with all the science and breakthroughs we've made and will make in the future, there will still always be more that we don't know than we do know. Do you really think all the accounts of supernatural occurrences throughout history are lies and hoaxes? Even if only one per cent of them are true, the amount of unexplained things that have happened is staggering. It's not likely that a dream did this to you, in fact it sounds silly, but who's to say it didn't? Maybe you're in that one per cent dear"

Ariadne watched the old lady's mannerisms become more pronounced and more excited. Whether what she was saying was true or not, she definitely seemed to believe it. Ariadne wondered what had happened in this lady's life that brought her to this point. Most people would have dismissed it all. She was almost advocating it.

As if sensing she'd said too much, the old lady began the lengthy process of standing up.

"I think I've taken up enough of your time, dear", she said as she strained to get herself up.

Ariadne, stunned by the idea that another person might actually believe a dream could attack the dreamer, watched the lady slowly totter to the door.

Just before leaving the room, she turned around and faced Ariadne.

"Some of the things that you mentioned have happened to people throughout history, dear. Thousands, maybe hundreds of thousands, of people have experienced similar things. Looking at it like that, maybe it isn't that unbelievable that sometimes a dream can go further than we're used to. Maybe, sometimes, they can burst into our real lives too"

The lady paused, as if unsure whether to continue.

She made her mind up, and left the room without another word.

Thirteen

"I want to go home! Please!"

It was the fifth time he'd asked in the space of twenty minutes, his eyes pleading with his captor, his face contorted into a grimace of pain. He trembled as he asked, scared of the response. Terrified that the answer would be a resounding 'No!', and that his torment would continue for another eternity.

His captor held his hand lovingly, as she had done every other time he'd asked the question, and gently stroked his face.

"But you are at home, sweetheart. This is your home. I'm your wife"

If his confused mind made any kind of connection, his eyes certainly didn't show it. He held onto her hand, squeezing for dear life knowing that she – as his captor – was the only one who could save him from this turmoil.

It was her turn to plead.

"Why don't you remember me, Alexandros? It's me, sweetheart. It's Maria"

She swallowed the pain – as she had done so many times before - and tried to give a comforting smile in spite of the heartbreak she felt. It was something she'd never quite got used to in the few years since his diagnosis. She knew that she never would.

"How about some tea?", she asked, using a tactic she'd learned from a kindly health visitor. Reassure then change the subject, she always said. Let the person know you're there and you love them, then change the subject so they stop focusing on whatever scary things they're feeling.

Sometimes it worked, sometimes it didn't. That seemed to be the story of dementia summed up in one phrase.

The mention of tea seemed to trigger something this time and his face softened slightly. The confusion was still in his eyes, but some of the panic seemed to dissipate.

"I like tea... My mum used to make coffee for dad though. My wife used to make me tea. She was lovely, although she never visits"

She restrained the urge to scream "I'm here! What is *wrong* with you?"

Not that she hadn't tried that before. When he'd first stopped recognising her, she tried doing just that. She'd screamed at him telling him who she was, about their daughter Ariadne, even about that stupid cat that he used to love feeding. She'd hoped that somewhere in his diseased brain the words would get through.

They never did.

There were moments when he seemed to recognise her, times when she knew the love in his eyes was coming from recognition, not just mere happiness at this stranger who'd brought him some food, or helped him shave. Real, true recognition that she was his wife, the mother of his child.

His face suddenly brightened.

"Did I ever tell you when I was little and the tea urn nearly fell on me?"

"No, that sounds terrible, sweetheart! What happened?"

As he recounted the story, she nodded enthusiastically, as she had done every other time he'd told it. It was something his mind kept going back to, a 'happy place' as some therapist somewhere would probably call it. She saw the light come back into his eyes, and the broken smile creep back onto his face as he described how the urn nearly fell on him but he'd moved out of the way at the last minute, smashing a vase in the process.

She watched him as he spoke, becoming animated and excited, childlike. Everything about him seemed to be becoming childlike nowadays, which didn't sit right with her. He was getting older – they both were – he should've been getting wiser, more distinguished. Of course he'd get more confused, everybody gets more confused as they get older. They'd start forgetting where they put things and taking longer to find where they'd parked the car. That felt like a lifetime ago with Alexandros though. That's how it'd all started, then the real confusion came, and the real memory problems. Not just forgetting where the car was parked but forgetting he brought the car out at all. Then forgetting well-known routes. Then forgetting how to drive.

She thought back to the weeks they'd spent waiting to see the specialist, then the days they spent afterwards waiting for the diagnosis. In his more lucid moments, they'd discussed the practical things – Power of Attorney, making a will. They'd been to support groups together, read book after book on the subject, attended talks by high profile neurologists and geriatricians, and essentially done everything they could to prepare themselves.

But, as she found out, there was no way to prepare yourself for this. The torturously slow decline of the person you love, the adjustments you make to the things you say, the things you do, the way you feel. The constant doubts about whether you're doing things the right way or making things worse. The guilt – so much guilt – every time your anger flares or you feel irritated. Wanting to run away from the stranger in front of you and into the arms of your lover, knowing they're the same person, but knowing they will never be the same person again.

As the tear rolled down her cheek Alex stopped his story, and looked at first puzzled and then concerned. He shifted closer to this stranger, wanting to help her. He wished his wife were here, she'd know what to say to this person. He was never very good with things like this, but Maria - she was an expert. She could make anything better. He missed her terribly.

He said the only thing his mind gave him to say.
"It's alright", he mumbled, "don't worry"
He clumsily put a hand on her shoulder.
Seeing his kindness, and the man he was – the man

he never would be again – made Maria cry even more. The tears streamed down her cheeks, and her shoulders heaved.

"It's alright, don't worry", he repeated.

A flash of something crossed his face and he gave a chuckle. He knew what would make her feel better.

"When I was little, a tea urn nearly fell on me. Shall I tell you the story?"

Maria nodded but it was no good, she could feel the emotions becoming uncontrollable and knew she would soon be in floods of tears. Completely inconsolable. She stood and, without a word, left the room. Alex didn't need to see her like this. She would take some time for herself then go back. All she needed to do was put her happy face back on, and start again. He wouldn't remember her tears, which was possibly the only consolation she could take from this horrific situation.

She went to the bathroom and ran the cold tap, turning it to its maximum position. She cupped the water in both hands and splashed it across her cheeks, allowing the cool liquid to calm her burning eyes. She wondered whether it was time to go to another support group and get some help. She was just so *alone*. The one person she wanted to speak to about this was Alex – and he was the one person she couldn't speak to about it. He could always make things better with just a hug. A real, sincere, genuine *hug*. Not the floppy armed thing he does now with a vacant stare, wondering who the stranger is that is grabbing him. She missed her husband. She missed her Alex.

As she watched the water running down the plughole, a mini-whirlpool sucking everything in its path into the murky blackness, she thought of her life doing the same. What was left now? They were all rushing to their inevitable deaths like so much water down the drain. And just as clean, running water is life-changing to some and seemingly meaningless to others, so were their lives. An old man gets dementia. Meaningless. Your husband gets dementia. Life-changing.

She had Ariadne, but then she was so far away. If she would only come and stay for a while maybe Alex would remember her. Even if the recognition only lasted a moment, maybe it would trigger something deeper in him and they could be a family again.

She thought again about what Ariadne had said about the dream. Did she know something? Was that some kind of a test to see if her old mum would give her more information?

She thought not. Ariadne wasn't like her friends' daughters in that way, she'd always been open, honest. If she knew something then she would've just said it outright. No, it wasn't a test.

A vague thought tried to enter her mind, but she managed to block it. The emotion came through – an unnerving feeling – but the meaning itself was hazy. She wanted it kept that way. Whatever it was, she didn't want to know.

She turned off the tap and watched the last of the water swirl down to the depths. She looked up at the mirror above the sink and studied the old, tired lady looking back at her. When did she get so *old*? How did life become this nightmare?

The thought brought her back to Ariadne's own nightmares. Something about them made Maria uneasy. It wasn't normal to have those types of dreams. Maybe once or twice, but not for this long. Something was happening.

Then the thought that had been trying to infiltrate her mind finally broke through, powerfully and completely.

Maybe Ariadne is remembering.

Fourteen

For the second time that day, Ariadne realised she was being watched by a figure in the doorway.

She gasped and momentarily tried to get up, hurting her neck in the process.

The figure held both hands up in a defensive gesture.

"Sorry Miss Perasmenos, please, don't get up. I'm PC Hall, and this is PC Morgan. We're with the Metropolitan police. Is it alright to come in and ask you some questions please?"

He stayed at the door, as if hesitant to come in without a formal acceptance. His partner, a lady who was smaller but somehow broader than him, also stood just behind the threshold.

Ariadne tried to gather her thoughts. She'd been thinking about the old lady and what she'd said about the dream. Even if she had been exaggerating about how often unexplained phenomena occurred, the fact that she'd even mentioned it meant that Ariadne couldn't be the only one. Even if only one other person in the world had experienced the same thing that she had, at least it meant she wasn't alone.

It was an encouraging thought, but also a worrying one. If she could be held down in a dream and physically suffer the consequences in the real world, then where were the limits?

The old lady's words ricocheted around her head.

Sometimes, we just have to accept that we don't know...

"Miss Perasmenos?"

She felt a flush of embarrassment as she realised the police were still waiting.

"Sorry. Yes, please come in"

"How are you feeling?", the male officer asked as he walked in. He had harsh features, a sharp chin and pointed nose, but he smiled as he asked the question. His eyes suggested to Ariadne that he genuinely cared about her response.

"I'm ok, thank you. A bit groggy but I think they must have given me some kind of medication"

"Well, you did experience quite a traumatic incident as far as I've been informed. I'd like to ask you just a few questions, but we can always come back at another time if you're not feeling quite right"

"No, it's fine", Ariadne replied, "I'd like to help however I can and just put all this behind me"

The officer looked at his female colleague, who pulled up a plastic chair and sat by the bottom end of the bed. They'd obviously arranged this earlier on – he'd do the small talk, she'd ask the questions. Ariadne wondered if maybe she wasn't as friendly as him. Good cop, bad cop, and all that.

"Hello there", she said with a smile as broad as her shoulders, "now I know you've been through quite an ordeal sweetheart, but we want you to know that we're here and that we'll do everything we can to make sure nobody can hurt you. So if you're worried that by speaking to us you're in any way compromising yourself then you really needn't be. We're here to make sure that whoever did this won't get away with it, and won't do it to anybody else. Is that ok?"

The way she spoke reminded Ariadne of a presenter on a children's television show. She thought to herself that if this lady was being the bad cop then she wasn't doing a very good job of it. She'd almost managed to out-friendly the first officer.

"Thank you", she said, trying to match the friendly tone, "that's definitely ok"

The officer took out her notebook.

"Now, I just wanted to ascertain what happened last night. We were called to your house, and when we got there it appeared as though there'd be an assault. Could you tell us a bit more about that please Miss Perasmenos?"

Ariadne wasn't sure where to begin. She didn't truly believe that her friend had done this, but that thought had spent a very long time concealed under a veil of denial. She could see the truth of it, that Anthony would never hurt her, but she didn't *want* to recognise it. After all, where would it leave her?

But she was in the position where anything she said might somehow incriminate him. Her denial wouldn't only be a way of keeping her own fears at bay, it would actually impact on another human being. Not just impact, *crush*.

In her mind she saw a cartoon-street with a caricature of Jackson strolling along, whistling. There was no noise but, like in a comic, there were musical notes in a big white speech bubble emanating from his mouth. The camera in her mind zoomed out and three men down the road were struggling with a rope leading up to a pulley and a grand piano. The piano swung in the breeze eights floors above the street where Jackson was walking. She saw herself standing with an oversized pair of scissors, capering around the men, taunting them and miming that she would cut the rope. Her close friend would be either crushed or spared depending on what she chose.

"I…fell asleep", she began, "and I must have had some kind of nightmare. I thought I was awake and that he was pinning me down –"

"Sorry", the officer interrupted, "when you say 'he' do you mean Mr Anthony Jackson?"

In her mind her fingers flexed hard on the scissors, clasping them shut and cutting the rope. The piano sped towards the earth and Jackson underneath.

She had a choice to make. Time to decide.

"No", she said quietly, "it wasn't him. It wasn't Anthony"

She looked up and saw the sadness in the police officer's face.

"Sweetheart, you don't need to be scared. He won't be able to hurt you, we'll make sure of that"

"No, it's not… I'm not protecting anyone. It really wasn't him. It wasn't Anthony"

Actually speaking the words aloud was bittersweet for Ariadne. The sense of relief she'd felt at acknowledging the truth about her friend and sparing him was at the same time tinged with fear. If the only other human being in the house hadn't hurt her, then who – or what - had?

The officer turned and looked at her colleague, who had been standing back slightly, presumably to give the impression of a safe, confidential space for Ariadne. He took a couple of steps forward and gave Ariadne a sympathetic look.

"If that's what you're telling us, then that's absolutely fine. But, just to reiterate what PC Morgan here said earlier, we will protect you. There is no need to be afraid, Miss Perasmenos, I promise you"

Ariadne almost wanted to say it was Jackson again. The temptation to blame him, to aim at someone and attribute all this to that person, became stronger. The easiest thing to do would be to pretend it was him, to both herself and the police. But it wasn't him. She knew it wasn't.

As the old lady had said, maybe she was in the one per cent of cases that were truly unexplained and where something supernatural had happened. As scary a thought as that was, she knew that blaming Jackson wouldn't be right. The realisation gave her an anchor of sorts. A solid base rooted in the truth. It made her feel protected in an odd way, even though the only logical conclusion if Jackson hadn't attacked her was that someone – or something – in her dream had.

She chose her words carefully when she spoke.

"It wasn't Anthony, honestly. I can't really remember what I said last night, but it wasn't him. If it was, I'd tell you but, it just wasn't"

The male officer nodded slowly, almost disappointed with the response. His colleague spoke again, asking Ariadne the question that she was dreading.

"You have a number of superficial injuries on your upper chest Miss Perasmenos. If Mr Jackson didn't do that, then do you have any idea what happened?"

Ariadne swallowed hard, wondering how to phrase the thoughts that had been swirling around her mind. She had two choices, tell the truth about the nightmares, or make something up so they wouldn't think she was out of her mind.

They looked at her expectantly.

"I've been having these dreams, and I... I had one last night and I don't know how but, maybe that had something to do with it. I don't, I'm not sure. That's the honest truth. And I know how that sounds. But I also know it wasn't Jackson. And I'm not saying that because I'm scared of him or any of that. I've known him for a while and he wouldn't do that. I can see that now. Clearly"

She'd decided that telling the truth earlier had made her feel stronger, so telling the truth again should have the same effect.

She was wrong, and suddenly felt incredibly stupid. For the second time today, she'd felt like a child trying to convince her parents of some lie, hoping they wouldn't get angry.

"So", PC Morgan began, "you're saying that your dream did this to you?"

Ariadne didn't get the impression that she was being rude or condescending, more that she wanted to clarify exactly what she'd been told.

"I don't know. But, maybe something else was in my room"

"You mean someone?"

"Sorry?"

"You mean someone was in your room. You said something"

"Did I?"

Ariadne looked at the other officer who nodded in agreement.

The stupidity she'd felt earlier took on a whole other dimension now.

"Sorry, I'm…tired"

PC Hall's phone rang.

"Sorry…", he mumbled as he stepped out of the room and answered the phone. PC Morgan watched her colleague leave, then turned back to Ariadne

"Miss Perasmenos, we took some samples from you last night, I'm not sure if you remember?"

The memory returned to Ariadne suddenly and completely. They'd taken a swab from her cheek and picked things from under her fingernails. They'd taken photographs of the marks on her too. The nurse or whoever it was had explained that they might need those things for evidence, and she kept asking if Ariadne had been sexually assaulted. It was all coming back to Ariadne now.

"Yes", she said, "I remember now"

"Well, some of that might come back and tell us a different story about what happened last night. In fact, that is probably the forensics lab calling my partner now. So if you don't remember what happened then that's fine. We can always come back and speak to you another time. But it's important that you tell us everything at this point, so we know how to go forward with things"

PC Hall walked back in and stepped over to his colleague. He aimed a quick smile in the direction of Ariadne, but seemed to be trying to avoid eye contact. He leaned down and whispered something to PC Morgan. Her eyes moved from her notebook and up to Ariadne, then quickly down again. She nodded, and PC Hall stood back up.

"Miss Perasmenos, that's all fine", PC Morgan said.

She put her notebook away and stood.

"I think maybe we should leave it there for today. Maybe you should rest, sweetheart"

Her concern was starting to grate on Ariadne, as was the whole cloak and dagger show that was going on. Yet again her mind flashed back to an image of her as a child, with the adults not telling her the whole story. This lady was even calling her sweetheart - just like her mum.

"But...what? I thought we were talking?"

PC Morgan turned from the door.

"We've got everything we need now. Thank you very much for your time Miss Perasmenos"

Ariadne didn't want them to leave, she wanted to make things clear.

"It wasn't Anthony", she blurted, "Ok? I appreciate everything you're saying but I would really like that to be clear. It wasn't him and I don't want to press charges or whatever the procedure is. He's very much innocent, and however much rest I get the things I'm saying won't change"

The officers shared another look. It was the male officer's turn to speak now.

"That's fine Miss Perasmenos, thank you for your time. We're sorry to bother you. I hope you feel better soon. Please try and get some rest"

Ariadne sensed a change in his tone. They'd both sounded different since PC Hall had come back in. And the way they were looking at her, was it...pity?

"What was the phone call about?", she asked.

Another shared look between the officers, another sting of confusion for Ariadne.

"It's all fine, Miss Perasmenos. Please don't worry. Thank you for your time"

He smiled and, with that, both officers stepped out of the room.

***

Anthony lay on the rock-solid bunk and looked up at the ceiling.

For the first time in his life, he wished he was friends with a lawyer. He knew some from work, but they were all in medical law, none of them would know about criminal proceedings.

Although, he thought wearily, they were bound to know more than him.

Nobody had mentioned a phone call yet. On television if someone was being questioned or arrested they got a phone call, didn't they? He couldn't remember, and didn't think there'd be any point asking for one anyway. What exactly was he going to do if they said no? And had he actually been arrested? He was sure they said something about being 'held for questioning'. Maybe he only got a phone call if he'd been arrested.

He didn't know.

What he did know was that even if he did have lawyer friends to call, he didn't really want anybody at work to know about this if he could help it. Not only to protect himself, but also for Ari. They'd think she was crazy. Although at this time she was probably thinking the same about him.

The memories of the previous night came back to him and he closed his eyes.

The police officers had left him in the little cell for hours now. One of them told him to "Wait here please, sir", as if he had some choice in the matter. That was the one who'd made a big show of bringing in the kitchen knife from Ari's house. It was in a clear polythene bag, and Anthony could see black dust and blood on the handle. Faint fingerprints stood out in the dust.

His fingerprints.

He wondered why they bothered calling him 'sir'. He thought back to those reality TV shows with cameras following the police around – he'd watched a million of them last year. It amazed him how effectively some of the police officers on those programmes had been able to say 'sir', but give it a very real subtext of 'you lying scum'.

Not that the officers who questioned him had done that, in fact they'd been quite nice considering that he was there on suspicion of assaulting a traumatised young woman in her own house while she slept.

Working for a regulatory body, he understood the need to go through everything and investigate before making a decision. He'd recounted everything to them, right down to the dreams Ariadne said she'd been having. They listened, but didn't give anything away. For all he knew, right now they could be making preparations to let him go, or making preparations to torture a confession out of him. They had very strong poker faces.

He suddenly felt very aware that he didn't.

Oddly, he had managed to remain quite calm, and was quite proud of the way he'd managed to keep himself together. Although with the amount of therapy he'd had over the past year he shouldn't really have been surprised.

Even when they'd explained that they'd put bags over his hands to "preserve the evidence", and made a crack about him having being caught 'red-handed', he'd still kept pretty calm.

In fact, he thought, given everything that had happened last year, and with Ari last night, then the actual arrest and questioning, he was coping quite well. Although that was another thing he'd learned last year - sometimes there's no choice but to go into survival mode. He had to cope. It was that or lose his mind.

He heard a cringe-inducing sound of metal on metal, and quickly sat up. The door slowly swung open and one of the officers who'd questioned him the night before stood in the doorway. Anthony couldn't remember his name, but thought it might be Morgan, although that might have been the female officer. He wasn't good with names at the best of times. And last night most definitely wasn't one of those.

The police officer beckoned Anthony over.
"That's it", he said curtly, "you can go"
"I can go? Where?"
"Go where you like, sir. We're releasing you"
"You're... Why?"

"Let's just say there's evidence that might bring some things into doubt"

"So, you believe me?"

The officer squared up to Anthony, his chest bumping into him. His tone didn't change, but his body language seemed to darken.

"I didn't say that, sir. And if we do find out that you've been lying this whole time and that something untoward happened, we won't be happy. Are we clear on that, sir?"

Anthony nodded. He wanted to protest his innocence and prove he didn't do anything, but this didn't seem like the time or the place for him to make a stand. He wondered if there ever was a time or place to answer back to a police officer. He thought probably not.

Ten minutes later he stood outside the police station. With the more immediate concerns – namely, his liberty – out of the way, his mind went straight to the only other thing he'd been thinking about all night.

What had *happened* to Ariadne?

Fifteen

The doctor was on his way apparently, although Ariadne had heard that one before. A few times.

She began to wonder whether nurses deliberately told their patients that doctors were on their way every so often, even when they weren't in the building. Maybe it was a way of giving people hope, or just a way of trying to whip up a frenzy of excitement. Like some kind of marketing campaign to build tension before the big event. She imagined doctors standing 'backstage' – the hospital staffroom – and getting all the nurses huddled around them for the big speech.

"Right, get 'em ready! It's nine a.m, so start telling them from now until this afternoon that I'm coming in a few minutes, then by the time I actually do turn up they'll love it. Putty in their hands, baby! It'll be like I'm a rock star!"

She laughed out loud at this, which was unfortunate given that the doctor had actually just stepped into her room.

He was young and had a clean-cut look. Apparently being groomed was part of the Hippocratic Oath now. He looked to Ariadne like a former boy-band member. Or possibly a current one.

"Feeling better, then?", he asked pleasantly with a knowing smirk on his face.

"Sorry! I was… I was just thinking about, um…"

Don't say rockstar, don't say rockstar…

"About something I saw on television the other day. It's silly"

She gave a smile, and the doctor gave one in return.

"Well, it's always nice to see patients smiling anyway"

He looked like a schoolboy when he smiled, she thought, all dimples. There was something cheeky about him, although that wasn't necessarily what a person looked for in a medical professional.

He pulled up the plastic chair which was still where the police had left it, and sat down. Ariadne half-expected him to turn it the wrong way round, sit on it, and strike a pose.

"Right then Miss Perasmenos, I'm here to give you a bit of an update and to generally see how you are. There certainly seems to be nothing wrong with your sense of humour, so how is everything else?"

As he looked at her, Ariadne realised he was actually very good-looking. Her cheeks got hot and she suddenly wondered whether she looked alright, and how her head looked with the bandage on.

She felt a surprising twinge of guilt at this, as if this was somehow unfair to Jackson.

Her mind flashed to the previous night, which opened a floodgate of guilt at all that had happened, removing any positive emotion that might have been there.

She hoped her friend was ok, she really did.

The doctor was still waiting for a response. She really needed to stop spacing out like that.

"I'm ok thanks, although I still don't know why my head is bandaged. I don't remember being hit on the head"

"You weren't actually. According to the police, you fainted and hit your head on the floor. Well, the floor and shards of broken glass unfortunately. So we had to remove the glass fragments, and then give you a few stitches. It'll probably be sore for a while I'm afraid, but it's nothing to worry about"

A vague memory came back to Ariadne now. The glass had fallen from her hand and smashed on the floor, so she must have fainted shortly after that and landed on the broken pieces.

She suddenly had a strange moment where she not only remembered dropping the glass, but actually *remembered being reminded* of her dream in the hotel. A memory of a memory.

What a mess all this was. And now she'd got

Jackson involved.

"Did the police speak to you at all?", she asked, hoping for news about her friend.

The light in his eyes seemed to dim slightly at this question. He answered cautiously, as if wanting his response to be measured.

"They did. I believe they spoke to you too. It seems as though you decided not to press charges, and they also decided not to pursue the matter due to their evidence. Is that right?"

Ariadne hadn't been told about any evidence they'd found.

"What evidence? Did they find something at my house? One of the officers mentioned the forensics place or something"

"I think", the doctor paused, searching for the right word, "it was more the physical evidence that they were looking at"

"What do you mean the physical evidence?"

The doctor shifted uncomfortably in his seat.

"We took…last night when you came in we took swabs from your fingernails and I believe the police also took some evidence from the gentleman at your house. Mr Jackson, was it?"

"That's right. Anthony Jackson. But he didn't do anything"

"That seems to be what the police have concluded as well. They swabbed Mr Jackson and found specks of your blood under his fingernails, although nothing that led them to believe that he attacked you. They also looked at the swabs we took from your fingernails"

"And?"

"They…they found not only your blood but also some skin"

"Skin? Whose skin?"

"They found some of your skin"

"What does that mean?"

Another pause.

"Miss Perasmenos, the person that attacked you most likely wouldn't only have blood under their fingernails, they would also have skin too. So the police don't think Mr Jackson did this to you anymore. They think that, well…it's a theory. But they think that maybe…"

Ariadne understood.

"They think I did this to myself?!"

The doctor gave a hesitant nod.

It made sense now. The phone call that the police officer had taken, the abrupt end to their visit. The looks of pity they'd given her. *Pity*. They thought she'd attacked herself. First Doctor Illari though she was talking to herself, now this doctor thought she'd been scratching and tearing at her own skin.

"I didn't make this up!", she blurted.

"I'm just telling you what they said Miss Perasmenos. I'm not making a judgement"

"But, they think I did this to myself? For what? Attention?!"

"No, no. The impression I got was that they didn't feel there was enough evidence to go forward. That's all"

"So they must think I did this to myself?"

"I don't know Miss Perasmenos. All I can tell you is that you haven't exhibited any signs that might indicate that you are at risk since you've been here. We're not worried about you in that regard, and in fact you're free to go home if you wish. In saying that, I would like to give you the telephone number of a colleague of mine who may be helpful to speak to. No pressure there at all, but that way you've got his number if you need it "

His words hung in the air between them.

Ariadne felt the tiredness weighing on her. It hung around her neck, physically forcing her shoulders down. She was tired. Too tired to fight anymore.

The doctor leaned closer.

"Miss Perasmenos, let's just say you did this to

yourself in your sleep. And I'm not saying that's what actually happened, but let's just say for argument's sake that it might be a possibility. Maybe it's because you're under a lot of stress, or maybe it's for some other reason, who knows? But surely, on the whole, it's a good thing? It means your friend didn't attack you. It means the police won't charge him with something he didn't do"

It also means, Ariadne thought wearily, that no matter where I go, or what I do, I'm not safe from *him*.

She suddenly heard a loud cackle echoing and ricocheting off the walls of the corridor. A demonic laugh, rushing down the sterile halls of the hospital and hurtling towards her. Rather than tapering off as it bounced its way down the hall, it seemed to get louder, roaring towards them in that small room, shaking the very foundations of the hospital, and knocking the doctor off his chair. He looked up at Ariadne with the same expression of fear and confusion she'd become so accustomed to seeing in her own reflection.

The noise threatened to deafen both of them.

There was blood coming from the doctor's ears now and he whipped off his coat, wrapping it around his head. Just as Ariadne was about to raise her hands to her ears to protect her own eardrums from bursting, the deafening roar abruptly stopped.

Ariadne looked at the doctor, who was still sat on his chair as he had been only moments ago. He was wearing his coat, and there was no sign of any blood from his ears.

Ariadne suddenly felt quite sick.

Sixteen

Anthony was feeling pretty pleased with himself. Without a map or a specific address, he'd been able to find Ariadne's house from memory alone.

He stood at the corner of the road and looked at the property, the memory of the previous night crashing into him like a tsunami. The first time he'd approached this house, he'd felt awkward, clumsy. That was nothing compared to the feeling of dread that overcame him now. The house didn't look inviting anymore. The front door was no longer welcoming, but intimidating now.

There was a huge black mark where the police must have used some kind of implement to force open the door. It looked like a black iris, coldly and dispassionately staring at him. Daring him to get closer.

He felt a clawed finger of ice slither down his back. It didn't race down like a drop of water, but moved slowly. Purposefully. As he had done the night before, he reached around to feel what was causing the chill but could feel nothing. In a few seconds the sensation passed.

The eye was still staring at him.

He sensed that he was looking at the house now in the same way that Ariadne must see it. Her home, her safe haven, not safe anymore. The walk towards it no longer the steps to a sanctuary from the outside world, but the slippery slope down into a more sinister one. He felt a wave of pity for Ariadne. What must it be like to be scared of your own home? Your own bed?

He felt an overwhelming tiredness. Another parallel with Ariadne, he thought. He was determined to find her. If she had ever needed a friend, it was now.

He hesitated. What if she did need a friend, but didn't want *him*?

He remembered the look in her eyes the previous night. She didn't think he was innocent then, why would she have changed her mind now?

He suddenly realised he'd been standing and staring at the house for some time now, and began to feel conspicuous. He needed to either keep going, or turn around and leave.

He made his decision and walked to the front door, all the while wondering how his friend would react, and whether she would even be there. He seemed to remember she had fainted as he was being dragged away, so maybe she was in hospital, or with the doctor, or with her family. She could be anywhere, but he had to at least *try* to find her here.

He walked up to the door and hesitantly pressed the doorbell. He avoided looking at the eye, but felt it's gaze on him.

He waited for a few seconds, then tried again.

A creeping, uneasy sensation began to slither around his chest, although he couldn't quite place why.

When Ariadne didn't come to the door, he knocked instead.

Still nothing.

He crouched down and looked through the letterbox to see if there was any movement in the house. He saw a shadow sweep across his vision, and in that same instant he suddenly knew he was being watched. And not from the eye this time, but from inside the house. It was an odd feeling, as though someone – or something – was evaluating him. Sizing him up.

Another shadow crossed his vision, this time travelling in the opposite direction to the way it had previously moved.

The odd feeling passed.

The watcher had turned away.

He let go of the letterbox - which clattered down loudly - and jumped up.

Had he started actually seeing things? He thought of Ariadne and how her own sleep-deprivation had been affecting her.

He stepped back and looked up at the house, as though Ariadne may be at the window, waving at him. As he stood in the middle of the small driveway, staring upwards at the windows, a thought occurred to him.

Ariadne hadn't called the police last night, as far as he knew, and he obviously hadn't.

Which could only mean one thing. One of the neighbours had.

No wonder he felt uncomfortable, and as though somebody was watching – they probably were! A relief flowed through him, cooling the fear that had burned within him, although not extinguishing it – he still had the nagging feeling that the watcher had been in the house and not outside.

He looked around at the houses on either side, and across the road. There was no movement of curtains, no fingers being pointed.

He suddenly felt very hot, and foolish for thinking that this was a good idea. What if the police had still been here? How would that have looked?

He walked hurriedly back to the tube station, smiling at himself and his paranoia.

If he knew that Ethel – Ariadne's scared neighbour – had been watching him with a telephone in her trembling hand since she heard the letterbox slam shut, he would've walked even faster.

Oblivious to this, he thought about where to look next for Ariadne, although his mind kept going back to the shadow in the house. The feeling he'd got that it was somehow watching him was so real it was hard to ignore. What if some demonic presence inside the house had been studying him? For all he knew, it had been.

For all he knew, it still was.

***

Anthony felt better as soon as he reached the

familiar surroundings of the London tube network, which was a sensation he never thought he'd experience. At least he knew this place, however disgusting it might be. The dirty seats, the noise, the crowds. There were no shadows that made you feel watched here, no phantom ice droplets falling down your spine. This was real, busy London life, there was no room for anything else here.

It wasn't rush hour so he was able to get a seat, although there were other people in the carriage this time so he wasn't alone. As he allowed himself to relax, he thought about what to do next. Ariadne wasn't at home, at least he didn't think she was, so maybe she was at a hospital somewhere. Either that or she was with her parents, although her dad was ill so it was unlikely her mum would be able to drop everything and pick her up. They lived hours away too, which made it even less likely.

The train was still above ground, so he took out his smartphone and logged onto his work database. In less than five minutes he had the list of all the possible hospitals Ariadne could have been taken to from her house, as well as their contact details. There were some benefits to working for a healthcare regulator, he thought, although admittedly not many.

While logged on he thought he'd better send an email to his manager, explaining his absence. The best thing he could come up with off the top of his head with was that he was ill and had been asleep so had only just had the chance to use his phone. A terrible excuse, he knew, but he had other things on his mind. He'd deal with work tomorrow, or the next day, or whenever. After last year, they were pretty lenient with him where absence was concerned anyway.

All he cared about right now was finding Ariadne, making sure she was alright, and ensuring that she didn't still think he had anything to do with what happened last night.

As the memory of the previous night returned the train rushed underground, causing a roar in the carriage and, unusually, a momentary blackout.

In that moment – but only for that moment – Anthony would have sworn he heard a burst of laughter.

Seventeen

The nurse brought Ariadne's nightclothes into the room and left them on the chair.

She smiled as she walked away, although Ariadne could tell her heart wasn't in it. This was probably hour number ten of a twelve hour shift, she thought. Ariadne doubted *she* would have been smiling either.

Her attention was drawn to the pile of folded clothes on the chair. So much negative emotion imbued in such simple garments. Nightclothes, usually a symbol of comfort, rest, pampering. Now they were torn, destroyed. As if ripping apart Ariadne's peace wasn't enough, he had to decimate her clothes too. Not to mention what he did to her flesh…

She felt a pressing need to focus on something else.

She looked around the room but her gaze was drawn back to the clothes.

Ariadne was surprised to see that they'd been cleaned and pressed. She began wondering whether there was some kind of laundry in the basement or something, and whether the nurses would sometimes secretly do their own washing. One of the drawbacks with working for a healthcare regulator was that she now doubted *everybody* in hospitals and surgeries everywhere.

She supposed there must be a laundry, how else would they clean all the sheets and gowns? Unless the police had cleaned everything after looking for evidence and whatever tests they would have done? Although she doubted the police would have clothes dry cleaned.

No, it must have been the hospital. And surely they had to wash the gowns, because they couldn't re-use them, could they? That would be disgusting. Who would want to wear a gown that somebody else wore in hospital? What if they'd died in it?

An icy draft billowed through the room.

She thought back to being at school. Somebody would feel a chill and the other kids would chant about how somebody had "walked across your grave". She'd joined in so as not to be singled out, but she'd never understood what the words could possibly have meant.

She felt like she might have an idea now.

The nurse came back in, this time carrying another, smaller pile of clothes.

"Hello there", she said as she efficiently put the new pile on top of the old. For a second it surprised Ariadne that the nurse was so willing to go near her nightclothes and had actually nonchalantly touched them, as though the rest of the world should be as scared as she was.

The nurse stopped as she saw Ariadne's face.

"You alright, love?"

"No. Yes. Sorry... could you please... this might sound strange but could you please take those nightclothes away for me?"

The nurse didn't look impressed.

"We don't usually dispose of clothes for patients, love"

"I appreciate that, but it's just that..."

Just that what? I'm scared of my clothes?

She took a deep breath.

"I was attacked last night while wearing those clothes", she continued as matter-of-factly as she could, "so I would really rather not have to take them with me"

The nurse's face softened. Ariadne thought she looked almost apologetic.

"Oh, love", she said as she scooped up the pile, "I didn't realise. No worries. Consider them gone!"

In the time it took Ariadne to say "Thank you", the nurse left the room.

Ariadne lay in the bed, thinking about what she needed to do before getting ready to be discharged. Something niggled at her. It was a strange feeling, almost the same way she'd felt before the water in her shower had turned to blood. Something was amiss.

She looked around the room. Everything seemed fine.

Her heartbeat suddenly rocketed, and she felt as though the breath had been knocked out of her. She was starting to recognise the feeling as the beginnings of a panic attack, although she would never give it that name.

She jerked up in the bed, her hand on her chest as though somehow able to slow her heart rate through sheer pressure and willpower. She tried forcing herself to relax, which she was coming to realise was as impossible as forcing yourself to sleep.

After a couple of minutes her breathing had returned to normal, although the uncomfortable feeling still remained. She was so tired she couldn't discern what was important anymore. She never knew if the things her subconscious picked up on were big problems or not. Maybe she had forgotten to buy pasta, or written the wrong phone number on her contact details at work, or hadn't put the cat food away in the cupboard. She'd learnt that her reaction to something was not necessarily a gauge as to how important it was. Just because she'd had a panic attack, didn't mean there was any reason to panic. In fact it was starting to seem that just the opposite was true.

Regardless of all that, she knew that here, in this room, something was not as it should be.

She thought about going home but realised that wasn't the source of her anxiety. It was definitely a source of anxiety, but this was something else.

She went through a mental checklist – home, work, Jackson - but couldn't work out the cause of this current unease.

Her eyes fixed on the pile of clothes sitting on the chair, and she realised.

She had been brought in by the police in her nightclothes. She hadn't brought any clothes with her to the hospital.

Where had they come from?

Ordinarily this wouldn't have been a cause for panic, but she was already on edge, her senses already too acute, too sensitive to things happening around her. It didn't take much for her to be pushed into that familiar hypervigilance where the smallest movement became the pinnacle of dread and fear.

She suddenly felt tearful, not so much because she was scared about the clothes – in fact intellectually she knew there must be some rational explanation - but more because she realised her emotions were not her own anymore. They – and consequently *she* - were being blown by the wind, going wherever it wanted to take them, and she was the one who had to deal with the consequences.

She hoped the nurse would come back and explain where the clothes had come from. Surely that would at least give her some consolation.

She reached to press the call bell.

"Hello Ari"

She looked up and saw Jackson.

Her gratitude must have shown on her face, as his expression changed from concern to relief in a millisecond.

He didn't move.

He'd planned a speech about friendship and how it could survive anything, and how he hoped she realised now that he would never hurt her. Deep down he was also quite looking forward to telling her how cleverly he'd worked out what hospital she was at, as well as not only the ward but the room number too.

"It was you"

His face dropped as he misunderstood what his friend was saying.

"No, Ari. Please. Look, I had nothing to do with any of it I swear. You have to believe me. I don't know what happened but I would never-"

"The clothes, I mean", Ariadne said, realising her poor choice of words, "Not... last night. You brought them, the clothes"

It took him a while to understand what she was saying. He nodded.

"Yes. I brought them. Actually I bought them, so they probably don't fit very well, and I probably missed cutting off a couple of the tags too. They seem to put tags everywhere now. Have you noticed? It used to be just one tag per garment, now they put about three in each. Has theft of clothes become some kind of epidemic?"

She smiled, not at what he was saying but at why he was saying it. He was trying to make them both feel better, and she found that she did. The familiarity of her good friend went some way to soothing the panic she had been feeling mere moments ago. The dull anxiety still pecked away at the back of her mind, causing intermittent palpitations and shallow breaths. But there was a warm, comfortable feeling that seemed to smooth over all of this.

She knew he would never hurt her. She couldn't believe she ever thought that he would.

"Thank you, Jackson. And, I…"

She looked into his eyes, and he understood.

"I know, Ari. It's ok"

He walked over to her. Not tentatively this time, but assuredly. He knew she wouldn't flinch. They embraced and Ariadne let out a breath she felt like she'd been holding for months.

"Jackson, I'm so sorry", she said as the tears began to fall.

"I know, Ari. I know"

"I'm just so scared"

"I know Ari, but I'm here. It'll be ok, I promise. It'll be ok"

And, now that her friend was back, Ariadne actually allowed herself to believe that a little.

Eighteen

After being officially 'discharged' from hospital – which essentially consisted of being shown the exit – Ariadne was allowed to go home.

Not that she was going to stay there for very long, Anthony had called Doctor Illari and arranged for her to spend the night at the sleep clinic.

She was going to be wired up to machines, recorded by cameras and sound equipment, and monitored by heat sensors.

As far as restful sleep was concerned, she didn't think it looked likely.

She sat in the reception area with Anthony, waiting for the bus that would take them to her house. She wanted to pick up some clothes – although Anthony had proved to be a scarily good judge of women's clothing sizes - and make sure Harry hadn't either died or destroyed the place. He wasn't the most settled cat, although she wondered if those types of cats actually existed anyway.

She looked at the people sitting around her, and wondered how many of them might have trouble sleeping, or may have got to the point where they didn't like their own homes anymore for some reason. It was strange when she thought about it – nobody really knows anything about the people they meet in life, even the people they see every day at work. When her dad had first been diagnosed she'd had this feeling too. She remembered walking down the road, looking at each person who passed by, and wondering whether any of them had to deal with the same thing she was dealing with.

At one time she wanted to find a support group. Not to actually join and participate or anything, but just to know it existed. Just to know that the things she was going through were being felt by other people, even if she never got to meet them.

Her thoughts turned to what other things the people around her might be going through. She was in a hospital, so their problems were probably pretty serious. Maybe some of them had trouble getting around, maybe some had diseases and conditions that needed constant monitoring and treatment.

Maybe some of them only had months, or weeks, or *days*, to live.

She knew she should feel something, that this should somehow put her own problems into perspective. And it did on an intellectual level, but that was all. She still felt dread whenever she thought of falling asleep, terrified by what new horror might be unleashed upon her. Her heart still raced, her breathing still became shallow, her stomach still plummeted through floor. The intellectual side of it wasn't the problem, it was the emotional side that affected her.

For the first time last night she'd been physically assaulted during the nightmare. For all she knew maybe she did only have days to live. She didn't know, and that was part of the problem too.

Nietzsche once said that if a person knows the 'why' of their suffering then they can bear almost any of the 'how'. Ariadne thought that if a person knew the 'how long' of the suffering it'd make it easier to bear too. If she knew there were five nightmares left, and that they'd scare her and maybe even cause a few more cuts, then she could probably handle that. But there was no way of knowing what was going to happen.

Things were escalating.

The fear had spread rapidly too. It had started with fear of falling asleep, then progressed to fear of her bed, then fear of being at home at all. It was strange how that worked, she thought, and how quickly too. She'd actually become afraid of being afraid of going to sleep.

The bus arrived and everybody got up and made their way onto it. Some people had help in the form of wheelchairs and sticks, others had friends and family there to hold their arm and guide them onto the vehicle.

As the bus pulled off, somebody suddenly gave a loud burst of laughter, causing both Ariadne and Anthony to jump. Ariadne took comfort in the fact that other people on the bus had been startled too, so the sound must have been real this time. Although at this point her definition of real was being redefined by the day.

"Somebody's having a good time", Anthony commented.

"Surely nothing is *that* funny though"

"You never know, I've been known to make people howl with laughter sometimes"

Ariadne looked at him doubtfully.

"Not intentionally though, Jackson. Sorry to be the one to tell you and everything"

"What?! That's rubbish. I made Kate laugh like that the other day"

"Kate?! She laughs at everyone's jokes, that one. Every joke a man makes anyway. And I hate to break it to you but you're wasting your time with her, she's taken"

"Wasting my ti- I wasn't trying to *do* anything Ari, I just made a joke and she laughed! There was no agenda!"

Ariadne gave a smirk and looked out of the window.

Anthony thought for a moment.

"And taken by who?"

Without missing a beat, Ariadne responded.

"Everyone"

Anthony laughed and shook his head.

Ariadne felt glad for the office talk. It was possibly the only normal thing she had left.

***

Anthony was surprised with the speed at which Ariadne walked to the house and opened the door, seemingly ignoring the black mark and slight dent on the front. There was no need for her to disable the alarm, it hadn't been reset since last night. He kept expecting her to be less hurried, and take things in. Although, he thought, maybe she just wanted to get it all over with.

Maybe she didn't want to remember.

Anthony began to think that maybe his own experience here had made him feel anxious about coming back too.

Harry didn't do his usual rushing to the door thing, and for a while they thought that he must have escaped when the police had come in. They eventually found him curled up behind the television.

He looked up at Ariadne, who thought he looked confused and angry but, above all else, hungry.

She cajoled him out from behind the television with some food, and then emptied his litter tray, which predictably wasn't in the best condition. Not that it was usually in great condition, but she could tell that Harry had obviously been stressed through the night and during the morning.

She suddenly realised she had no idea what time it was. She looked at her watch and saw it was just after three in the afternoon.

"What time is the sleep clinic expecting us?", she asked Anthony, who seemed to be preoccupied by the door for some reason.

"Um, about seven I think. It's the floor above where you met him the first time, so we'll find it easily"

"Ok"

Ariadne noticed that Anthony went back to apparently staring through the front door. He was sitting on the sofa but had positioned himself so that he was staring directly at the letterbox. Every so often he would look up and then across the room.

"Are you ok?", she asked. Maybe he wasn't ready to have come back here so soon. It hadn't even occurred to her that this might be difficult for him too. They'd barely even spoken about the police taking him away.

"I'm fine", he said, turning and giving possibly the least convincing smile Ariadne had ever seen. "I'm just looking around"

"At what though?! Surely you've seen doors before? Maybe… maybe we shouldn't have come back together so soon"

"No, it's fine Ari. I was looking through the letterbox when I came round to find you earlier. I was just looking at the angles and reflections and stuff. Nothing important"

He didn't want to tell her about the shadows he'd seen. It'd only scare her. It was doing a good enough job of scaring him.

Ariadne gave a sceptical nod and turned back to the cat. She watched Harry's little head move back and forth as he hungrily ate the food, and she thought about how much she loved *her* house. It was cosy, familiar, and hers. A surge of anger ran through her as she somehow seemed to remember that this was her house, and not anybody else's. She wasn't going to be chased out or allow panic to take over. That familiar feeling of being in the arena returned to her, empowering her. This is where the battle is fought, she thought, and where she would win.

She'd go to the sleep clinic tonight, but she'd come right back here tomorrow.

Her thoughts turned to Harry. She'd planned on dropping him off with Ethel, her neighbour, but she began feeling hesitant about that now. She wanted a concrete reason to come back in case her will didn't hold. If Harry needed to be fed, she'd have to come back home. Maybe she should leave him in the house.

She suddenly felt both selfish and foolish at planning to use Harry like that. She couldn't stake *his* life on how *she* might feel tomorrow. She decided she would leave him with Ethel.

"Will you watch the cat while I clean up this glass?

And I need to get some things together for tonight too"

Anthony turned from the door.

"Sure. Do you want me to come upstairs with you?"

"No thanks, Jackson. I don't know whether you'd be able to keep your hands off!"

Anthony turned red and Ariadne realised what she'd said.

"No! I meant... Not because of last night. I was trying to make a joke. It wasn't about last night. It wasn't... Sorry"

Anthony smiled, but Ariadne could tell he'd been struck by her words. She walked over to him, realising he was overdue an apology. She stood in front of him and looked him directly in the eye.

"I know you had nothing to do with last night, Jackson. I trust you. In fact if you weren't with me I probably wouldn't have been able to even come back here today. I don't know what's going on but I know it's nothing to do with you. I feel safe with you, Jackson. I am just so sorry for last night. You've been so great and I've put you through all this. Thank you for being here, Jackson"

Anthony reached out and took her hand.

"I know Ari. It's ok"

"But it's not though is it", she protested, "I didn't stop the police, I accused you of attacking me... What am I doing? I'm trying to be strong, but I'm not. I'm not strong enough, Jackson. I can't do this"

The lump in her throat and flow of her tears caught Ariadne by surprise. Another emotion, blown by the wind.

"You *are* strong Ari. You've just been through a lot, that's all. I can't imagine the things you've experienced over the last couple of weeks, but you're getting through it Ari. And that's because you're strong"

"I'm not strong", she said. "Strong people don't cry and aren't scared of going to sleep. Look at me! Look at the stitches in my head and the cuts on my neck!"

He took her hands in his.

"Ari, you're not a mess. Look at me. You're not. And you *are* strong. All the help you gave me last year was... I couldn't have got through that without you, and I'm not going to let you go through this alone either. I'll protect you, Ari, I won't hurt you"

He pulled her into his arms and squeezed her to him. She flinched and broke away as the cuts on her chest squashed against him.

She tried to reposition her body and hug him again.

"Ow!"

She quickly pulled back.

"Sorry Ari", he said sheepishly.

They tried again but Ariadne had to break away once more. They stood opposite each other and made eye contact. Ariadne gave a small grin.

"What?", Anthony asked.

"I thought you said you wouldn't hurt me?"

He registered the mischievous look in her eye.

"Yeah, well, I thought you wanted me to keep my hands off you. But you just keep throwing yourself at me!"

She chuckled, and went to playfully hit Anthony's shoulder. She missed.

Anthony laughed now.

"What was that?!"

"I was trying to hit you!"

"You didn't try very hard, I'm at most a foot away from you!"

"Fine!"

She threw her arm forward again, somehow managing to not even get as far as his shoulder this time, but instead landing a light punch on his jaw.

His eyes widened with the shock of it, and he burst out laughing.

"What was that?!"

Ariadne couldn't answer. She clutched her stomach while attempting a futile attempt at giving a coherent apology through her laughter.

It amazed both of them how quickly they'd gone from despair to elation, not just within twenty-four hours but within twenty-four seconds.

Ariadne wiped her eyes, which had been shedding tears of a different kind now.

Harry looked up, unimpressed with these strange giants that kept selfishly interrupting his life, and went back to his food.

The room was filled with their laughter now – the joyous noise creating a cocoon, a safe space which would protect them. It was laughter that declared that they were alive, that they were happy, that they couldn't be touched by anything.

They both knew that nothing had been particularly funny, but they welcomed the release from all of the drama and tension that lay behind them.

If they knew how much more of it lay in front, they would've stopped in a heartbeat.

Nineteen

Alex sat in his favourite armchair, Maria – poor, exhausted Maria - sat across the room from him. It hadn't been a good day.

She'd begun wondering recently whether he even knew that was his favourite chair anymore, or if he just sat in it because he'd got used to it.

One of the things she'd learned through dealing with his illness, was that he'd started to rely more and more on familiarity and routine. He always used to sit in that old chair because it was the most comfortable, but if for some reason he couldn't, then he would've just sat somewhere else. Not sitting in that chair would have irked him slightly.

Now it would panic him.

Maria watched him as he sat in front of the TV, staring at the quiz show which he used to love. Again, she wondered whether he still loved it, or even knew what it was. Maybe he liked the music, and recognised the sound effects as being familiar. They'd play a heartbeat very quietly, more a vibration that an actual sound. Then, as the contestant would think about their answer, the volume and speed of the heartbeat would increase. The idea was to cause the audience at home to begin feeling uneasy, to build tension so that they wouldn't change the channel.

She wondered whether he recognised the noises somewhere in his mind and found comfort in them. Not that he seemed to give much of an indication if he did.

They used to play a little game with each other with these television shows. Whenever a new contestant arrived they'd try to guess details about their lives. Maria always thought it was silly, although that might have been because Alex always guessed correctly. She'd tried playing it again with him recently, but he hadn't responded.

She'd call out 'teacher!' or 'retail manager!', and he'd look at her as if trying to work out what in the world she was talking about.

Then as if trying to work out who she was and what she was doing in his house.

He sometimes surprised Maria by calling out a correct answer to one of the questions. It was as though all the information in his head had been shaken up, and all the pathways that allowed him to retrieve it were mixed up too. When he got an answer right, she thought that maybe it meant that when the information was shaken up, and when the pathways were mixed, some of them might coincidentally have found each other again. Which meant he could sometimes retrieve the right information, and sometimes have a perfectly normal conversation.

That was one of the most difficult parts for Maria to cope with. If her husband was gone, that would be one thing, but every so often he was there again. Not always just for a moment either, sometimes for half an hour or so. He'd be Alex again, the man she married. She always said the best times she had with Alex now were the times when he was him again, before the confusion and distress and problems came crashing back.

They were also the worst times, cruelly reminding her of precisely who she'd lost.

On television, the host was introducing the next contestant. Maria wanted to call out 'Pharmacist!' but knew there'd be no point. Alex wouldn't understand.

After the obligatory introductions and 'hilarious' anecdotes – he wasn't a pharmacist, he was a dentist, which Maria felt was close enough to be proud of - the quiz began.

The first few questions were too easy for Maria and her mind drifted. She began thinking again about the conversation she'd had with Ariadne. That particular unwelcome thought returned to her.

What if Ariadne is remembering?

But she couldn't be, it wasn't possible. Surely if she was going to remember then it would've happened by now? Although, in saying that, there was all that business the other week…

Alex's chair creaked as he sat forward and leaned towards the television. Maria's attention was drawn to the sound of a rapid heartbeat coming from the television. She wished they wouldn't do that anymore. She was already on edge, she didn't need manufactured tension in her life too.

The host had his serious face on, so the dentist must have answered quite a few correct questions and be at the big money ones now. The dentist had leaned forward in his chair too, and Maria wondered whether Alex was copying him when he had shuffled forward, or was in some way getting absorbed in the programme.

The host began to ask a question about rivers around the world. He asked slowly and purposefully, with a gravity that suggested the dentist's very life depended on a correct answer.

As the dentist began talking about seas and expanses of water, Maria realised that Alex hadn't had a drink since breakfast. His unfinished glass of water still sat on the little table next to his chair.

"Alex", she called out.

He didn't hear. Or at least he didn't respond if he did.

"Alex, darling", she tried again, "your water. You need to drink"

He turned his head slowly, as if taking in his surroundings for the first time, which in a way maybe he was. He looked blankly at Maria, who pointed to the glass and repeated that he needed to drink.

He nodded almost imperceptibly, then began to turn back around. His gaze passed the television this time and settled instead on the little table next to him.

Maria felt a flutter in her chest as she hoped that her husband might be able to understand and drink something by himself this time. His coordination had been getting worse recently.

The heartbeat started getting louder and faster on

the television. The low, regular rumble came through the speakers. Maria couldn't tell whether it was actually increasing in frequency or volume, or whether that was her own heart beating. It certainly felt like it was.

Every time Alex did something, some basic thing that he'd done a million times before in his previous life, she felt that same flutter in her chest. It was as though if he could do this thing, whether it was picking up a glass, or holding a spoon, or using the remote control, just this *one thing*, then it would mean that he was still in there somewhere. Yes, it stung being reminded of what she'd lost, but at least for a few seconds he'd be here again. The time after those few seconds was horrific, but at least that brief period of time would have existed. Maria and Alex would be a normal married couple, just watching television like all the rest.

She watched as Alex reached over and tentatively clasped the glass. There wasn't much water left in it so she wasn't particularly worried that he would spill it. She was more concerned he wouldn't pick it up at all.

As he lifted the glass to his mouth, Maria dared not breathe. She just watched, as her husband slowly brought the glass up to his mouth. The heartbeat was definitely getting louder now, she could tell. Her own heart started beating to the same rhythm. She didn't look away from him.

Alex hesitantly drank from the glass with a trembling hand, draining the little bit of liquid left in it. He looked over at Maria. His facial expression didn't change, but she noticed something in his eyes. A look of recognition maybe, possibly even pride.

At the same time, the dentist in the quiz must have got the question right because an almighty cheer came through the speakers, filling the room with applause and excited shouts.

Maria wanted to shout too. She wanted to hug Alex, to run over and throw her arms around him and scream "Well done!", but she knew there was no point. It might scare him, or make him even more anxious than he had been all day today. In any case, she knew that people with dementia don't learn to repeat behaviours that they get praised for like other people do. She could congratulate him all day but it wouldn't mean he'd drink by himself again next time.

She smiled at him as he lowered the glass, enjoying the moment of having her husband back. Some might think it was a small victory, being a grown man and being able to take a drink from a glass all by yourself. Those were the people who had never seen this illness before.

Alex looked at the little table, then back at the glass in his hand. He looked down the other side of the chair, as if searching for something. He turned towards Maria with a bewildered look, and her heart sank as she realised he didn't know what to do next. He'd finished with the glass, but wasn't sure where it should go again. She watched him as he looked from the glass to the floor, to the table again, then back to the glass, then to the television.

Then, using his free hand he slowly opened the pocket on his jumper, and carefully slid the glass in there. The pockets were huge, and so the glass had no trouble fitting into it. Maria wasn't worried that it might break.

She only wished she could say the same about her heart.

Twenty

The soft light of evening had given way to the blackness of night by the time they reached the sleep clinic.

The receptionist had greeted them as they entered, and Anthony grinned slightly as he realised his friend's description of the receptionist had been incredibly apt. She did indeed look like she belonged in a library.

She gave them a warm smile that, along with the pictures on the wall and marble tablet behind the reception desk, immediately took Ariadne back to their previous meeting. It seemed like a hundred years had passed since she'd last been here, it definitely felt like it anyway.

The receptionist informed them that Doctor Illari wouldn't be attending tonight as he had a prior engagement, but would review the results as soon as he could. Ariadne felt a tug of disappointment at that, although she supposed that given the last minute nature of her recent appointments with him, she should probably just be grateful for the help he could give.

"He also left some forms for you to fill in please, dear", the receptionist continued, "they shouldn't take long. Then our nurse will ask you some questions and take your blood pressure. I'll also tell Derek you're here too. He's the technician who'll set everything up for your polysomnogram"

Ariadne and Anthony shared a look.

"Sorry, the polysomnogram is the sleep study. Well, actually that's not quite accurate, is it? The polysomnogram is the result, really, although we use the same word when we talk about the study itself too. That's all it is. Sorry about the jargon"

Ariadne noticed that Anthony was nodding vigorously while the receptionist was talking, as though he was a fellow clinician taking in vital information. Ariadne herself wasn't too bothered about what things were called, she just hoped they'd be effective enough to get to the bottom of what was happening to her. During the journey to the sleep clinic the lethargy and tiredness had hit her all over again. She'd even found herself having episodes of microsleep again.

At the moment all her body craved was rest, and all she wanted to do was sleep.

Unfortunately, that was also the only thing she was afraid to do.

***

The next hour or so went by in a fog of strange and slightly absurd experiences.

Ariadne had initially seen the nurse, who had run through an unnecessarily long list of questions. She frantically scribbled the responses on a large legal pad, missing nothing. The whole experience only took fifteen minutes, which was fortunate because Ariadne felt like she was going to fall asleep after two.

The bulk of the last hour had been taken up by Derek preparing her for the study.

They'd provided her with a pair of pyjamas, the colour of which could only really be described as seasick-green. The top half had two neat little slits on the front, and the bottom half had two more at the legs. Ariadne hadn't asked what they were for, although she was sure she'd be told soon enough.

Derek then began what he called 'the PSG Preparation chuckling to himself as he said it. On realising that his audience were offering nothing but polite smiles, he silently put on his gloves and began.

He started by carefully unwrapping the bandage from Ariadne's head, and then taking various measurements. Every so often he'd stop and dot a part of her scalp with what looked like a marker pen but felt like a knife. The experience wasn't pleasant, and had reminded Ariadne of her dreams more than a few times. He then used some kind of paste – which felt like sandpaper - to scrub her skin at the points he'd marked.

"This is to get the grease off so the electrodes attach properly", he casually explained, "we wouldn't want them falling off in the night. Although if they do, we can always reattach them while you're asleep. Don't worry"

The thought of a stranger sneaking into her room and attaching anything to her head would ordinarily have worried Ariadne, although the tiredness had her fully in its grip now. She was at that stage where words floated around her, occasionally sinking in but often just sailing by. Life became smoke at times like this – drifting and swirling around her, ethereal. She wasn't fully awake, but not completely asleep either. It was a kind of primal state where her body craved rest only and seemed to discard every other impulse. Even hunger and thirst seemed to diminish.

She was glad Anthony was in the room with her. His presence felt comforting, and she knew it wasn't only attributable to the fact that his was a familiar face. She was staring to rely on having him around, although was too tired to even begin to analyse what that might mean.

Derek described the electrodes they were going to attach to her head, proudly remarking that they were gold-tipped. Apparently that was a big deal in sleep clinic circles, although once again Derek found his audience looking decidedly unimpressed.

He paused and gave a look which said 'tough crowd' before continuing.

Next, he attached the small electrodes under Ariadne's chin and behind her ears. The paste he used didn't hurt as much this time, which Ariadne thought must mean that either her head was becoming desensitised to all the various knocks and scrapes, or that Derek took instruction very well.

He taped the last few electrodes to her upper chest and legs, expertly sliding them into the slits in Ariadne's pyjamas. She did her best not to flinch as some of the electrodes brushed against the cuts on her chest. That particular part of life - pain - wasn't like smoke at all and couldn't be ignored no matter how tired she felt.

"Sorry, there. Nearly finished"

He expertly placed a sticky pad to the centre of her chest which would monitor her heart rhythm. Anthony looked away for a moment as Derek had to lift her top slightly to hand the pad to Ariadne under her clothes. She took it and stuck it onto her chest. Having a pad there was a strange feeling, and it adhered almost as strongly as the leg wax she used.

"There we are. All finished. We used to tape microphones to peoples' necks too you know, but we've upgraded everything so the ceiling microphones will pick up any sounds. We're not using a thermistor either – that normally goes up your nose to measure temperature changes – so that's good too. In a way, you're pretty lucky"

That was one word for it, she thought.

Derek connected all the wires to a box, and explained that all the measurements would be sent through to the next room, where he would be monitoring everything.

"I'm here all night, so we won't miss anything. Are you staying here too, Chief?"

It took Anthony a moment to realise Derek was talking to him.

"Yes. I mean, if that's ok?"

He looked at Ariadne, who nodded slowly. She looked almost dazed at this point, and felt it too.

"Of course its ok, Jackson", she said vacantly.

He turned back to Derek.

"I can just sit in the waiting room if I'm allowed"

Derek gave an excited chuckle.

"Of course you're allowed! But sit in with me Chief!"

He gave Anthony a hard slap on the shoulder.

"Thanks", Anthony replied, giving Ariadne a

confused look. He began to wonder what it must do to a person to spend endless hours in a small room watching other people sleep.

Derek leaned nearer to him.

"Although I have to warn you Chief, it's not all glamorous working at a sleep clinic, nothing like the films"

Anthony's earlier question had apparently been answered.

"OK. I'll lower my expectations", he said with a wink.

"No worries", Derek said, completely missing the irony and giving his new best friend another hearty slap on the shoulder.

Ariadne just watched them with a slightly glazed expression on her face. She just wanted a bed to lie in. The constant adrenalin rushes and anxiety had worn her down. As much as she feared sleep, she also craved it. It was like being in a burning building, in a room full of smoke. The knowledge that the next breath would consist of toxic smoke wouldn't stop the desire to breathe, or the eventual automatic inhalation. Sleep was a need, just like breathing. No matter what it might bring, it had to be done.

She wanted to sleep for as long as possible here too. As long as she was being monitored then she was safe, it was something she wanted to take full advantage of.

She brightened slightly as a thought occurred to her.

"Is there anything I could take", she asked Derek, "to make sure I get a good night's sleep?"

"You don't look like you need anything, there, if I'm being honest. Also, we're not allowed to give any kind of medication. There have been some bad incidents in the past"

"Like, side effects?"

Derek wasn't making eye contact anymore.

"Not…side effects, exactly. There was an incident some years ago when one of the people we were studying was having night terrors. Do you know what they are?"

Ariadne nodded, Anthony didn't.

"You don't know, Chief?"

Derek stood straighter now, and when he spoke it was with much more authority.

"I suppose the easiest way to describe it is like a nightmare, but much worse. People generally open their eyes in the middle of it, there, and look around in this crazy kind of way. They're not just afraid Chief, they're *terrified*. Like an animal in one of those nature documentaries being chased by a lion and about to get torn to shreds. Terror. Some of them scream or shout or wave their arms around, or hug their knees to their chest like they're trying to prevent an attack. Who knows what they're seeing in there, but it's nothing good. You can't comfort them or help them, you just have to wait until they wake up. And when they do, get out of the way, there, because they're likely to still be panicked which means they'll come out swinging. I've seen it a lot"

Anthony nodded.

"So, what happened?", he asked.

Derek gave him a quizzical look.

"The side effects?"

"Oh. Well, we were monitoring this man a while ago who said he suffered from night terrors. Except he couldn't sleep while he was here. I mean, eventually he would've done but we didn't have time to wait. We only had one study room at this point, so we had to make the most of it. He was vomiting because he was so scared too, poor guy, so we gave him medication to help him sleep"

Derek's eyes glazed over, as if he was seeing the incident in his mind all over again. Ariadne thought he had the look of someone who'd replayed this story over and over again mentally, but hadn't necessarily spoken about it much.

Like herself, and her own dreams, she thought.

Anthony spoke.

"So what *did* happen Derek?"

His eyes refocused as he came back into the room.

"He got trapped. A night terror could last maybe an hour at most, this one went on for two. And he couldn't get out of it. So we don't give medication"

Ariadne felt like a piece of the puzzle was missing. She looked at Anthony to gauge his response, which seemed the same as hers. She turned back to Derek.

"Two hours?", she asked, "But…I mean, that doesn't sound that bad. I mean, no, it sounds bad. It sounds horrible. But, you look like somebody died"

His head jerked up, and he looked Ariadne directly in the eye when he spoke.

"He did. It only lasted two hours because that's when he died. Probably would've lasted five times that, but the stress of the night terror was too much for him, there, and his heart gave out. He was trapped in his own personal mental and physical torture for two full hours. Every horrific thing that he'd ever seen or experienced or imagined must have happened to him in that night terror. Every single thing. And it would've felt so real his body wouldn't know the difference. It literally ended up killing him"

Derek looked from Ariadne to Anthony, whose concerned face mirrored her own.

"We can't give any medication", Derek said solemnly, and left the room.

Ariadne didn't feel particularly tired anymore. Silence hung in the room between her and Anthony like a third presence.

"Well", he began, "that was intense. He didn't even call anybody 'Chief' for a few seconds"

"It was", she replied, her gaze fixed somewhere miles away.

Anthony took his friend's hand, which seemed to snap her back into the present. Her body didn't move, but her eyes focused on him.

"I'll be here, Ari"

She squeezed his hand.

"I know. Thank you. And not just for this

Jackson… I can't imagine what I put you through last night with the police, and-"

"Ari, stop. We've been through this. It's alright. You're going through something horrible right now and I'm going to help you just like you helped me when I needed you. I'm not going anywhere. Police, or no police"

This time it was Ariadne who instigated an embrace, albeit one at arm's length to minimise any pain it might cause her chest. She was also trying to be careful not to rip any electrodes or pads off either.

The hug felt good, she felt protected again.

"Although… you know", Anthony said, "the 'no police' option would probably be better…"

She smiled and suddenly realised how kind his eyes were when he looked at her.

An hour later, as she lay in the bed in the clinic and was drifting off to sleep, it was that embrace and that look which she remembered. Of all the warm experiences that she ran though her mind as a way to relax, that was the one to finally give her the permission she needed to let go.

Ariadne fell asleep.

Twenty One

Derek had described the 'nerve centre' of the sleep clinic in such a way that Anthony had half-expected an enormous door to slide open with a hiss, revealing a multi-levelled expanse of glass and chrome. The area would be filled with monitors and specialist sleep equipment that was being tended to by the world's top scientists.

In reality, Anthony had seen toilet cubicles that were bigger than this room. And probably more comfortable.

Derek walked in first. On the left side was a small desk on which sat a laptop. There were around eight cables running from it to various other machines. There was also something that looked like a polygraph machine, as well as one of those heart rate monitors Anthony had seen on just about every television medical drama from the last three decades.

Above the desk on brackets were two small monitors attached to the wall. They looked older than Anthony, and as if they were ready to collapse at any given moment. Anthony recognised the image on the first monitor as the bedroom where Ariadne was now sleeping. He felt a skip in his heartbeat as he saw her looking so still and calm. She looked more at peace than he'd seen in a long time. He hoped it would last, but suspected it probably wouldn't.

It took him a moment to work out what the other monitor showed. He decided that it must have been a view from directly above Ariadne's bed, but recorded with a different type of camera. It seemed to be one of those cameras that recorded only heat. The various reds, blues and oranges made the whole scene look quite psychedelic.

On the right side of the room was a filing cabinet, and it was obvious to Anthony that any occupant of the office could either sit at the desk or open the filing cabinet, but couldn't actually do both at the same time.

Derek must have seen the unasked question on his face.

"We don't need to use that stuff very much, Chief. Most of it is just archived papers. Take a seat"

He motioned to the two chairs. One was a faux-leather office-type chair with worn out armrests and padding missing from the seat. The other was a fold up chair that Derek had obviously set out for his guest.

Anthony sat on the fold up chair, even though it meant shuffling awkwardly past his host. The seat was surprisingly comfortable, and Anthony – suddenly aware of being exhausted - exhaled as though he'd just ran a marathon.

"Long day, huh Chief?"

"Long month"

"Yeah, I know what that's like"

Derek took his own seat next to Anthony and began typing. Anthony watched as he brought up screen after screen of diagrams and graphs, readouts and displays. He navigated them with an ease that told Anthony he had been doing this job for a very long time.

"Looks like your girlfriend hasn't had a great time of it either", Derek continued.

"Oh, she's not my girlfriend"

Derek stopped typing and looked at Anthony.

"No?"

"No. We're just friends. We work together. Just friends"

Derek turned back to his computer and resumed typing.

"Could've fooled me, Chief. She's definitely into you anyway. And the way you look at her... Looks like more than friendship, Chief!"

He chuckled heartily. When Anthony didn't join in, he turned around and gave him a quick slap on the shoulder.

"I'm joking, chief! You look so serious!"

"She's been through a lot. That's all. I just want to

be there for her. That's it"

"She touches your arm a lot though, you have to admit"

"She also had me arrested"

Derek's smile faded and was quickly replaced by a sheepish expression. He was silent for a minute, as if considering what to say next.

"Ok, Chief. But for what it's worth, I still think she likes you. Anyway, let's get this equipment set up"

As he continued opening newer and flashier screens on the computer, Anthony began thinking about what he'd said. There was no real way to know whether Ariadne liked him more than just as a friend. Everything was too confused at the moment, the water too muddied. Even if she liked him more than a friend now, maybe that was only because she was so scared all the time and needed *someone*. Once this was all over who knew how she'd feel?

Another question bubbled to the surface from the depths of his unconscious.

Who knew how – or when – this would all be over anyway?

He thought about everything that had been happening, and decided this might be the opportunity to get an expert view on it all. And there seemed no doubt that's what Derek was.

"So", he began, "have you seen all of these things before? The voices and all of that?"

Derek nodded, but didn't take his eyes off the screen.

"Not necessarily the voices, but sleep paralysis isn't new. People have been suffering from it for centuries, there. They wake up, can't move and panic. Some of them even say they feel like they're being watched or there's something in room with them. It's scary, but it's pretty common"

"What about the scratches?"

He stopped typing. He was all business again, Anthony noticed.

"That's a bit trickier, chief. Some people have reported waking up with welts and scratches on their body, and they don't know where they're from. Most of the time they're doing it themselves to be honest."

"Is it... is it possible that Ariadne did this to herself?"

Just asking the question felt like a betrayal.

"It's possible. There have been incidents of people scratching and hitting themselves. People sometimes even attack the person they're in bed with"

A cheeky grin formed on his face and he turned to Anthony.

"What?", Anthony asked, sensing his host was about to say something inappropriate.

Derek's smile dropped.

"Nothing, Chief. Never mind"

He continued typing.

"So, people actually do this to themselves?"

"Sometimes, not all the time. Some people start wearing mittens to bed, there, and still wake up with scratches. I've never seen anything like that here, but the stories are out there. Who knows what's true and what isn't? One thing I've learnt from working here is that there's more stuff we don't understand than stuff that we do"

"But what about the voice? Did Ariadne put on the voice herself?"

"Chief, you're asking me questions I don't know the answers to. If you're asking whether it's possible, then yeah, it is. Only last week there was a case where a man was in a coma for a month then came out talking in a Nigerian accent even though he'd been born and raised in Newcastle. His family tree was all Newcastle, no connection with Nigeria at all. But somehow he was able to change his voice so completely you'd think he was brought up over there. I studied psychology, so I've heard about things like this before too. So yeah, it's possible your friend put on a voice in her sleep, there, just like it's possible a person's accent can change overnight. But, you know, doesn't mean it happened"

"You studied psychology?"

There was a tone of scepticism in Anthony's voice. Derek picked up on it.

"Yes, I studied psychology Chief! Did you think I just turned up the day of the interview, there, and gave Doctor Illari a winning smile?!"

Anthony allowed himself to laugh at this.

"Sorry Derek, no.. I didn't mean to… I'm tired and stressed that's all"

"Is that cos you're worried about your *girlfriend*?"

He turned and gave Anthony a wink.

Now they both laughed.

"Ok, Chief. Let me be honest here. I know about this case. I know about your arrest. All of it. And I can honestly say that there's nothing there that can't be explained by psychology. Literally, nothing. Yeah it's weird, and yeah it's scary, but it's all explainable. I don't know if that makes you feel better or not, but there it is"

Anthony thought carefully before speaking again, and when he did his voice was quiet, almost conspiratorial.

"What if", he said, "what if I saw something too?"

"What do you mean? You saw something? The other night, there, with the police?"

"No. I went to Ariadne's house to find her, it was after the other night. She was still in hospital but I didn't know that obviously, so I went to her place. I looked through the letterbox and there were…"

"What?"

"Shadows"

"Shadows?"

"Shadows"

"What do you mean shadows?"

"What do you mean what do I mean? Shadows! You've been *outside* this building, I take it?"

"Yeah, Mr Smart Man, I've been outside and I've

seen shadows. Why is that weird? They're not exactly rare"

"Her house was empty and I saw shadows. Like people were in there. And I felt, I don't know, watched"

Anthony suddenly wished he hadn't said anything.

"You felt wat-"

"Look, I know it sounds stupid, ok? But Ariadne keeps talking about a shadow man in her dream. I go to her house and see shadows moving in an empty place. I mean, surely this can't all be explained by psychology? She's not crazy Derek, and neither am I"

Derek stopped typing and was silent for a minute. He looked at the monitor but didn't seem to be looking at anything in particular.

He clicked his fingers.

"The cat"

"What?"

"Her cat! She's got a cat, yeah? Cats move around. Shadows. And you felt watched? To be honest, there Chief, if I went back to a place where I'd been arrested a day earlier I'd probably feel pretty watched too. Mystery solved"

Anthony shook his head. Logically, it made sense, but there was still something not quite right.

"No, there are other things too. Like, I thought I heard laughter, and Ari kept saying the shadow man laughed. It's...ah forget it"

He turned to the monitor now too, and watched Ariadne sleeping. He thought about everything she'd been through, and everything *he'd* been through. It couldn't *all* be explained by psychology. There was too much going on, too many similarities between things he'd felt and things Ari had felt.

"Ok", Derek began, "maybe there is something else going on. I don't know. I'm just here to analyse your friend's sleep, and look for anything irregular. These monitors and all this equipment is going to give us more information about what's happening. You know about the five stages, yeah?"

Anthony's blank look answered the question.

"The five stages of sleep?"

"I work for a healthcare regulator, Derek. The only stages I know about involve people being struck off or suspended"

"Point taken, there. You know about REM sleep though?"

"I know it exists. That's when you dream isn't it?"

Derek shifted in his seat slightly, and again adopted his 'professional' voice.

"Ok, there are basically five stages of sleep. They go from one to four, and then the fifth is REM. These five stages come in cycles, and each cycle lasts about an hour an half to two hours. Your REM sleep in the first few cycles each night are generally pretty short, but as the night goes the length of the REM increases. You with me so far, Chief?"

"Yes. Five stages equals one cycle. And the last part of each cycle is REM sleep"

"Exactly. So stage one is pretty light. You kind of drift all over the place, in and out of sleep, and it won't take much to wake you. Have you ever been falling asleep and suddenly jerked awake like you've been electrocuted?"

Anthony recognised that as something he'd experienced a number of times. He'd wake up, startled and wondering what had just happened.

"Sometimes", he said.

"Right, so the times that happened to you, you were in stage one. You feel like you're falling, there, then your whole body jerks. It's weird, and can scare the crap out of anybody you're sleeping with too"

He gave a wink which Anthony could only really describe as 'sleazy'.

Not getting the response he'd hoped, Derek continued.

"Anyway, that's stage one. Stage two is pretty dull, your brain waves get slower but no jerking or freefalling.

You can tell when stage three begins – well, someone monitoring you can - because your brain waves slow right down and you get these incredibly long waves called delta waves, but they're mixed with faster waves too. Then at stage four it's pretty much delta waves only. To be honest, a lot of people reckon stages three and four are the same, and group them both as one. I like keeping them separate though, the more specific you can be about these things the better. That's what I think. Anyway, we measure all this with that weird looking thing over there"

He motioned to the machine that Anthony had earlier thought looked like a polygraph.

"It looks like a lie detector", he said.

"It does actually, and there are some similarities I suppose Chief. With this, at any given time we can see what stage of sleep your friend is in. Welcome to the world of electroencephalography. Pretty cool, huh Chief?"

Anthony nodded and found himself genuinely impressed with Derek's knowledge.

"Ok, so after stage four we get?", Derek asked, the teacher testing his student.

"REM sleep?", Anthony asked, slightly worried about getting the wrong answer and missing out on the gold star.

"Yup! Very good there Chief. Actually, let's go back a step for a minute, you might find this interesting. Stage four is considered deep sleep, so there's no eye movement and no muscle activity, okay? Also, at this stage you have a hard time waking someone up. It's here where kids might wet the bed, or adults might go for a little sleepwalk, okay?"

"Ok"

"It's also here", Derek continued, "where you might find night terrors"

"So, if Ari gets to this stage-"

"She will get to this stage, Chief"

"So when she gets to this stage, we have to watch

and see what happens?"

"We don't have to. Everything's being recorded and timed, so we can match the stage of sleep with anything strange we see happening on the screen, or anything your friend tells us when she wakes up"

Anthony took a minute to absorb all this information.

"So what about stage five then? REM sleep"

Derek shifted excitedly in his seat.

"This is my favourite part cos fun things start happening here. You start breathing more rapidly and not as regularly, your muscles are paralysed and your eyes jerk around all over the place. If you want to know where sleep paralysis lives, it's here Chief. Your brain actually *paralyses* you – think about that, our brain paralyses us *every single* night. It does this so we don't start trying to get up and act out our dreams in our bedrooms, which is a good thing. But..."

He paused for effect and raised finger.

"When there's overlap between this stage and waking up, then your brain might get confused and keep you paralysed for a while. On top of that, at this stage your heart rate gets quicker too, your body can't regulate its temperature effectively anymore, and your blood pressure goes up. You with me so far? Imagine it Chief, imagine waking up paralysed in the middle of the night with your heart racing and being either unbearably hot or painfully cold. Not nice, Chief, especially if you've never experienced it before and haven't got a clue what's happening"

Anthony looked to the screen and at Ariadne. He tried to imagine what she must have been going through the past few weeks, but found he didn't want to think about it anymore. It made him too uncomfortable to contemplate poor Ariadne in that house, alone, being tormented night after night. Whether it could be explained by psychology or not – and at this point he still thought not – it was torture for her.

Derek put a consoling hand on his shoulder.

"She'll be ok, Chief. We'll find out what's going on. This is what we do"

Anthony didn't move his eyes from the screen. He knew it was impossible but thought for a second that he could see Ariadne's eyes flickering underneath her eyelids. The camera was too far away to pick up a tiny detail like that, but he could've sworn he saw it. Maybe she was dreaming.

He just wished he knew what she was seeing in there.

Twenty Two

A corridor.

An endless tube stretching into infinity, the floral carpet indicating that this is some horrific house, stretched and skewed. The lighting is poor but lining each wall are a thousand doors, all identical.

Then, a feeling. One of those feelings that tells you something is undoubtedly true, even though you have no idea how you know.

The feeling travels in pulses through the body, as though being enthusiastically pumped through the circulatory system by the heart itself.

The message is clear - one of these doors will lead to freedom, safety.

None of the others will.

A noise from behind, heavy footsteps. Starting quietly but then increasing in both volume and speed. The chase is on now. The attack imminent.

The adrenalin flows as the heartbeat rockets. Another attack is coming, it's inevitable.

Unless…

Unless I can find the right door.

A door coming up on the left is slightly ajar, but that would be too obvious. The door needs to feel like the right one, not just be the most convenient. That one is probably a trap, who knew what new evils would lurk behind it? A gentle push of the door, and Pandora's Box would open, unleashing unimaginable and irreversible horrors.

So which door is the correct one?

A voice can be heard from somewhere. Rapid shouts. Not angry, more of a warning. Maybe a warning about the doors? Or maybe it's supposed to sound like a warning, but is actually a threat? There is no way of knowing anymore.

Legs getting tired now, heart racing, breathing

getting difficult.

As he finally fell to the floor, defeated, Alex Perasmenos felt his pursuer's hand grab onto his shoulder, and suddenly understood what was being said.

"Please sweetheart! Stop!"

"Leave me alone!", he shouted, as he squirmed to get away. There were more doors, one of them had to lead to freedom. She couldn't keep him trapped here any longer.

The pursuer shouted again, her voice breaking this time as though she was crying.

"Where are you trying to go, sweetheart? It's two o'clock in the morning!"

She broke down and cried now, her hand falling from his shoulder and joining her other hand to cover her face.

He turned and looked at her, registering the wrinkled hands over the face, and the shoulders heaving with every tear. There was something familiar in her voice now. Not threatening, or even warning anymore. Just familiar. He started to think maybe she wasn't trying to hurt him. He still didn't know who she was, or where they both were, so he knew he still needed to tread carefully. He looked around and saw a light fitting that he used to have in his old house. The place he lived with Maria.

He thought about Maria a lot. He desperately wished she'd come and save him from all this.

He stared at the woman kneeling next to him on the floor, her face still in her hands. He could still hear her crying, although it seemed to be quieter now. Maybe she wasn't so sad anymore.

He put his hand on her shoulder, which seemed to make her cry even more for some reason. He didn't know why, he was just trying to help. Why had she started crying again? And why were they sitting on the floor?

"You'll catch cold", he found himself saying to her, "it's cold out here"

This seemed to mean something to the lady. She

took her hands away from her face and looked at him.

"It is cold isn't it, Alex?"

How did he know her name? No matter, she'd stopped crying now and he was feeling a bit chilly too now she mentioned it.

"Yes, it is", he said.

"Shall we go to that room at the end? It's warm in there. That's where your bed is"

Maria chose her words carefully. That's where their bed used to be, but not anymore. For longer than she could remember she'd been sleeping in the spare room. It meant he wouldn't wake up and be scared at the stranger lying next to him, but at the same time meant that she was close enough to hear him if he got up or needed her in the night. He'd been walking around at night a lot recently. He was getting worse.

He nodded at the lady and stood up, reaching out a hand to help her too. She took it gratefully and allowed him to help her up.

Alex Perasmenos would never know how much that gesture meant to his wife. As far as he was concerned, he was helping an old lady to stand. As far as that old lady was concerned though, her husband was showing her a kindness like he always used to. For that brief second Alex was the gentleman she'd met and fallen in love with. The gentleman she'd married.

She led him to the bedroom, thinking about how often she used to do that when they'd first got married. She'd take his hand and the two lovers would walk upstairs, giggling and excited. It was a lifetime ago, never to happen again.

She helped him into bed and waited for him to drift off before leaving the room. It didn't take very long for him to fall asleep, mainly because he hadn't slept properly for months. Neither of them had. She knew it wasn't falling asleep that was the problem, it was waking up an hour later and not knowing where he was.

As she lay in her bed, listening out for any noises and looking to the corridor for any signs of movement, she wondered how long it would be before she had to wake up and rescue her husband again. If she was lucky it would be a couple of hours, if she was really lucky it'd be three.

Her thoughts turned to Ariadne. She realised that she hadn't spoken to her for a while, and missed their exchanges. She'd give her a call in the morning. She hadn't even asked poor Ariadne how she'd been sleeping recently. Her focus had been Alex, not her daughter, and certainly not herself.

Her focus was always Alex now.

She thought about that man again, and how his widow had waited for twenty years in vain for him to wake up. She couldn't imagine what that was like. Waiting for two decades for the love of your life to come back. She wondered what was worse, seeing a person that you love asleep for years and then losing them, or seeing them like Alex and then losing them anyway. At least the widow could remember her husband as he was, not as a scared and confused version of himself.

The guilt began burrowing into her. It did that sometimes, sneaking up on her and telling her she was bad for thinking things, or evil for wanting some part of her old life back. The truth was, there wasn't much more that she could physically or emotionally do for Alex. As carers went, she was perfect. There was no room for improvement.

She ignored the guilt this time —sometimes she could, sometimes she couldn't – and went back to thinking about the man in the coma.

Not for the first time, she didn't think she'd sleep very much for the rest of the night.

Twenty Three

Even though he hadn't realised, it was a year ago to the day that Anthony had gone back to work. He'd had almost five months on leave after what Human Resources euphemistically called 'the incident'.

This amount of time off might have seemed excessive to those around him – specifically the office gossips - but the truth was that 'the incident' was essentially the last straw.

Anthony's problems had been a lifetime in the making.

As a child he'd always been more anxious than his classmates, without always knowing why or where the anxiety had come from. As he got older sometimes things would affect him so deeply that they'd cause him to switch from his baseline of 'anxious' to full-blown 'panicked'.

That was one of the reasons he'd been so proud of himself at the police station, it was one of the few times in his life he'd managed to get control of his anxiety and prevent a full-on panic attack.

He realised that there didn't seem to be any specific pattern or common thread running through the things that would trigger an attack. Sometimes it was an event at work, sometimes an exchange with someone on the tube, and sometimes even just sitting and thinking about his life would tie him up in so many knots he wouldn't know what day it was.

The event that finally tipped him from anxiety to an almost total breakdown happened at work. One of his registrants had turned up for a hearing and apparently decided that the whole investigation was Anthony's fault. It wasn't. Anthony was just the paper-pusher, the middle man between the practice committees and the registrants themselves.

It had all happened almost by chance. The

registrant – a muscular mental health nurse named Connor Burgess – was causing a scene at reception just as Anthony was walking out to lunch. Not having witnessed any of the previous shouting, when Anthony was asked by Connor if he knew a man named Anthony Jackson, he simply responded by saying "That's me".

At which point Connor floored him with a single punch, and proceeded to use his midriff as a football. It had taken three security guards to restrain him until the police arrived.

Anthony had never been a violent person, like most sane people he tried to avoid physical confrontations whenever possible. The resultant shock and trauma of the attack made him spiral rapidly into a deep depression. He became not only wary of leaving the house, but also found himself incredibly scared of other people. It'd taken five long months of tears, therapy, and support groups to get him back to some semblance of normality, and even then he knew he'd never be completely the same. To his private shame, even now whenever he went to lunch he used a different door to the one he'd used that day.

On the recommendation of one of his therapists, he tried to keep safely exposing himself to things which made him feel apprehensive. So he'd spent a lot of time watching documentaries on gangs, war, killings, and anything else which would normally cause his anxiety levels to increase.

He'd found the programmes on gangs the most difficult to watch, mainly due to the senselessness and ferocity of the violence. He'd experienced all too well how quickly violence could flare up in the real world, and the illusion that we are all protected by some sort of unspoken social etiquette that nobody would dare disobey had been shattered along with his ribs.

The serial killer documentaries were the easiest for him to watch, maybe because serial killings were so rare and there was never any real-life footage of any violence being committed. The gangs had seemed to film everything. He soon realised that aside from the biography of the specific killer, most of these programmes gave pretty much the same information, so he got used to them quite quickly.

He also began to learn some things.

The first thing he'd learned was the 'Macdonald Triad', otherwise known as the serial killer triangle due to the three childhood traits that formed the points of it. These traits were apparently shared by a huge number of serial killers, and each documentary trotted out the same information as though imparting great wisdom to the viewer. Anthony knew the traits by heart now - bed-wetting, cruelty to animals, and starting fires. Of course, the information was useless until someone actually started killing, otherwise it meant locking up a child for the rest of their life based on behaviours that could – but wouldn't necessarily – mean they'd turn out to be a danger to society.

The second thing he remembered was the information about post-mortems and how they could help pinpoint the exact method of killing. Stab and gunshot wounds were usually – but not always – fairly straightforward, but it was the rarer ones which fascinated Anthony. Some victims had little red flecks around their eyes known as petechial haemorrhaging, which could be used to show evidence of strangulation. The name had always stuck with Anthony as he once had a teacher called Mr Pete Teakle who, he imagined, would have had an even rougher time at school if his student's had known about this phrase.

Then there were the various bruises and ligature marks which were sometimes found around the neck, which could be used to ascertain with frightening accuracy just what type of material was used to strangle the poor victim.

It was this type of bruising that Anthony's mind violently flashed back to as he stared in disbelief at the marks appearing on Ariadne's neck.

Only moments earlier, he had been sitting with Derek, talking about how hungry he was and if anywhere was open to get something to eat. That was when an alarm had sounded.

Derek had nonchalantly flicked a switch.

"That's the EEG I told you about. Delta waves, Chief. Your friend is having a dream"

Derek had casually leaned back onto the hind legs of his chair and stretched, glancing up at the small monitor at the same time as Anthony.

Derek nearly fell completely backwards off his chair now, and frantically pin wheeled his arms in an effort to straighten himself, all the while not taking his eyes off the monitor.

Ariadne was jerking and convulsing on the bed, as though she were being repeatedly defibrillated by some invisible force.

Anthony grabbed Derek's shoulder frantically and watched, frozen and in disbelief, as his friend jerked and jumped on the bed.

In an instant the two men ran from the office to the bedroom, Anthony calling his friend's name as he ran, his mind flashing back to the horrors of the other evening.

Derek wrenched the door open and ran in, switching on the lights and rushing over to Ariadne.

"Ariadne! Miss Perasmenos!", he shouted. He tried first to shake her awake, and then when that proved fruitless he tried to restrain her at the shoulders to stop her from harming herself.

Anthony ran to the foot of the bed, and tried in vain to hold Ariadne's legs down. She kicked ferociously, as though trying to free herself from some invisible bonds.

"Ari!", Anthony shouted, "Wake up! Ari!"

Her eyes remained closed, but her face was contorted into a grimace of pain. Her fists – white at the knuckles - were clenched tightly but remained firmly at her side, even though her upper arms were intermittently whipping upwards. It was as though she was being restrained at the wrists, and fighting to get free.

Derek pushed down harder, fearing that she might dislocate her shoulders through the violent spasms.

It was at this point that Anthony noticed the red marks appearing on Ariadne's neck and his mind flashed back to the documentaries. The marks were indicators of a brutal strangulation, yet with nothing external apparently inflicting them.

"What do we do?!", Anthony screamed at Derek, who followed his gaze to Ariadne's neck.

Large red welts were appearing and patches of skin darkened into bruises.

He returned the question with a look of panic which immediately told Anthony that any theories of psychology as the cause of this had gone out of the window.

An alarm still sounded from somewhere. As Anthony used his bodyweight to push down on Ariadne's ankles and restrain her, he thought it sounded like a screech. Then it became more staccato, almost a rat-tat-tat.

Then, a cackle.

The adrenalin surging in him, Anthony screamed at Ariadne. In a single fluid movement, he let go of her legs, rushed to the top of the bed, and grabbed her face.

He leaned over and shouted into her ear.

"Ariadne! You have to wake up! Do you understand? You have to wake up!"

Her face had turned red and she gasped now as if struggling to breathe. Anthony's own breath caught in his throat and his stomach plummeted to the floor as he saw tiny red flecks –*petechiae* - appearing around Ariadne's eyes. He could hear a faint wheezing coming from her mouth, even though nothing visible seemed to be choking her. The marks on her neck became a deeper red colour now too, tinged with a darker blue.

Derek joined in the chorus, both men shouting as loudly as they could in an effort to wake Ariadne.

Suddenly, as though a switch had been tripped, she stopped choking and thrashing and was still.

Silence.

Anthony and Derek looked at each other, the unspoken question hanging in the air between them.

What is *happening* here?

A horrific grin creeped onto Ariadne's face. Both men then stood and watched in horror as a thin but definite cut snaked its way slowly across Ariadne's collarbone. The blood seeped from the fresh wound and dripped lazily down towards the bed.

As the blood reached the sheet and began soaking into the cotton, Ariadne's limbs began thrashing again. Small flecks of blood flicked into the air, some landing on Ariadne's face which was still fixed with that sick grin.

The panic took hold of Anthony completely now.

"Ari! No!", he screamed.

Derek, still trying but failing to restrain her by the shoulders, gasped at the new horrors he was witnessing.

"He's killing her! Do something!", Anthony shouted at him.

Derek let go of Ariadne's shoulders and did the only thing he could think of. He slapped her hard across the face.

Her eyes opened and she gasped as though emerging from a near-drowning, lurching forward and sitting up.

She swallowed massive gulps of air as if having finished a marathon. Anthony put his hands on her shoulders

"It's ok, Ari. I'm here"

She turned and looked at him, but her focus was somewhere else. She turned her head back towards the door and stared at a point somewhere in the far distance.

The room was silent except for the fading sound of the alarm, and the irregular rhythm of Ariadne's harsh breathing.

Anthony took a tentative step back. The blood on Ariadne's wound ran down her chest now, the red liquid pooling in the crease of her pyjamas at the waist.

"Ari?", Anthony asked quietly, his voice not much more than a whisper. "Are you ok?"

She never shifted her gaze, even when she finally spoke. When she did, her voice was quiet as though matching Anthony's, but her speech was clear. Both Anthony and Derek were in no doubt as to the four solitary words she said next.

"I saw his face"

Twenty Four

Dr. Illari arrived within an hour of Derek's frantic telephone call.

He walked into his office and saw them all sitting solemnly, as though witnesses to some unspeakable horror. Anthony had moved one of the armchairs next to Ariadne's chair and was holding her hand. Derek sat behind the desk, jumping up out of the chair as he saw his boss enter the room. The doctor didn't notice, his face was that of a man both concerned and intrigued by what he had been told. He hurriedly took off his coat and walked over to Ariadne.

"Miss Perasmenos", he said, trying desperately to avoid staring at the marks on her neck, "I must apologise for my absence this evening, although as I am sure you can appreciate I had not anticipated that I would be needed"

Somewhere in her mind, Ariadne sensed that she should probably be comforted by the doctor's voice, but she felt nothing but a vague numbness.

"It's ok", she said quietly and with no emotion, "I don't think it would have made a difference anyway"

He shared a look of concern with Anthony, then retrieved a fold-up chair from behind the door and sat opposite them.

"Would you like to tell me about the dream?", he asked Ariadne gently.

She absent-mindedly shook her head, then answered as dispassionately as if she were reading from a script.

"It was the same as always, he was chasing me then came after me in his car. Except this time he didn't hit me with the car and when he'd caught up with me, we were inside it instead. I was his passenger and he was strangling me as we drove"

"Where were you going?"

"I don't know", she frowned as she tried to retrieve the memory. "At the start of the dream I think I was driving by myself, and then…"

She gasped as the memory scorched through her mind, violently and suddenly.

Anthony placed his free hand on her shoulder.

"It's ok Ari. You're safe now", he said. "Do you remember what happened next?"

She closed her eyes as she answered.

"He was in the back seat at first. I was driving. He swung his arm around the headrest and started strangling me. Then somehow he was at the wheel and I was in the passenger seat. But my arms and legs were paralysed again and he was still choking me. Somehow he was driving even though both his hands were on my neck. After that, he had some kind of blade. That's when he cut me. He drew the blade along here..."

She traced the outline of the cut on her collar bone with her finger. She remembered Derek using antiseptic wipes and some kind of paper strips to seal the wound, and she could feel the slight bumps of the paper now. It wasn't deep, more like a long paper-cut, but the fact that it happened at all terrified her.

In an instant the fear came flooding back, and the terror and horror knocked into her like a freight train. Any defences she'd put up were knocked down now, exposing her to the harsh reality of what had happened.

"What is *happening* to me?", she screamed out as she began to cry. Any numbness had vanished totally now, replaced with an overwhelming hybrid of sadness and fear.

Anthony turned towards her and she instinctively reached out to him with her arms open. He embraced her, mindful this time of not squeezing too hard because of her wounds - old and new.

"We're going to find out, Ari", he said consolingly, looking at Doctor Illari for some kind of confirmation on that. The doctor didn't look so sure but somehow managed to prevent his doubt from seeping into his words.

"Of course we will, Mr Jackson. You have nothing

to worry about, Miss Perasmenos. We have the recordings and data from last night, and we will do everything we can to find out what happened and how to stop this"

None of the assurances made Ariadne feel any better. She was beginning to think she needed an exorcist, not a sleep expert. Her mind returned to the old lady in the hospital and what she'd said about unexplainable things happening.

"Dr", she asked, wiping the tears away with her hand, "has this happened before? I mean, that you've experienced?"

He paused for some time, considering his response.

"I have heard stories like this Miss Perasmenos, but never anything that has been taken seriously by much of the scientific or medical communities. I have to say, I myself have not seen anything like this and so cannot corroborate any of the reports in existence. In fact I'm not sure how much credence to give them at all. But, Miss Perasmenos, we've seen plenty of sleep disorders here, and occasionally a person might wake up with a bruise or mark on them and not know how it got there. There's always the possibility that it's psychosomatic, but it's not an area that I have had much experience in I'm afraid. It's just not that common"

"What about cuts?", she asked, trying to prevent the tears from returning, "Could the cuts from the other night have happened like this one?"

She pointed at her neck as she spoke, but stopped short of touching it again. Anthony noticed her hand was shaking.

"It's... possible Miss Perasmenos", the doctor said cautiously, "The mind can convince the body of many things, even injuries. When we feel stress, we might feel sick. When we're happy, we probably have an abundance of energy. Similarly, if your dream is vivid enough then maybe your body believes that what is happening is real, to the point where it manifests the injury onto itself"

Ariadne didn't think he sounded particularly

convinced.

"But you haven't seen this before?"

"No, I'm afraid I haven't, but if we discover that there is no alternative explanation, then we might have to work on the basis that this too could be psychosomatic"

Ariadne wasn't sure how to feel about this, although she didn't think there was a correct way to deal with any of it. She held on tight to Anthony.

"I think there is an alternative, Doctor", Derek suddenly said.

"Oh?"

"Doctor, me and the Chief here saw what happened. Something did that to her. It was holding her arms so she couldn't move, and then... did that to her neck. I know what you're thinking, but think about how many years I've been doing this –*we've* been doing this. This has gone from sleep disorder into... I don't even know. Some people find small bruises when they wake up, yes. We've both read the journals and seen the reports. But cuts? This is... it was an attack, Doctor"

The doctor visibly bristled at this.

"Derek, I think we should review the recording and see what happened, then we can decide what we think happened and how to proceed. Now is not a time for ghost stories"

It was the first time he had used that word, and it hung heavily in the air amongst them.

"Doctor", Derek continued, "before all of this happened, I was telling the Chief here how all of the things that have happened can be explained by sleep disorders and psychology. I mean, sleep paralysis on its own is enough to terrify most people, there, and just watching a night terror is bad enough, let alone being inside one. But I'm not convinced there isn't more to this Doctor. There was a purpose behind this. It felt different"

"It felt different? And how many times have you been in the room with a patient, Derek? Maybe what felt different was the fact that you weren't behind a door watching on a monitor. You were in the room while all of this was happening, manhandling the patient no less"

"We had to go in, Doctor. We were restraining her so she didn't dislocate anything, there. We weren't doing anything wrong. It's not like we caused that cut"

Doctor Illari didn't respond. Ariadne sensed that this wasn't the first time they'd had this type of conversation.

"I don't know Doctor, I'm just saying", Derek continued, more cautiously, "maybe something else is going on here. Something that we don't quite understand yet. That's all I'm saying"

The doctor turned to Ariadne.

"Miss Perasmenos, I'm sorry that you're having to listen to this. Derek here seems to have forgotten that we are doctors and work by the rules and parameters of science"

He looked directly at Derek.

"Science, Derek. Not voodoo. If we are unable to find an adequate explanation for these events then we will of course review the situation and come to a decision. Until then, we will look over the evidence we have - and by that I mean the recordings from Miss Perasmenos' house the other evening as well as the data from tonight – and cast our objective and scientific minds over it all. I hope this is clear, Derek?"

It was apparent to them all that this wasn't a question.

Derek nodded, his shoulders slumping slightly.

"Ok, Doctor. Maybe I could've waited for a more appropriate time to voice my views, there. I'm sorry, Miss Perasmenos. Sorry, Chief. I'll go and get the recordings together"

He left the room, carefully avoiding eye contact with Doctor Illari.

The doctor turned back to Ariadne. This time his voice *was* calming to her.

"Miss Perasmenos, you have been through an

extraordinarily difficult time, and I don't just mean tonight, I mean with everything that's happened recently. You have my clinic at your disposal if you wish to stay and try to sleep, we have another bedroom if you'd prefer to rest in there. Alternatively, I can make arrangements for a car to take you home, or to take you to a hospital if you would like them to look at your neck. It is entirely up to you"

There was only one place Ariadne wanted to be now. A safe place, somewhere she was always able to go to in a crisis. Somewhere she probably should have gone to when this all started.

"I think I should take up my mum's offer to go and stay with her. It'd do me good to get out of London"

The doctor nodded.

As she spoke the words an odd feeling swept over her. It was as though her parents' house was where she was headed all along. As though there'd be some kind of answer there and this would end, one way or another.

Doctor Illari organised a car to take her home, and assured her that he would review all of the information they'd collected and let her know what he found.

As she travelled in the back of the cab, she watched the streets of London as they woke up and began a new day. Deliveries were being made to various shops, employees with bunches of keys opened doors and shutters, a few people in suits wandered around nursing cups of coffee. Amidst the excitement and promise of a new day, she sensed a strange and unfamiliar feeling.

He wasn't grinning anymore.

Twenty Five

Ariadne felt strangely hopeful walking back into her house.

Anthony had gone home to pick up his car so he could drive Ariadne to her parents' house. She had thought that entering the house alone might have made her feel scared, and was surprised to find that she was feeling quite positive.

At first she thought it was because she was out of that clinic – not to mention out of that nightmare - and going back to somewhere familiar. Her home, her territory. This didn't feel like the full explanation though, especially since it hadn't truly felt like it was *her* territory for weeks now.

There was something making her feel better, stronger.

It wasn't until she began walking upstairs that she was able to place it. As she ascended, her mind drifted back to the time when she had walked up the stairs and felt some kind of presence. The memory of it made her realise why she now felt more positive.

He was weaker now.

And not just because she'd seen his face, although that was certainly a part of it. The creature had a face. She knew who she needed to beat.

There was another reason for her optimism though - he didn't want her going to her parents' house. The fact she was going to arrange to do just that made her feel more in control. Something that *she* was going to do was negatively affecting *him*, weakening him even. And it felt good.

She reached the top of the stairs and walked towards the bedroom door. The dread feeling she had begun to experience – the knots in her stomach, the slight nausea, the weak feeling in her legs – were all much less now. Still there, but weaker.

Like him.

She got to her bedroom and began packing a bag. She didn't know how long she'd be with her parents, but wanted to be ready for at least a week. She contemplated calling the office but didn't have the energy, she would deal with it when she could. They knew she'd fainted and had been taken to hospital, so they probably wouldn't have expected her back yet. It wasn't as if her line manager or Eddie had been concerned enough to bother calling her either. She had bigger problems to deal with.

She picked up her mobile and dialled her parents' number. She carefully and slowly placed the phone between her ear and shoulder so she could pack her clothes more quickly, although still being careful not to put any pressure on her injuries.

As the phone rang, she thought about her home. The house and this room were tainted with blood, and the memories of the dreams – if they could even be called dreams, she didn't know anymore – seemed to echo around the small space.

The phone rang longer than usual before her mum answered.

"Hello?"

"Mum. It's me"

"Ariadne! Oh sweetheart, it's so nice to hear your voice. I've been meaning to call you but things... Well, your dad's been having some more problems. So how are you sweetheart?"

"I'm ok mum. I'll tell you about it when I see you. I was thinking of maybe coming to stay for a little while if that's alri-"

"Oh Ariadne! Of course! Oh, it'd be so nice to see you. And your dad would love to see you too"

Her mum's voice was breaking slightly. She sounded choked, as though trying not to cry. Ariadne stopped packing the bag and allowed the phone to drop from her shoulder and into her hand. As she raised the handset back to her ear, a jolt of adrenalin shot through her.

"Mum? Are you ok?"

"Yes, sweetheart. I'm just so glad you're coming home"

Her voice broke completely now, and she began to cry.

"Oh Mum, what's wrong? Is everything ok with Dad?"

"He's just so confused all the time sweetheart. He doesn't even know I'm there anymore. How can you forget so many years of marriage just like that? He remembers other things from even before we were married, but he doesn't remember me"

"I know mum, but it's the illness. He's still in there somewhere. He still loves you"

"I know, sweetheart, I know. It's just so hard"

"Oh mum..."

"Look, don't worry about me, I'm just feeling a bit emotional. I haven't really slept. You just get here safely, alright sweetheart?"

"I will do mum. Don't worry, ok? We can have a nice long talk when I get there and you'll feel better. There's someone I want you to meet too"

She immediately regretted her ham-fisted attempt at casually introducing Anthony. Her mother responded immediately.

"What do you mean?", she asked, seeming to perk up slightly, "like a boy? When did you meet a boy? Which boy?"

Ariadne was reminded of a child she'd seen in a park some time ago. He'd fallen over and grazed his knee, and was inconsolable up until the point his mother had mentioned ice cream. In a second, the tears were dry.

"He's someone I work with mum. He's helped me a lot and, I don't know, he's been really supportive. He's going to drive me up to the house if that's ok? I thought

Harry probably wouldn't appreciate travelling on the train so a car would be much better for everyone"

"Of course it's ok! I can't believe you never mentioned a boy. All this waiting then suddenly there's a boy! That's really cheered me up Ariadne!"

"Mum, he's just a friend"

"No he's not! I know you Ariadne. A mother knows the difference between her daughter telling her something, and her daughter *telling* her something. And you just told me something, sweetheart. What's his name?"

"Anthony"

Then the question she knew was coming.

"Is he Greek?"

"No, mum, he's not Greek. Can we just.. you'll meet him when we get there"

"Does he like Greek food? I can make something for you when you arrive"

Ariadne knew better than to argue.

"I think he does... Mum, I really just want to stay a few days and take some time to relax. I want to see you and Dad. Let's not make this about anything else, ok?"

"OK, sweetheart"

Ariadne had been waiting for her mum to mention the dreams, but it looked like she wasn't going to, especially now that she'd mentioned Anthony. She'd planned a whole conversation that looked like it wasn't going to happen.

Unless she prompted it.

"Mum, you know I've been having those dreams?"

Her mum hesitated before responding.

"Oh, don't worry about them sweetheart. We can talk about all of that when you come up"

Ariadne's brow furrowed as she wondered about her mum's choice of words.

"Well, just so you know, I seem to have got some scratches on me, so I don't want you to be worried when you see me"

Maria felt her heartbeat quicken.

"What do you mean? Who scratched you? What's this got to do with the dreams?"

"I don't know who, Mum. I've had more nightmares recently, and this time I've woken up and there have been scratches and... look, it's fine. It looks worse than it is, but I just want you to know mum"

"I don't understand"

"I don't either. I told you about that man and the dreams and everything, and being run over and all that. Now I keep waking up with scratches and things"

"Have you told the doctor?"

"Yes. Well, I stayed at a sleep clinic bu-"

"What?! You didn't tell me that"

"We've only just got back. Didn't you wonder why I was calling you so early? And why I'm not on the way to work?"

Maria couldn't remember the last time she needed to know the specific time. Maybe one of Alex's appointments or the quiz show that he liked to watch. Everything just seemed to merge together recently. Did it really matter what hour of the day something terrible was happening?

"I didn't think, Ari, no", her mum said, sounding despondent again, "just get here as soon as you can, sweetheart. No more talk about chefs and dogs"

Ariadne frowned as the comment struck her.

Maria closed her eyes.

"Why do you say that?"

"I'm just saying", she said hurriedly, "no more talking about horrible things, just get here when you can"

"No, but... you mentioned dogs and chefs. I didn't say that"

"You did. You told me the other day!"

"Yeah, but just now I didn't mention either of them, and you mentioned both. You went weird the other day when I mentioned it too. Why would you remember that, mum?"

Maria didn't respond. Ariadne could hear her

breathing and could picture her panicking as she desperately searched for something convincing to say.

"Mum?"

"I don't know sweetheart. Just get here and we can talk about it if you want. Alright? I'll see you in a few hours"

Maria hung up.

Ariadne just stood by the wardrobe, still holding the phone to her ear. She began to wonder just what was going on.

She finished packing her bag and went downstairs to put Harry in his box. Four hours in a car probably wouldn't be that much fun for him, but she couldn't very well leave him here.

She had a curious feeling that she wouldn't have to put up with all of this much longer, that this whole ordeal was somehow coming to an end.

Although just what that meant was anybody's guess.

Twenty Six

Maria made up the bed in the second spare room with the intensity of a Marine. She *knew* she shouldn't have said anything to Ariadne. Why had she been so specific? She could've just said 'dreams' or something, she didn't have to mention the chef and that stupid dog.

She sighed mournfully. There were so many other things going on at the moment, how was she supposed to cope with it all at once?

She worked quickly and quietly, smoothing the sheets and ensuring the corners wouldn't be out of place in an nineteen-fifties hospital. She was being careful not to wake up Alex too. After all the excitement of last night, he needed his sleep. Although, as she was painfully aware, so did she.

As she plumped the pillows with too much force, she began considering what to tell Ariadne. Or whether to tell her anything at all.

After all, what good would it do? It wasn't as if this was all happening merely because she didn't know. Surely there must be another reason for all this? The whole thing defied explanation. Maybe the first few dreams made sense in a way, but going on for so long? And scratches? What was all that about?

Maybe it was Harry. She'd warned her about having a cat in the bedroom. Who knew what would happen if the cat started crawling all over her, and clawing at her in her sleep. Of course she woke up with scratches!

It had nothing to do with her not telling Ariadne. No. It was something else.

A coincidence, that's all. Nothing more, nothing less.

No need to say anything to anyone.

She continued making the bed. The soft, white duvet felt cool against her hands and arms, and she realised she was using much less force this time. The poor pillows had taken the brunt of it, apparently.

Her thoughts turned to the other part of the conversation she'd had with Ariadne.

Anthony.

Maria smiled.

It was about time she found someone and settled down, even if he wasn't Greek. As she kept telling Ariadne, London was no place for a girl on her own. And she wasn't a girl anymore, but a woman.

A woman who wasn't getting any younger.

A woman whose mother was looking forward to some grandchildren.

Maria hoped it would work out. With all the stress of looking after Alex it was nice to have some good news for a change. Everything had been dark and bleak for so long.

The faintest hint of guilt tugged at her.

Not that she minded looking after Alex, of course. After all, he was her husband.

Is her husband.

Yes, *is* my husband, she thought. Her use of the past tense caused the guilt to tug harder.

She focused her attention on making up the bed again. She thought about Ariadne again and all she'd been through recently. Hopefully this boy would help her to-

There was a loud crash from outside and she rushed to the window.

The refuse collectors were heaving boxes and dustbins, clattering them all over the place. It took a few moments for her heartbeat to settle back to normal.

As she stared out of the window, she felt her gaze being inexorably drawn to the driveway. It was as if some puppeteer held the string which controlled her head, and was intermittently pulling it so she couldn't quite be free of the view of the drive. She tried to avoid it, but found it becoming increasingly difficult. A thought came to her now, repeating in her mind over and over again.

Maybe Ariadne has a *right* to know…

She turned away from the window and continued making the bed.

Twenty Seven

Ariadne hesitated at the kerb before stepping into the car.

Anthony leaned across the passenger seat and craned his neck to see her through the open window.

"Are you ok?", he asked, noticing the scarf she'd wrapped around her neck and upper chest.

She nodded as she quickly jerked open the door and sat in the passenger seat.

"It's just that, the car...", she said.

"I know. Don't worry, I'll drive carefully"

"I don't mean your driving, I mean-"

"I know!", he said with a chuckle.

Her concerned look gave way to a smile. She felt the corners of her eyes crease and hoped the make-up she'd used to cover those red spots hadn't smudged.

"Very funny", she said, carefully pulling the belt across her chest.

"Are you ok with that belt? We can stop and buy you one of those fluffy pink things if you like? Not only will it feel softer, but you'll be the coolest cat on the motorway"

Ariadne pointed to the backseat.

"I'm fine, thanks. I wouldn't want our other cool cat to get jealous"

Harry apathetically looked out of his travel box. Unless they were bringing him food, he wasn't particularly bothered about the giants.

"So", Anthony said, "are you ready?"

"I'm ready"

"Are you sure? It's nearly four hours of motorway and the food at the services can only really be described as 'interesting'..."

"I'm sure, let's go"

"As you wish, madam"

He pulled away from the house and Ariadne felt a slight rush of adrenalin. In some odd way, she felt like she wasn't being passive anymore, that she was no longer in the role of victim. Yes, she was scared, but she was still going forward. She wasn't retreating, that's just what a victim would have done.

She was bringing the fight to him.

Him.

The shadow man, no longer faceless. She knew nothing about him other than what he looked like, and that he was tormenting her. She didn't even know if he was a real person. Although she supposed he must be. He felt real enough to her.

"-on or something?"

Anthony's voice brought her back into the present.

"Sorry?"

"Shall I put some music on or something?"

"If you want. I don't mind really. Maybe we could listen to the radio. I feel like I haven't heard any news for ages either"

He clicked on the radio and tried to find a station.

"To be fair, you've been a bit busy recently Ari. Oh, did you call work?"

"No, I haven't since I fainted. I just can't face it. I know that sounds silly, but I'll sort it out when I get back. Were they ok with you taking time off?"

"Not really. But given how much annual leave I've still got to take they can't say much. I also reckon that they think I'm liable to need therapy again at any given time, so Eddie's probably worried about saying no"

"Good old Eddie. I still can't believe he took that job. He used to be nice before he started managing everything"

"I know! He was the first person I met when I started and had to sit in on hearings. I really liked him back then. He said I could come to him anytime, blah, blah, blah. Now he spends all his time trying to trip people up so he can fire them!"

Ariadne laughed.

"Have you noticed how he asks you to confirm your signature on something before he starts shouting at you about it? He's watched too many courtroom dramas! Of course it's my work, my names on it! You don't need to get me to say it 'for the record', your honour!"

"We need to get out of that place, we really do"

"We will at some point. Hopefully sooner rather than later"

They both physically relaxed now they were talking about work. It brought a feeling of normality into what was most definitely an abnormal situation.

Ariadne fidgeted in her seat, and Anthony noticed that she kept pulling the belt away from her neck and collarbone. He was going to suggest that she unclasped the seatbelt for a while, although stopped short when he realised that would probably be insensitive given the dreams she'd been having.

"We can stop and buy something to put under that if you want? Seriously, I'm not joking. I think there'll be services coming up in about ten minutes, we can stop if you like?"

"Nah, it's ok. It's more annoying than anything. I tried wearing a polo neck to give some padding, but it just made me itchy. I'll be fine"

"Ok"

She gave him a smile. He glanced at her from the road and smiled back. They held each other's eyes a moment longer than usual.

"Thank you, Jackson. And not just for driving either. If it weren't for you I'd be a complete mess now"

"No you wouldn't. You're tough Ari. I'm just glad I could be here for you"

"I am too"

Neither of them spoke for a while. Anthony seemed overly focused on the road now, and his body language looked slightly less relaxed. He seemed nervous. She was going to make a joke, but stopped herself. She didn't want to detract from the genuine appreciation she'd voiced.

She allowed her mind to drift and realised that, ironically, she felt safer in this car than she had in a long time. It was an odd sensation. She thought that logically she shouldn't feel safe in any car because of the dreams, but she felt safe here. There was only one reason for that.

Jackson.

He somehow managed to make her feel protected, even though she didn't quite know how she could even be protected from all this. He'd gone from her close colleague to her strong protector in a matter of days.

Life can be strange.

She thought about him meeting her parents. He knew all about her dad, although she wasn't sure he really understood that dementia didn't just mean forgetting things. She hoped her dad wouldn't be too bad when she saw him. It always worried her, and the few times she'd gone up to see them since his diagnosis had been pretty difficult. It was as if a new piece of him was missing every time she saw him. Like a jigsaw being taken apart. She wondered how many pieces he could afford lose before there was nothing left.

Life can be strange.

She began playing with the radio tuner, hoping to find some music she liked, or at the very least something that didn't make her feel old. After three minutes of flitting from one station to the other, and being subjected to nothing vaguely approaching music, she found a song she recognised and actually liked. She looked at the LCD readout and saw it was a jazz radio station. So much for not feeling old. She left it playing though, it filled the car with a kind of warmth. It was comforting. Now everybody was singing the blues, not just her.

She lay back and tried to relax into the seat. The tiredness was back now, she could feel it. Sometimes it weighed her down as if from above, but this time it felt like something was *pulling* her down instead. As though the chair was somehow gently soothing her muscles until they were jelly, then lightly drawing them backwards. Like slipping into a warm pool, the water taking her weight and allowing her to just float. To just relax.

She allowed the jazz song to fill her ears, her head. As she listened to the off-beats of the music and the pained voice of the singer, she began to wonder what constituted 'jazz' exactly, and whether there were any rules to it. She vaguely remembered hearing a television presenter say that if you had to ask that question, then you'd never know. As if it was some exclusive club that you had to be born into.

The slow beats and off-keys swirled around her head, soothing her, allowing her to drift further and further away. The motorway noises dissipated until they were nothing but a vague and unnoticeable background noise. Sometimes Harry's purring vibrated through her when he was asleep on her lap. The sensation in the car was similar but somehow amplified, as if the vehicle itself was purring and vibrating, creating a whole body massage from within.

She began to hear a soft voice, almost a whisper, coming through the speaker and taking on the soothing qualities of the music. Like a summer breeze whistling through a humid night, the voice glided along, through the musical notes and into her soul.

She thought it might be another singer or a radio DJ, but then she began to recognise her own name.

"Ari-ad-ne…"

She kept her eyes closed.

She didn't feel threatened - the voice sounded friendly, there was no malice behind it. She vaguely heard the voice saying something else but couldn't make out what it was. She strained to listen, trying to tune out the ever-softer and near-silent ambient noises of the car.

As though meeting her in the middle somehow, all at once the voice became stronger, but not necessarily louder. It was more like the other sounds had faded, giving the voice the opportunity to be heard.

"You won't be the same again, Ariadne"

Her first thought was that she might have misheard, but the voice came through again, unmistakably uttering the same phrase. She strained to listen further, all the while keeping her eyes closed as though this would somehow make the voice clearer.

"Don't open this door"

There was an urgency to the voice now. It still wasn't threatening, more of a plea. A friendly warning.

Which served to make it all the more unnerving.

A sudden curiosity swept over her. She wanted to know why she shouldn't go, and just what exactly would change. She already had the sense that the shadow man didn't want her to go to Liverpool, but she didn't think the voice was his. She couldn't place why, but it didn't *feel* like him.

She wanted to communicate with the voice, to find out whatever or whoever it was, and what it wanted to tell her. In her mind, she asked one question.

Why?

The car violently swerved underneath her, and she jerked open her eyes. Anthony was straining at the wheel, trying desperately to regain control of the vehicle. The veins in his neck bulged as he fought against the unseen force jerking the steering wheel back and forth, swerving the car all over the road.

"Ariadne! What's happening?", he screamed as the car careered into the middle lane.

"I don't know!", she shouted, "it must be the voice"

He looked at her then, and in that second she knew.

"You heard it as wel-"

The sudden jolt of the car stopped the word in her throat as they skidded across the slow lane and headed uncontrollably toward the embankment.

Ariadne saw Anthony slamming his foot against the

brake, and watched in horror as the pedal didn't budge. He leaned into the steering wheel then, frantically trying to stop them from crashing.

He failed.

The car slammed through the barrier and smashed into the grassy hill beyond. Ariadne screamed as she saw Anthony's neck jerk at an impossible angle, slamming his face into the steering wheel. His head bounced backwards like a basketball, smashing into the headrest which such force that it was knocked off the back of the seat.

The seatbelt crunched into her ribs and collarbone, a lightning rod of pain searing through her as she suddenly couldn't breathe. As if some creature had its arms around her in a vice-like grip, squeezing and stopping her lungs from working. For a split second an image of the old woman in her dream flashed into her mind.

As the windscreen shattered, spraying them both with glass, she closed her eyes tightly in anticipation of what might come next.

She realised they had stopped. The impact was over.

She looked over at Anthony, who was slumped forward over the steering wheel, his neck twisted so that he was facing his friend. The light had gone out of his eyes.

She heard an horrific scream come out of her throat, seemingly of its own volition.

With a trembling hand, she reached over to him, and then jumped as he suddenly sprang up. A marionette whose strings had been pulled by some unknown force. She realised with a cold terror that he wasn't her friend anymore, but a lifeless travesty of what was once a human. The side of his face was a mess of crushed bone and pulped flesh, and Ariadne saw that one of his eyes had been completely destroyed, as had a number of his teeth. The voice that came out of his mouth wasn't his own, it was the voice she'd heard only moments ago coming through the radio.

"This", it said, "this is what would happen"

His mouth clumsily opened and closed, manipulated by a puppeteer. His tongue lolled uselessly around, and there was no movement of any muscles. He was a ventriloquist's dummy now, and Ariadne thought she knew just who was operating him.

The creature's remaining eye rolled towards something behind Ariadne, and she turned just in time to see a car skidding along the road and slamming into them with a horrific smash.

Ariadne opened her eyes and lurched forward against the seatbelt as Anthony tried to concentrate on driving.

"Ow", she said as the seatbelt cut into her sore chest.

"Ari?", he asked, "Are you ok? Were you asleep?"

It took her a few moments to compose herself.

"I… Yes, I must have been"

Anthony was trying to keep his eyes on the road, while at the same time attempting to look over to make sure his friend was alright.

"It's ok, Ari. Shall we stop somewhere?"

She didn't have to think about the answer.

"No", she said defiantly, "I'm ok. Let's keep going. Let's just get there"

The dream had galvanised her resolve. This would not continue. She was going to end this.

Whatever it might take.

Twenty Eight

Four hours, two stops and one unfortunate 'incident' with Harry's bowels later, they arrived in Liverpool. Anthony had hoped he'd see the Liver building or drive through Liverpool central on the way, but Ariadne's parents' house was in a place called Maghull, so much to his disappointment they hadn't passed any of that. The only thing to see was a hospital for the criminally insane, but he didn't feel like getting his camera out for that.

Ariadne hadn't fallen asleep in the car again. She'd spent the time playing with the radio, talking to Anthony about work, talking to Harry. Anything to stay awake.

There had of course been long periods of silence when neither she nor Anthony had spoken to each other, but they hadn't been awkward. They'd worked together long enough to be comfortable together in silence.

Until recently, at least.

She had noticed that Anthony seemed to be trying to make any silences as short as possible though, presumably to save her from her own thoughts. Or sleep.

She'd used some of the journey to brief Anthony about her dad. She wasn't sure herself what to expect, but she just wanted to ensure that if her dad acted strangely Anthony wouldn't take it personally. As she listed the types of things he might say or do, she wondered just who she was actually preparing – Anthony, or herself.

They pulled up in front of the drive, which Anthony noticed sloped quite steeply up to the house. It gave the property a slightly imposing feel, he thought. Before he'd had a chance to lift the handbrake, Ariadne's mum was standing by the passenger door, motioning excitedly for Ariadne to wind down the window.

Ariadne opened the door.

"We're getting out mum!", she said, stepping out of the car, "we don't need to talk through the window!"

"Oh, stop it!", Maria said.

She went to hug Ariadne, but stopped short. Her face dropped as she saw the marks on her daughter's neck. Ariadne mentally chastised herself for taking off the scarf during the journey and forgetting to put it back on again, although she also allowed an inward sigh of relief that she'd used the make up around her eyes.

"Mum, don't do that look. I told you, I'm ok, it's fine"

"You don't look fine sweetheart. Between you and that dad of yours... I don't know"

She shook her head woefully and pulled her daughter forward for a hug, being careful to press into her too much.

"It's good to see you mum"

"You too, sweetheart. I'm so glad you're here"

Anthony stepped out of the car and began walking around to them. Maria leaned closer to Ariadne.

"Does he know about your dad?"

She nodded.

"Yes. I told him"

Her mum gave a bittersweet smile.

"Thanks sweetheart"

She turned to Anthony, who was walking nervously up to them.

"And this must be the young man I've been hearing so much about!"

"Hello Mrs Perasmenos. It's very nice to meet you"

"And you!"

She gave him a brief hug, nodding her approval at Ariadne over his shoulder. It occurred to Ariadne that a wink and a 'Wahey!' would've been more subtle. She didn't nod back and instead rolled her eyes and left them to it.

She went and retrieved the Harry-in-a-box, sitting him down on the drive. She could feel him moving around in there, and heard little meows of hunger.

As she unlatched the little door and took him out, he gave what she definitely recognised as a meow of annoyance. He clearly wasn't a fan of being caged.

"I know, I know, but you're free now Harry. And look who it is!"

She carried him over to her mum, rubbing the underside of his chin with her finger. He started purring and lifted his head. All was forgiven apparently.

"My little Harry! There he is!"

Maria reached over and scooped him out of Ariadne's arms. He purred louder than ever as she took over stroking duties.

"He definitely isn't that friendly with me", Anthony offered.

"Well, it took him a while to like me too, didn't it my little Harry? Yes! It did, didn't it!"

Maria was doing her best baby-faces at Harry, who seemed to have decided to just keep his eyes close and enjoy the massage.

"Shall we go in mum?"

"Yes! You must be ravenous after that journey. If you and Anthony go and sit at the table, I'll go upstairs and get your dad"

"Ok. Thanks mum"

"No problem sweetheart"

Maria carried Harry – who seemed to be in some kind of trance now - into the house.

"Thanks Mrs Perasmenos", Anthony called after her.

"You're very welcome, Anthony"

Ariadne went to retrieve her bag from the car, a smirk on her face. Anthony noticed her expression.

"What?"

"Ooh, thank you Mrs Perasmenos!", she said in the campest voice she could muster.

"I was being polite!"

"It was a bit snivelling wasn't it?"

"Snivelling?! I was being respectful to your mum! You could learn something from me, Miss P!"

She retrieved her bag and began walking to the house.

"Whatever you say, Mr J…", she called out over her shoulder.

Anthony laughed, closed the boot and followed her up the steep drive.

As Ariadne walked inside the house, a million happy memories of childhood flooded her senses. She saw the staircase that she used to run up and down without a care in the world, and the living room where she spent so many happy evenings. The house even smelled the same. She felt something she hadn't felt in a long time – relief at being home. She put her bag down in the hall, and led Anthony into the dining room.

She smiled, completely oblivious to just what she was walking towards.

Twenty Nine

While Harry got acquainted with a new sofa to sleep on, Ariadne helped her mum bring the various dishes and bowls over to the table.

Anthony had offered to help, but Maria had refused to let him do anything. He was their guest, he didn't have to lift a finger. Ariadne had hoped she might be seen as a guest too now, but apparently her mum had other plans.

"How much food did you make, mum?!", Ariadne asked as she brought yet another bowl to the table.

"Oh stop it! It's nice having lots of people to cook for. I'm allowed to spoil my daughter and her friend, aren't I?!"

Ariadne gave her mum a look, and Anthony could tell he must have missed a conversation somewhere. He was glad he hadn't been in the kitchen.

Ariadne sat down next to Anthony as her mum walked out of the room.

"Sorry, Jackson", she said.

"And stop calling him Jackson for crying out loud", Maria called out. "The man's name is Anthony"

She poked her head back around the door.

"Isn't that right, sweetheart?", she asked Anthony with a wink.

"That's right, Mrs Perasmenos", he said enthusiastically, "I've told her before but she just doesn't listen. What can you do?"

He held his palms-up and shrugged in a gesture of mock defeat.

"Nothing, sweetheart. And I've tried, believe me!"

Maria and Anthony laughed at the shared joke. Ariadne gave him a playful slap on the arm.

"You've got comfortable pretty quickly! And no ganging up! Where's my dad? He's always on my side"

As if on cue, they heard slow, unsure footsteps

coming from the staircase and turned. From where Ariadne sat she could see her dad's feet, and she watched as he slowly appeared one step at a time. She first noticed his slippers – the same ones he'd had for about as long as she could remember. Then she saw his pyjama bottoms, then a glimpse of the base of his dressing gown. With a horror more real than any dream could possibly match, she saw how much he'd changed from the strong man she used to know. His pyjamas hung off him awkwardly and when she finally saw his face, it was gaunt. A skull with a thin sheet of skin stretched over it. His expression was one of pure, focused concentration. As if the very act of walking down the stairs could only be achieved through a massive force of will.

He reached the bottom step and slowly looked round towards the dinner table as though moving through treacle. As his eyes met Ariadne's, his facial expression changed from frustrated concentration to pure joy.

On seeing his smile, she recognised her father again.

"Ari!", he called out. "Is that? Is that Ariadne?"

"Yes Dad, it's me!", she said as she rushed over, blinking back the tears.

She gave him a hug, being cautious not to squeeze too hard in case she hurt either her father or herself. She could feel how much weight he'd lost since the last time she'd seen him. There was a slight pressure on her bruises now, but she didn't care. She wanted to squeeze her daddy as hard as she could.

"Why didn't you tell me Ari was coming?", he called out to the kitchen.

Maria came out with a salad bowl in one hand and a pan of something that looked like mashed potato in the other.

"I did sweetheart! I've been telling you all day!"

"No", he said defiantly, "I would've remembered. How could I forget my Ari?"

He took an unsure step back and looked at his

daughter. The pride in his eyes was unmistakable. It was the same look he used to give her when she'd done well at school.

"Oh Dad, it's so good to see you. How are you?"

"Me? I'm fine. Didn't your mother tell you?", he looked over at Maria, "Didn't you tell her?"

"Tell her what?"

"We're going on holiday in a couple of weeks. We're doing a tour of the United States. I haven't been there for years"

Ariadne looked over at Maria, who closed her eyes and gave a slow shake of her head.

Ariadne understood.

"That's really good Dad. You can tell me about it later", she said, barely able to contain the sadness from leaking into her tone.

"Ariadne has brought someone for you to meet, Alex", Maria said.

"Who?"

"A friend of mine Dad, you'll like him"

She led him over to the dining table, where Anthony sat nervously watching the exchange.

"This is Anthony. He's my friend"

Anthony stood and held out his hand.

"Very nice to meet you Mr Perasmenos. You have a very lovely house"

Alex stared at Anthony as if trying to place where he'd seen him before.

"You're not one of those nurses are you?"

"No, I'm a friend of your daughter. We work together"

Alex shook his hand cautiously.

"Good. I don't like those nurses. They treat me like I don't know what I'm doing. The sooner they leave the better"

Maria came over and took Alex's hand.

"We can talk about that later Alex. We should eat"

Alex gave Anthony another cautious look, then allowed Maria to guide him to his chair.

She sat him down at the head of the table, and carefully rolled up his sleeves. She took a napkin and began tucking the corner into the top of his nightshirt.

"No", he said in a hushed panic, "I don't need it"

"Alex, you do need it sweetheart. You always have it"

"No! Please. The nurse"

He indicated Anthony with his eyes, and gave an uncomfortable smile when Anthony looked over and accidentally made eye contact with him.

Anthony looked away quickly, pretending not to notice. He calmly rolled his sleeves up and began tucking his own napkin into the top of his shirt. He then put his hands in his lap and waited, all the while being careful not to look over at Alex again.

For a moment nobody moved, as Alex seemed to be weighing something up in his mind. It amazed Ariadne how clearly she could read her poor dad now. He'd always been strong and able to hide his feelings, now his every facial expression seemed to telegraph his thoughts. It made her think of a child who hadn't yet learned to hide their feelings as a survival mechanism to get through life. She felt a crushing sorrow. Her dad's naivety made him more vulnerable than he would ever have the insight to realise.

She watched as her dad visibly relaxed, and allowed Maria to tuck the napkin into his shirt.

Ariadne took Anthony's hand under the table and mouthed him a quick 'thank you'. She couldn't remember a time when she'd felt so grateful to another person for a kindness they'd shown.

After Alex said grace – which Ariadne was surprised he was able to remember and recite perfectly no less - they began passing plates around to each other and dishing up food. Every so often Anthony asked the name of a particular dish, and Maria took great pride in telling him. Alex was more talkative than normal, he was mercifully having quite a good day, and even told a few stories about the village where he grew up in Cyprus.

If Ariadne had been surprised at her dad's ability to remember a prayer, his ability to remember detailed stories and events from the past left her open-mouthed. A few times he'd corrected Maria about details of stories she had told, even though he wasn't able to reliably tell them what he had done earlier that day. She also wondered about the United States holiday and where that came from. Maybe he'd seen something about it on television, or maybe it was just the first thing that had popped into his confused, damaged mind.

"How was your drive up here then?", Alex asked Anthony, for the second time.

"It was fine thanks, Mr Perasmenos"

"You've got a very nice car. I used to have a nice one too before the accident. The replacement one wasn't so good"

Ariadne looked up, her mind flashing back to her dream. The crash on the embankment, her dead friend as a sick marionette.

"What accident?", she asked.

"When my daughter was little she had a crash"

"What? *I'm* your daughter. What do... Mum, what does he mean?"

"Nothing, sweetheart. He's confused that's all. Nobody had any accident"

"They did", Alex protested, "right outside there. You can still see the dent in the tree!"

Ariadne turned to the window and squinted, trying to see if it was true. She trawled her memories, trying to remember any kind of accident. She came up blank.

"How old was I when this happened, Dad?"

Maria stood now.

"Sweetheart, he's confused. Nothing happened"

"It did!", he protested again. "Don't you

remember? The dog?"

Ariadne felt a jolt of adrenalin shoot through her, turning her veins to both ice and fire simultaneously. She suddenly felt both too hot and too cold.

She forced herself to stand and suddenly felt very faint.

"Mum. What is going on? Did I hit a dog? Is that why you mentioned a dog?"

"*I'm* the one that mentioned a dog!", Alex said.

"No!", Maria said.

Ariadne could tell she was panicking now.

"Mum?"

"Ok! Yes, you hit a dog. Ok? We didn't want to tell you because you'd be upset. OK?"

"What?! Why didn't you tell me when I was telling you about the dreams?! That's why you acted all weird when I mentioned the dog!"

"Oh sweetheart, what difference would it make? It wouldn't stop you dreaming about it, would it? Why would I tell you?"

"That's not the point mum", Ariadne said, "you should've told me"

Maria exhaled and rubbed her weary face with both hands.

"Ok. I should have done sweetheart. I'm sorry, ok? Please, let's just finish eating and have a nice day. Please let's not spoil it. We can talk about it later if you like. Ok?"

Ariadne looked at her dad, and then at Anthony who was beyond nervous now.

She reluctantly nodded, if only to spare any further distress to everybody else at the table. She sat back down, which was a relief as she wasn't sure how much longer she could stay upright without fainting.

Maria sat down too, and an awkward silence hung in the air as they slowly starting trying to eat again.

Ariadne tried to retrieve the memory. There was nothing. She had no recollection of having an accident, let alone hitting a dog. It must be more than coincidence that she'd been dreaming about a dog though, surely? There must be more to it.

She looked over at her mum, who seemed intent on avoiding eye contact.

Alex was the one to break the silence. He leaned over to Ariadne.

"You didn't hit a dog, Ari", he said and gave her hand a pat.

Maria looked over.

"Ok Dad", Ariadne said.

"Do you believe me?"

"Yes Dad, I do. I didn't hit a dog"

He smiled, satisfied, and leaned back.

Maria nervously looked at Anthony.

"So, Anthony, tell us about you. Where are you-"

She wasn't able to finish her question. Just like Ariadne had done when she awoke at the sleep clinic, Alex interjected with four short words which changed everything.

"You hit a man"

Thirty

When bad things happen in life, we all do one thing. Sometimes we do it as soon as the bad thing happens, sometimes later on, but we all get to it eventually.

We romanticise yesterday.

We find ourselves yearning for our 'old' life, holding onto the irrational thought that everything was perfect back then. Idyllic. And that if we could just somehow have avoided today we'd still be living in that pain-free utopia.

We'd be happy. Even though we likely never were.

The most recent event always feels like the worst. The only advantage to it is that it causes our old problems to fade slightly. Yes, they're still there, and they still hurt. But at least we'd got used to them and were living with them. Then something new comes along and... how do we deal with *this* now?

Ariadne knew how she would deal with it. She would find out everything that she possibly could, in the hope that there was some flicker of sense to be salvaged from it.

In the seconds following her dad's outburst, Ariadne looked to her mum, whose face immediately told her that which she most feared - he was telling the truth. Maria had protested, and made excuses, and told Ariadne that her dad was just confused. *It's the dementia, sweetheart, that's all.* But Ariadne could tell. Far from protesting too much, her mum wasn't protesting enough. There was no conviction behind anything she was saying. Ariadne got the feeling that her mum wanted her to know what had happened but was just going through the motions of denying it because that's what she was supposed to do. She'd stood up again, and made a lot of noise, but Ariadne could see that her heart wasn't in it. Even her dad probably could.

After Maria had said her piece, she'd sat down, not daring to look up at her guests.

Ariadne just stared at her and waited for her to look up. After an uncomfortable, awkward silence, Maria hesitantly raised her head, finding herself face to face with her daughter.

There were tears in her mum's eyes.

"Mum. Please", she said. Her voice was soft but there was the smallest hint of steel behind it.

Suddenly, any pretence evaporated and Maria's face softened. It was as if the mask had been whipped off.

"Oh sweetheart, I'm so sorry. We just didn't want to tell you. It was all so...so sudden"

"See!", Alex said. "It's true! I told you! Didn't I tell them?"

He looked over at Anthony, who nodded and gave a weak smile.

"Mum", Ariadne continued, "just tell me"

Maria took a deep breath, exhaling through her nose and closing her eyes as if preparing herself.

"You were so young, sweetheart. Your dad was taking you out in the car and you were all excited. We used to have this pink booster seat – a bit of foam really –that we put on the passenger seat, and you'd just get so excited. Your dad used to let you sit on it and make driving sounds. You loved it Ari, it was something special that you did in the car with Dad"

She looked over at Alex and thought for a second that she saw a flicker of recognition in his face. Then, it was gone.

"Anyway", she continued, "your dad was taking you out one morning and, like he always did, he let you sit in the seat and make noises and be a bit silly and everything. It was sunny that day so he needed his sunglasses. So he came back in, and you..."

She wiped at her eyes with a napkin now.

"You somehow released the handbrake. The car was facing the house, so you must have started rolling backwards and you... A man that lived quite close to here was coming home from work. He used to work long night shifts, so he was just on the way home. And the car..."

Ariadne gasped.

"I killed him?"

"No sweetheart! No! You didn't kill anybody. They said that the way he fell meant that he hit his head on the road. The car actually didn't do much damage to him at all really, I think the only other thing was a broken arm, and that was because of how he fell too. It was just the way he hit his head. It...it put him in a coma sweetheart"

Ariadne felt the tears flowing down her face now, and she automatically reached out to Anthony, who put his arm around her. She nestled into him and wept.

"Maybe we should talk about this another time", Anthony said to Maria, "this is probably too much"

"Yes", Maria agreed, "it is. We should talk about this another time"

"No", Ariadne said, turning her head from Anthony's shoulder. "I want to know. Where is he now? Can I talk to him?"

"He....", Maria started to speak, but wasn't able to finish as her tears began to fall and her words caught in her throat.

Ariadne felt confusion alongside a rising panic. There was something she wasn't being told.

"What, mum? Why are you crying? You said I didn't kill him. What happened? Dad?"

"It was a dog, Ari. Just a dog"

He gave Maria an exaggerated wink, and she put her head in her hands and sobbed.

"Oh Ari", she said through her fingers.

"What mum?! Tell me!"

"You didn't kill him sweetheart!", she blurted, "he was in a coma for a long time"

"Mum! Did he die? Is that what you're telling me? Did he *die*?"

She didn't answer.

"Mum!"

Maria dropped her hands and looked at her daughter with a mixture of sadness and pity. She gave a single nod.

Ariadne stood now.

"But you told me I didn't kill him! I did! I killed him!"

"No, Ari!", her mum said, gaining strength from reserves she didn't know she had, "you didn't! It was an accident and he hit his head and went into a coma, but you didn't kill him. It was twenty years ago that it happened and he only died a few weeks ago, and it was his wife who made the decision. It wasn't you sweetheart"

"He had a *wife*?!"

Ariadne collapsed down onto her chair and put her head in her hands.

She wasn't crying now, she was wailing.

"He had a wife!", she screamed at nobody in particular.

Maria came around the table now and hugged Ariadne from behind her chair. When she spoke it was in between sobs.

"I'm so sorry sweetheart. We never wanted you to know. We wanted to spare you from all this. That's why we said you'd hit a dog and that was that. We've lived with this sweetheart, believe me every day we've lived with this, but you never had to. I'm so sorry"

Ariadne felt numb, she wasn't even aware her mum was hugging her. It made sense now. She was a killer. That's why this was happening. She deserved everything she got. She had a few bruises and scratches, but she was alive. His wife, his poor wife. What if her dad had been in a coma for twenty years? What kind of life would her mum have had? No life at all.

A sudden realisation struck her.

"He died a few weeks ago?", she asked.

"Yes, sweetheart"

"But that's when the dreams started"

Anthony could see where her thought process was headed.

"Ari, come on. You can't think that's related. You're just in shock"

"No, I'm not", she said in a measured tone, "my dreams started once he'd died. It's him. He's doing this. He's punishing me"

"Sweetheart, it was an accident. Nobody's punishing anyone. It's a horrible, tragic thing, but he's not even here anymore. He can't hurt you now"

"But it explains all of this. He died and now he's taking his revenge on me. Every night he's killed me. Think about it. He's even used a car!"

She gave an empty laugh bereft of any joy.

"Ari", Anthony said, "listen to me. You're in shock. I think we should take some time to-"

"I don't want to take some time! I need to sort this out. I need to.. I don't know what I need to do, but this needs to end"

"It's ended, sweetheart", Maria said, "it's over. He died. Maybe you saw the report about him dying on the news or in the paper, and that's why you've started dreaming about it. He was in the newspapers a lot back then, he was quite a famous chef in his ti-"

"He was a *what*?!"

Maria realised what she'd said.

"He was a chef?"

Maria nodded sheepishly.

Ariadne's shoulders slumped even lower as she realised how much more sense it all made now. The dog, the Chef, the shadow man.

Was the shadow his soul? Is that why he never had a face?

The chilling image of his countenance that had exploded into her dream at the sleep clinic suddenly flashed into her mind.

She had seen his face now, so did that mean that something had changed? Was he no longer a soul but somehow becoming more tangible?

Her thoughts suddenly stopped racing as she realised something.

She'd *seen* his *face*. Which meant there was a simple way of finding out whether the man her mum described was the same man from her dreams.

"Mum", she blurted, "I want to see what he looked like"

Her mum went to speak but thought better of it. She gave a weak smile, defeated.

"I might have a newspaper somewhere"

Which meant that she did. Ariadne knew her mum would hold onto something like that.

Maria silently stood, leaning against the table and pushing herself up with tired hands. She walked out of the room.

Ariadne watched her leave, saddened by the crushed way she shuffled up the stairs.

The room was silent except for the occasional sound of cutlery on ceramic. Alex had started eating again.

Anthony turned to Ariadne.

"Are you ok?"

She shook her head. She wasn't ok at all. She needed to do something, to make things right. Was she just supposed to forget any of this ever happened?

And even if she wanted to forget, she knew *he* wouldn't let her.

"Dad", she asked, "where did he live?"

"Who?"

"The chef?"

"What chef?"

She took a deep breath.

"The man I hit with the car a long time ago. Where did he live?"

"Round the corner"

"Where?"

Anthony's eyes widened.

"Ari, you're not actually going to go there? What for?"

"I don't know, but I need his wife to know I'm sorry. *He* needs to know"

"Ari, wait a minute, I can understand why you might want to do this, but I don't think it's a good idea to rush into it all. Especially right now. It might be best to just calm down and decide later. Take some time, and just sleep on it"

He winced as he heard the unfortunate phrase coming out of his own mouth.

"I can't sleep on it, can I?! What do you think he's going to do next? Look at what he's done already"

She yanked the collar of her top down, revealing her collarbone and the various scratches and cuts on her upper chest and neck.

"I need to do something before he kills me"

"Ari, he's not going to-"

"How do you know? You saw me at the clinic! Explain it! How else does this all make sense?"

Anthony thought about the conversation he'd had with Derek, how he'd said that everything up until that night at the clinic could be explained by sleep disorders and psychology. Then he remembered Derek's eyes when they saw Ariadne on the bed, and how he'd stood up to Doctor Illari and told him there was more to it than psychology.

He had no answer for Ariadne. So far, nobody had.

"If you want to go, I'm coming with you. But I think you should wait, Ari"

"Fine" she said, defiantly, "Dad?"

Alex had been trying but failing to follow the conversation.

"Yes?", he said cautiously.

"That man that I hit with the car a long time ago. You said he lived round the corner. Do you know what road?"

"Two roads that way", he pointed out of the window, "Opposite the church. The detached house with the double garage"

"Are you sure, Dad?"

He looked puzzled, as though Ariadne was being deliberately dense.

"Of course I'm sure, Ari. I've lived here a long time. You're starting to sound like one of those nurses"

Maria walked downstairs, and they watched her as she came back into the room as silently as she'd left. She was holding a newspaper.

She started handing it to Ariadne but paused halfway.

"You don't have to look at this. It won't change anything"

"We can't just pretend it didn't happen mum. I can't anyway. I need to make this right. I'm going to go and see the man's wife"

"What?!", Maria dropped the newspaper onto the floor, "Why?! No sweetheart, just let her be. *Please!*"

"I need her to know I'm sorry, mum. You must be able to see that. And maybe I am in shock" – she looked at Anthony – "or maybe I'm not thinking clearly, but I want to do this now. Before I start pretending everything's ok when it obviously isn't. I know what'll happen mum. We'll sit here and have a nice evening and be comfortable, and I'll feel slightly better and think I should wait and see tomorrow, but then what? What happens when I sleep tonight? What will he do then?"

Maria looked at the bruises and marks on her daughter's neck. She didn't believe any of this, but she knew Ariadne. If this was going to give her the closure she needed...

She nodded resignedly.

"Ok sweetheart. I still see her from time to time, she's a nice lady. Even after everything that happened, she never wanted you to get into trouble or anything. I can come too if you like"

"No, mum. That's ok. I feel like I need to do this alone"

Anthony stood.

"Ari, I'd feel much better if I came with you. I don't think you should go by yourself"

"Neither do I", her mum agreed.

"Look, both of you. It's fine. I know you think I'm not thinking straight but I am. It all makes sense now. I just need to apologise and explain what happened. She needs to know I'm sorry. I just… I feel like it'll make this all stop. He needs to know"

"Sweetheart, you keep saying that. He's not here anymore! And she knows what happened, she's known for twenty years! You should just leave it now. What good will it do?"

"I don't know, mum! It just feels like something I have to do. And something I need to do alone too. The worst that'll happen is it'll make no difference. But I need to try, do you understand?! I need to at least try to end this nightmare!"

Her attention was drawn to the newspaper on the floor. Her mum had folded it open on the page showing the photograph of the man. Ariadne saw it and immediately recognised the face. A new rush of adrenalin coursed through her body. She picked up the newspaper and held it to her mum.

"*This* nightmare! *Him!* He needs to know I didn't mean it! There's no other way to stop this. I just need to try"

Her mum held her hands up in a gesture of defeat. She went over and sat next to Alex.

Anthony moved closer to Ariadne, and lowered his voice. He took her hand.

"Ari, trust me. You're not in your right mind. I care about you. If anything happens to you… I know you feel like you have to do this, but you have to take a moment and just think about it. Please, just listen to me. We might not just be talking about an old woman here Ari. What if he's got kids? What if there are two or three twenty-something kids who don't know what happened? Then you burst in and announce that… And tell them what happened? How do you think they'll react to that? Stop and let's finish eating, or we don't even have to finish eating, but let's just stop all this for a little while. Ok? Put it to the side. Wait an hour or two, and then decide"

He gently brushed the back of Ariadne's cheek with his free hand. He gave her a smile.

"I'm not saying the great Ariadne Perasmenos is wrong by the way, I wouldn't dare. I'm just saying let's wait a little while. We've got the rest of the afternoon and all evening to decide. I don't want anything to happen to you Ari, and I will do everything I can to make sure you're ok"

She looked into his eyes and smiled as she realised that it now seemed as though both of them saw him as the protector. When he'd touched her cheek the anxiety and panic had dissipated almost instantly. She still felt anxious, but felt that she could control herself more now. The negative emotions were being smothered by the positive.

It felt good.

"OK", she said, "you win. But we have to talk about this later"

He nodded.

"Of course. And I bet you won't let me forget it either"

Maria felt a palpable sense of relief. Not only because her daughter had decided not to burst into the widow's house, but also because Anthony had been the reason for her decision. She did feel vaguely slighted that her words hadn't made the difference, but at least somebody's had. And the fact she hadn't slapped his hand away from her cheek could only be a good thing.

She just hoped Ariadne wouldn't change her mind later. About Anthony, or anything else.

Thirty One

After much persuasion, Anthony decided to stay overnight.

In truth, his protestations had all been put on out of politeness - he didn't particularly relish the thought of another four hour car journey. Especially without Ariadne. The more he thought about it, the less he wanted to do anything without Ariadne anymore.

After lunch, things had settled down somewhat. Alex had gone upstairs to sleep, and Ariadne and her mum had cleared the dishes away and begun washing up together. The mood in the kitchen had been tense at first, with neither mother nor daughter mentioning the events at the dinner table, or on the driveway all those years ago. They carried out the chores in silence, and Ariadne had found her mind wandering to her dad. She began to think about exactly how much he had changed, and noticed for the first time the toll it had taken on her mum too. She looked older, tired. The bags under her eyes were heavier, the lines on her face deeper. Ariadne hadn't noticed before but her mum seemed to gaze off into the distance occasionally, reminding her of her own episodes of microsleep. She wondered whether it was the difficult past her mum was seeing, or the difficult present.

She had made small talk in an attempt to snap her mum out of this reverie, asking about cousins and aunts she hadn't seen for a while. In no time their conversation blossomed from a cautious, stilted chat into a heart-to-heart between girlfriends. Mother and daughter had found their rhythm again, and the relief they felt was like a third presence in the room. Even when they eventually spoke about the accident, and Ariadne's dad, the third presence remained, mitigating the discomfort although not able to remove it completely.

Anthony had made himself scarce to give them a

chance to catch up, and by default found himself on cat-sitting duty, although that mainly consisted of being stared at with a 'you're still here, then?' look.

Reclining on the sofa, he'd dozed off a couple of times. The past few days had drained him physically as well as emotionally. Although, he thought, at least he was able to catch up on some sleep. Not like poor Ari.

The second time he'd woken up, he'd been surprised to find Harry curled up next to him, nestled against his leg. He could hear and feel the low purring, which soothed him off into yet another nap.

Soon after, Ariadne walked into the room.

"Apparently I'm not being a good host and should offer you a drin-"

She immediately stopped when she saw he was asleep, then smiled as she noticed Harry using Anthony's leg as a pillow. He was a real user, that one. She stood and watched the rhythmic rise and fall of his chest, feeling a strange jealously that he was able to sleep. There was a feeling of warmth there too. He was a good man. He'd helped her a lot recently, in fact more than just recently. She'd been there for him last year, and he was there for her now. The more she thought about it, the more she believed they made a pretty a good team.

Her mum casually walked past on her way upstairs, and gave her a nudge.

"Just friends, hey sweetheart?", she said with a smirk.

Ariadne gave her mum a nudge in return and smiled.

"I'm going to sort some things out for your father upstairs, so you two can have some time to sit here and…be unfriendly"

"Mum!"

Before Ariadne could say anything else, her mum gave a playful wink and disappeared up the stairs.

Ariadne shook her head and looked back at Anthony. She creeped over to the armchair next to the sofa, and slowly lowered herself down so as not to make too much noise. Anthony seemed to be in a pretty deep sleep if his snoring was anything to go by, but she didn't want to risk waking him.

As she sat, the tiredness descended like a cloak of lead being suddenly thrown over her, weighing her down almost painfully. Sometimes – like in the car - the tiredness struck as though she were attached to some heavy object and had been thrown into deep water, inexorably being sucked down into oblivion. This time it felt like it came from above. Whichever way it came upon her, the sudden tiredness was always completely out of her control, and was an overwhelming, dizzying sensation.

She thought about all that had happened since she'd arrived, and still felt raw about what she'd learned. Ironically, the fact that she was so worn out probably lessened the blow of finding out about the accident.

After she and her mum had started conversing normally again in the kitchen, she had consoled Ariadne, explaining yet again that it was an accident and that nobody was to blame. She said there'd been a Crash Investigator involved, and he had officially ruled that it was a tragic accident and nothing more. They'd taken the car and tested it on a slope with a similar gradient to the driveway. There'd been no problem with the handbrake or any other part of the car. The car manufacturer was in the clear, Ariadne's parents were in the clear, and so was she. It was an accident. A tragic, horrific one, but an accident nonetheless.

So why did she feel she was being punished?

By *him*?

Why did she keep sensing his presence and feeling as though she needed to make things right, if not with him then at least with his poor widow?

The voice she'd heard in the car came back to her now. Quietly, almost as if carried on the wind.

"Ari-ad-ne"

At first she thought she was imagining it, and shifted

in her seat in an attempt to jerk herself fully awake in case she'd drifted off. She placed a cushion behind her back, forcing herself to sit slightly more upright.

There was a brief silence, but then the voice returned, louder and more defiant.

"You'll never be the same"

She looked over at Anthony, who was still fast asleep. She wondered whether to wake him and tell him what was happening, but dismissed the idea. What would be the point? He wouldn't be able to hear it or do anything to stop it. He needed his rest. This was her battle.

It was at that point she noticed Harry. Specifically, his ears.

The voice continued intermittently, and every time it spoke, Harry's ears flicked slightly. As though he were picking up the sounds. As though he could *hear* the voice.

She thought it might be a result of her tired eyes or her sleep-addled mind. She didn't know which of her perceptions she could trust anymore. She picked a focal point on the sofa just behind Harry and kept still until the voice returned. If his ears moved, she'd see them twitch against the pattern on the sofa.

The voice returned even louder this time, and she saw Harry's ears unmistakably move.

He'd heard it.

She stared at him, wondering what that meant. Were her dreams really leaching into her real-life, becoming tangible? Real?

Or was it the other way round?

And if the voice was real, then did that mean the warning was real too? She'd previously thought that the revelation at the dinner table had been the focus of the warning, but then why was she still hearing it? It meant there was something else.

A cold terror gripped her.

It meant this definitely wasn't over.

The panic came back now, returning as suddenly as

the voice. A thousand insects scurrying over her body, digging and burrowing into her flesh, stinging adrenalin into her veins. Her breathing became shallow again and she felt an overwhelming sense of urgency.

Then, the voice again.

"Stop this, Ariadne"

Her eyes darted to Harry, just in time to see his ears move again.

There was a rustling noise from behind her and she froze, not wanting to know what fresh horror might be about to befall her. The sound continued on, becoming louder and more pronounced. An element of the noise reminded her of Jenny, her colleague, who would rip paper from her legal pad and loudly screw it up before throwing it in the bin with a flourish. It was the same noise - paper being scrunched and crumpled, but amplified a hundred times.

She realised that particular sound was never emitted at the same time as the voice, as if timed so that they would never coincide.

As if timed so that she would hear everything.

She forced herself to turn her head, wanting to confront the horror on her own terms. A strange tearing noise joined the cacophony now, and the sounds came as if on a loop. The voice, the rustling, the tearing.

She was facing what seemed to be the source of the noises, but saw nothing amiss. The dining table sat in the centre of the room next to a cabinet on one side and the sideboard on the other. The only other items in the room were a couple of vases and-

Her breath caught in her throat.

The newspaper.

It lay, folded and motionless, on the polished wood of the sideboard. Ariadne knew – she sensed – that the source of all of this was the newspaper.

At that realisation, the voice boomed Ariadne's name, startling her and spurring her out of her inaction.

She stood cautiously, and hesitantly stepped around the armchair and toward the sideboard.

As she creeped over, the volume of the voice and the noises rose. She heard her name being repeated, over and over, becoming louder with each utterance.

She realised there were other voices now too. They were whispers, filling in the silences between the main voice and the sounds of the paper. An unwelcome addition to the loop. Nothing was discernible but her name in the midst of the chants and chattering.

The adrenalin rushing through her body caused her to suddenly feel light-headed. Another dizzying sensation - this time unrelated to the sensation of falling asleep. She continued walking slowly toward the paper. Her steps were tentative and she unconsciously held her breath.

As she reached to pick up the yellowing, brittle newspaper, she fought to still her trembling hand. She cautiously gripped the paper as if handling a snake, lifting it and then carefully locating the page with his photograph.

In an instant the voice bellowed her name and the whispers exploded into shouts, punctuated now with intermittent screams. Pained, horrific howls of anguish. Victims of a thousand murders pleading for mercy that would never come. Ariadne winced as the pitch and volume became almost unbearable, reminding her of the demonic laugh in the hospital that knocked the doctor from his chair.

She forced herself to look fully at the photo, expecting it to be moving, expecting it to be bleeding from the mouth. Somewhere deep in her mind she'd imagined the print leaching from the paper and dripping onto the floor, forming a puddle from which the shadow man would rise, towering above her and grinning cruelly.

But it was none of those things. It was the same as it had been before.

Except, that is, for the eyes.

The eyes which had seemed so full of life the first time she'd looked now seemed murderous, pulsing with rage.

They may not have moved but they dripped with a demonic hatred, alive with anger but simultaneously undead.

Her hands shook uncontrollably, and she noticed that the photograph was not trembling with her. The print and various sections of the paper jerked with her unstable grip, but the photograph did not. It was as if the photo existed independently of her reality, unaffected by the physical world. The small square wasn't the border of a photograph now, but a portal to another world. An unspeakable place where he *exists*.

Ariadne was reminded of a series of small holographic stickers that she'd had as a child. They'd looked as though a piece of the real world had been neatly removed and trapped in a small rectangle. That's how his face looked now, three dimensional, poised to erupt through his portal and join Ariadne in her reality.

As if reading her thoughts, his eyes burned into her and he grinned. The grin that had become so familiar to her, so horrific, so *deadly*, now stared up at her in her family home. The message was clear – nowhere is safe. There is no sanctum, no haven from which to seek escape.

The screams and shouts of the voices reached a peak, shaking the foundations of the house and causing Ariadne's vision to blur.

She tightly screwed her eyes shut, closed the paper and threw it down on the floor.

The noises stopped, but her emotions did not

She kept her eyes closed, and crouched down to retrieve the paper. She folded it by touch with trembling hands, then leaned over and put it back on the sideboard, feeling her way.

She hesitantly opened her eyes and looked toward the sideboard.

The newspaper was just that – a newspaper.

She turned towards Anthony, who was still asleep and blissfully unaware of the terrors his friend was suffering. Harry was asleep too. Maybe he hadn't heard anything after all. She couldn't trust her perceptions anymore, that much was obvious.

Her heart raced and her throat was painfully dry. She trembled violently now, and the memories of the dream, the Chef, *him*, came flooding back to her. The images and sounds assaulted her mentally, emotionally, physically. The thoughts and suspicions which had been drifting around the edges of her mind now coalesced into a whole. Space dust forged by gravity into solid rock. Definitive, final.

This would never be over.

A cruel terror gripped her, this time curiously infusing her with a defiant strength. She knew what she had to do. It was inevitable. She had to take control.

She swiftly stepped past Anthony on legs of jelly, picked up her coat and left the house. She closed the door silently behind her, like a thief trying not to get caught.

This was going to end, one way or another.

Thirty Two

It took around ten minutes for Ariadne to reach the right road, which was approximately the same amount of time it took for her breathing and her heartbeat to get back to normal.

She'd based her journey entirely on her dad's directions, and felt slightly ashamed that she hadn't trusted that they would be accurate. Until she actually saw the church for herself she wasn't convinced that he hadn't been thinking of something else or misremembering. She realised now that his long-term memory was strangely unaffected, even though his short term memory was seemingly in tatters.

She turned a corner and found herself at the bottom of the road, looking for the house. From her vantage point she could view most of the street. The road was fairly straight, which was fortunate because it meant she shouldn't need to walk the length of the road to find the house.

She stood and scanned the properties around her. The houses were old but fairly well-maintained, and a number of them had carefully manicured lawns and neat little hedges in the front. A lot of time and money had clearly been spent on both gardening and topiary.

Her gaze fell onto a detached house with a double garage, the only one in the road it seemed as all the others had single garages. It was also directly opposite the church. Her dad had been incredibly precise.

This was it.

She'd expected some kind of feeling to come upon her, an acknowledgement from somewhere that this was the right place. After all, this house was once the dwelling place of the life she had ruined. At the very least she thought the voice would come back, either to warn or to taunt her.

But there was nothing.

It was a house, just like all the others on the street. The only difference was the garage, and that didn't look particularly menacing. The ordinariness of it all was almost disappointing. She wanted a showdown, a final fight that would end the nightmares, the voices, the wounds. Surely the setting for that would be somewhere more imposing than this small house in North Liverpool?

She began walking towards the property. With each step the memory of her nightmares – both sleeping and waking - seemed to become more vivid. This wasn't the street where she had seen the Chef, she knew that, but something about it started to *feel* the same. As happened so often in her dreams, the look of the place was at odds with how the place *felt*.

She remembered reading about dementia when her dad had first been diagnosed, and finding out about something called the Capgras effect. People sometimes wouldn't believe that their husband or wife were who they said they were anymore. They would acknowledge that the person looked the same, and spoke in the same way, and acted just like the person, but they didn't *feel* the same. Ariadne was having the exact opposite feeling about this street. It didn't look like the street from her dream, the houses were different and the road was not as wide, but it *felt* identical.

As she walked closer, she saw that the large driveway was empty, even though three cars could probably quite comfortably have been parked there. She remembered Anthony's warning that there might be more people at home, but judging by the driveway, this wasn't likely.

Not likely, she thought, but that didn't mean impossible.

Her mind started racing at what she might find in the house and her body responded by flooding her with adrenalin. She stopped and tried to catch her breath, realising that she had become too scared to think clearly. Every thought process vanished into the fog of terror in which her mind had suddenly become enveloped. Everything was blurry, confused.

She tried to focus on her breathing, all the while wondering about her dad's own thought processes and whether this was how he viewed the world now. Unable to cope with any more distress, she pushed the thoughts out of her mind. She waited a few seconds so as to compose herself, and rationalised that even if other people did live there, it was early afternoon and mid-week so anybody young enough to work was probably doing just that. It was likely that only Ariadne and the man's wife would participate in this reunion. If she was even at home.

Ariadne both wanted her to be there, but also be somewhere else. Anywhere else. She didn't want this confrontation, she didn't want any of this. But she knew, whether she wanted it or not, there would be another confrontation. *He* would make sure of it. At least this one would be on her own terms.

She resumed walking towards the property, and was suddenly struck by that familiar feeling of dread which so often smothered her as she walked to her own house. Her legs felt like they couldn't take her weight, and she again felt breathless. She fought to walk on this time. The assault of fear had physically weakened her, but it was also reminding her just what she was fighting for.

As it had done at her parents' house, the fear gave her a strange defiance. She didn't want to be scared of walking home anymore, or fearful of closing her eyes in her own bed.

No, she thought, this needs to end. Today.

She stood only a few houses away now and noticed how well maintained the driveway was, bordered with colourful flowers which reminded her of the florist's shop below Dr. Illari's clinic.

There were small gnomes along the driveway, frozen in their various pursuits. One was cheerfully pushing a small wheelbarrow, another was fishing, and another was riding a deliberately undersized bicycle. Their initially friendly demeanours didn't stay that way for Ariadne, and their fixed maniacal smiles coupled with their dead, unseeing eyes suddenly chilled her to the core. As she walked closer, she saw them in more detail, and their activities took on a more sinister quality. Their grins were also altogether too familiar.

In her mind she saw them as they were, beneath their façade. They were no longer gnomes, but imps. Gatekeepers of some unspeakable place where the shadow man resided. The place Ariadne may well have glimpsed in the newspaper.

She began to wonder now just what exactly was being pushed in that wheelbarrow – a corpse? A soul being ferried from this world to the next?

Her attention was drawn to the other imp who playfully held out a fishing rod with chubby little fingers. She began to consider the possibilities of what was attached to the end of the line. A worm? An amputated thumb? An eyeball gouged out during a never-ending torture?

And, if that was the case, what exactly was the imp hoping to catch?

She closed her eyes and inhaled deeply, trying to shake off the feeling and keep focused. These were nothing but tricks, games to stop her doing what she knew needed to be done. Same as the voices - not real, but seeming that way to scare her.

It wouldn't work, she thought, as the defiance rose up in her again. No more dreams, no more fear.

No more bruises.

As she began walking up the driveway, she felt the lifeless eyes of each imp burning into her as she passed. Somehow she knew the dead iris' were watching her, hate-filled, convicting her for her crime.

Her *crime*.

She had killed the owner of this house. Running him over yet never answering for it.

Her role as the victim in this situation was beginning to feel decidedly uncertain.

Somewhere in the distance, she heard the rev of an

engine. She froze, not daring to move until the sound had echoed into nothingness. She didn't know if it had even belonged to a real car. The lines between dreams and reality were becoming increasingly blurred.

She waited for a moment at the front door, remembering the words that were spoken to her in the car on the way up.

Don't open this door...

Did the voice mean this door? Is that why the warning had continued?

And where had the voice come from anyway? Was it a friendly warning as it had first appeared, or did the shadow man not want her to be here because this would somehow end his grip on her?

She thought about the feeling she'd had of him when she had first decided to come up to Liverpool, the fact that she could sense he wasn't grinning anymore.

He hadn't wanted her to come here, and so this is exactly where she needed to be.

Another thought occurred to her, emboldening her further. She *had* paid for her crime, she'd paid every night for the past few weeks. Of course she was the victim here. Look at what he was doing, what he would continue to do until...

Until what? He'd killed her?

She felt a jolt of adrenalin and pressed the doorbell.

This is exactly where I need to be...

In spite of the burst of determination, she still did not dare to look behind her. In her mind, the imps were growing larger, cracking through their thin shells and expanding, their red bodies pulsing with rage, oozing blood, poised to attack. Growing so large that their long shadows leeched along the floor and then up the walls of the house, like the dream in the hotel where Ariadne had stood in the lobby an eternity ago. The feeling was the same now, waiting for the door to open, the lift to arrive. Monsters behind her, escape in front.

But would it be an escape, or would she find herse-
"Yes?"

An old woman stood in the doorway.

Ariadne had half-expected her to look like the hag she'd seen in her dream, and was taken aback for a second by her appearance. Her face was kind, and her eyes looked sad, as though she'd seen too much. She looked more like the woman Ariadne had met in the hospital than the hag who'd attacked her.

She was suddenly very aware that she hadn't yet spoken.

"Um...hello", she said nervously. "My name is Ariadne Perasmenos. My parents live a few roads away"

The woman was smiling pleasantly, but Ariadne noticed something change in her eyes. It would've been imperceptible if she hadn't been specifically looking for it.

Recognition.

"Ariadne", she said slowly as if speaking the name for the first time, "is this about... Sorry, what is this about exactly?"

"Of course, sorry. I wanted to... "

As if totally losing control of herself, Ariadne was suddenly overcome with emotion. Tears pricked her eyes and she fought to stop her lip from trembling.

"I just want you to know that..."

Everything had happened so quickly she hadn't even really thought about what she was going to say when she got here. She felt an overwhelming sadness now that she was actually faced with the woman whose life she had so dramatically and irreversibly changed.

"I'm sorry", she said, no longer able to hold back the tears, "I just want you to know. I'm so sorry. I didn't know until today. I swear"

The woman put a consoling hand on Ariadne's arm. Her skin was warm and soft, comforting. She wondered if the woman had ever had children, or grandchildren.

"Shhh", she said soothingly, "it's ok. Come in and

we can talk properly. It's ok, Ariadne. It really is"

She stepped aside and motioned for Ariadne to come into the house.

As she walked inside the door, her defiance fled and she felt foolish for crying – surely she had no right, especially *here*? She would just explain and leave, that's all. She'd made this poor woman suffer enough. What kind of confrontation did she expect this to be?

She suddenly felt like the oppressor again. And not only had that man been her victim but now so was his poor wife. Not to mention his family, his friends.

She felt so consumed with guilt that she forgot that the woman had seemed to recognise her. So consumed that she didn't see the heavy padlock on the doorway which led off the hall.

And so consumed that she didn't notice the old woman glancing up and down the street before closing the door, smiling to herself.

Satisfied that nobody had seen.

***

Anthony's sleep was dreamless.

He'd woken up only once, when Harry had progressed from curling up beside him to curling up on his lap, but he'd quickly drifted off again.

Maria was still upstairs. She'd checked on Alex and found he was fast asleep on the bed, fully clothed. She stared at him for a while, enjoying how peaceful he looked. He wasn't trying to remember anything, or pretending to know something that he obviously didn't. He was just resting. There was a purity to it that she desperately missed.

She walked up to the bed and softly lay down next to him. Seeing Ariadne and Anthony together had made her realise how much she missed physical intimacy. The kind that she and Alex had always had until he started forgetting and acting out of character. Before he'd forgotten her.

She didn't want to remember any of that now.

While awake he sometimes didn't let her get close, but now he was asleep she could safely lie next to him free from the fear of rejection. She liked making the most of moments like these, because she never knew when he'd forget her again, or not be Alex anymore for a while. She dreaded the time when he wouldn't be Alex ever again.

She felt a calmness wash over her, a sense of belonging. The kind of emotions that can come separately from a variety of sources, but only come together in a perfect whole when you're with the one you love.

She thought about Ariadne, which she was surprised to find added to her sense of relief. She had never wanted to deceive her daughter, neither of them had. They'd only ever been trying to protect her. She had dreaded the day that Ariadne ever found out, but now that it had happened, she felt glad. The weight of the lie had been lifted from her shoulders, she just hoped it wasn't weighing too heavily on Ariadne's.

At the very least, it meant Ariadne could confront whatever memories she needed to confront to get past all of this. Now that she knew, she could come to terms with it in her own way, and move on.

Maybe even move on with Anthony, she thought. That wouldn't be so bad, he seemed nice.

She began feeling that she probably should've told Ariadne earlier, but when exactly was the right time to tell your daughter she'd caused a tragedy when she was young, and a man was in a coma because of it?

She snuggled closer to Alex, unconsciously trying to regain the calm feeling she'd felt earlier. She thought back to her conversation with Ariadne in the kitchen, and how they'd managed to recapture some of their own closeness that she was so afraid might be lost once Ariadne knew the truth.

Just before a deep and peaceful sleep took her away from the problems and worries of the waking world, Maria smiled to herself thinking about her daughter and her husband. It was the closest thing to happiness she'd felt in a long time.

Thirty Three

The old woman gestured for Ariadne to enter the front room ahead of her, and then shuffled along behind.

Ariadne stood just inside the doorway for a moment, looking at the space.

Delicate pastel colours had been used to decorate the room, and the wallpaper was an intricate design of flowers intertwined with their own stalks and leaves. The three piece suite was oversized, but not in a way that swamped the room. Rather, it added to the inviting feel. Everything seemed designed to be cosy, comfortable. There was an element of delicateness to everything, which seemed strange to Ariadne given the huge chairs.

The overriding feeling was that of being in a show home, a place designed to be pretty and perfect, but not necessarily used. It was clear to Ariadne that no man had lived here for a long time.

"Would you like some tea?", the old woman asked.

Ariadne noticed a china teapot, hand painted with an exquisite floral decoration. It sat on a small table which itself was covered in a fine embroidered lace. Ariadne had seen similar things when visiting relatives in Lefkara, a small village in Cyprus. She wondered whether that's where this woman had bought hers.

Two china cups, decorated in the same pattern as the teapot, had been laid out too. The whole pretty set seemed to have been prepared with the utmost care and attention to detail, as if waiting for some special visitor.

"Oh, I'm sorry am I imposing?", Ariadne asked.

"Not at all. You've come all this way, it'd be silly not to stay"

"But, do you have a guest?", she asked, motioning to the cups.

"Oh, no!", the woman said with a chuckle, "I always do that. So many people have been coming round and checking in on me that it's just become a habit I suppose!"

The old woman quickly looked away from Ariadne before shuffling over to the table and pouring two cups of tea. Her hands shook slightly, and Ariadne wasn't sure if that was an indication of her host's anxiety, or simply her age.

A wave of guilt swept over Ariadne. The woman had people checking up on her recently. Of course she had, her husband had died.

Ariadne had killed him.

"I'm so sorry", she said again, "I don't even really know why I'm here. I suppose, I just want you to know how sorry I am. I'm still trying to understand it all myself and I only found out a short while ago, and I needed to come and... I need you to know, I need *everyone* to know, how sorry I am"

She felt foolish again. It was impossible that this quiet, pristine living room could be in any way connected with the horrors she'd been experiencing. In contrast, she thought with a flush of shame, it must have been the scene of untold horrors for the bereaved woman sitting opposite her now.

First would have been the shock of the accident, the helpless floundering, the constant questions – why us? What am I supposed to do now? How can I go on with him like that? Futile questions remaining unanswered. Next would come the slow fading of hope as days turned to weeks turned to months turned to years. At first, friends and well-wishers would come round, bringing cakes, flowers, smiles and hope. They would soon tire though. Caught up in their own lives, too busy, not wanting to share in the tragedy. Maybe even avoiding the old woman as though she had some contagious disease. As though her poor fortune would somehow rub off onto them, infecting their own lives like an incurable disease.

And finally, after waiting and agonising and hoping in vain, she still lost him.

Ariadne wondered how many times this woman had sat in this little room, staring out of the window and wishing for things to be different. Never quite believing, but at the same time knowing that things would never be right again.

Unable to bear looking at her now, Ariadne turned and stared out of the front windows. She looked out through the frilly curtains at the gnomes. That's all they were from here - gnomes. Not imps, of course not. The only demonic presence in this room was the murderer who had got away unpunished.

"I'm not sure if you know", the woman suddenly began, "but it was very hard for me after the accident. It was hard for a very long time. But…"

She took Ariadne's hand.

"…it was a long time ago. I won't lie, I was angry at first. And of course now that Mark has gone… It's brought memories back, of course it has, but I'm alright. I've got my friends, and my garden. I'm alright"

The woman took a sip of her tea and shuffled back to her armchair. She looked relaxed now, as though she'd got something off her chest that had been festering for the longest time. She seemed almost happy that Ariadne was visiting.

Ariadne hadn't known the man's name until now. It must have been written in the paper but she hadn't noticed. The first time she looked she'd just been focusing on the man's appearance, and the second time she wasn't in a position to focus on much at all. She felt like this new knowledge should affect her in some way, or mean something, but it didn't.

Maybe, she thought, there was nothing now that could make her feel any worse than she already did.

They sat in silence for a while, both women exchanging polite smiles occasionally. Ariadne had no idea how to even act, let alone what she should be saying. Every so often she would think of something, but then stop herself. Nothing seemed appropriate. She was going to ask how long they'd been married, whether they'd had children, when the funeral had taken place. The only thing they had in common was the husband's death, but it wouldn't be right to ask questions about him. There was a black cloud hanging over it all. A cloud brought into their lives by Ariadne herself.

The old woman was looking at her almost expectantly, as though waiting for Ariadne to say a specific phrase or word. She searched her mind for the correct thing to say, sipping her tea every few seconds and trying to be a good guest all the while.

"I like your house", she offered.

"Thank you"

The woman smiled awkwardly. Ariadne smiled back.

More silence.

A thought occurred to Ariadne.

"Would you like me to explain? I mean, what happened?"

"I thought you didn't remember any of it?"

There was a slight accusation in her tone, although Ariadne quickly dismissed this as either her own imagination or sleep-deprived mind. She was starting to feel tired, although she'd got used to feeling exhausted as soon as she sat down anywhere.

"Oh, I don't remember. I just mean I can tell you what my parents told me"

"Your mother and father explained everything at the time. I understand. It was an accident"

Again, the woman's tone wasn't quite right. The things she was saying weren't tallying with the way she was saying them.

Ariadne sensed that something was awry with the house now too. Once again it was more of a sense than a concrete, logical thought, and she was unable to pinpoint the cause of her unease. There was something amiss though, something strange about this property.

She looked around the room again. It was pretty, and very feminine, but that niggling thought still scrabbled around in the back of her mind. The room seemed somehow too perfect. Almost staged.

"So you live in London?", the woman asked, interrupting her thoughts.

"Yes. In north London. I think that's where most of us Greeks live really!"

"I haven't been to London. What's it like?"

"It's nice. I mean, parts of it are nice. Commuting into the city every day can be a bit of a nightmare though!"

"A nightmare?", the woman asked in that strange tone again.

Ariadne looked directly at her now, and saw that her eyes had locked onto her own with a ferocious intensity.

"Yes", Ariadne responded cautiously.

"I've heard about that", the woman said with a slight smile.

"You've heard?"

"Yes. I know all about it. Your mother told me"

Ariadne put her cup down on the saucer, but misjudged the distance and caused a harsh cracking noise. It reminded her of a noise she'd heard recently, but she couldn't quite place it.

The sound reverberated around her head. She was getting a migraine and felt like she needed something to eat. Her head felt light.

"My mother told you? About my commuting?", she asked through a slight fog.

The woman paused, her eyes searching Ariadne seemingly for some sign. She stood, never taking her eyes off her guest.

"I remember Mark used to talk about London. He always wanted to work in one of the restaurants there. He was a chef, I'm not sure if anybody told you?"

Ariadne felt vaguely nauseous now, and her legs felt quite numb. She tried to stand up but wasn't able to raise herself. She felt pins and needles where her stomach should be.

The woman didn't wait for an answer.

"There was a particular restaurant he always spoke about. I think it was in the west end, or whatever it's called. Anyway, they'd won one of those stars and Mark always wanted to work there. He applied a few times but wasn't able to get in for some reason"

Ariadne felt the numbness rising from her legs and stomach, up to her chest and along her arms. It was as if the room was filling with liquid nitrogen in the same way her shower cubicle had filled with blood. Not boiling her this time, but freezing and deadening the nerves on the way up. Out of nowhere, and seemingly of its own volition, her mind registered that the feelings of extreme cold and extreme heat were curiously similar.

The old woman seemed not to have noticed. She was staring at Ariadne's eyes, as though trying to read her thoughts.

"So he looked elsewhere instead, and eventually found a few closer to home. There was one quite close to here that he really liked but never thought he'd be let in the door. Given that he couldn't find anything else, he took a chance and applied for the interview. It was more of an audition really because he had to cook for the owners rather than sit and speak with them. They really liked his food – everybody did wherever he cooked - and they invited him to carry out a couple of trial shifts for them"

The old woman walked effortlessly over to Ariadne – no shuffling now – and took the cup and saucer from her lap, carefully placing them on the table as she spoke.

"Anyway", she continued, as she casually walked over to the under stairs cupboard and called over her shoulder, "they asked him to do five shifts in total. Which he did, and very successfully too I might add. But then they asked him to do five more. I remember telling him not to, and that they were taking advantage, but he was insistent.

This was where he wanted to work, and you know what men are like, don't you Ari? Can I call you Ari?"

Ariadne was unable to speak or move at all now. Her body no longer belonged to her. She swivelled her eyes around and saw that the woman had retrieved a wheelchair from the cupboard. Through a haze she felt herself being lifted into it, her mind desperately searching for an explanation. How could this woman have drugged her? She'd been watching her as she'd poured the tea, and both cups had been poured from the same pot. There's no way she could have been expecting Ariadne to turn up.

How could she have known?

As if in answer, she sensed his grin.

As the woman spoke again, she began expertly and efficiently strapping Ariadne into the chair.

"Well, anyway *Ari*, he went through the motions and did all the shifts. He had to work all types of shifts at all hours. In fact, you'll like this, he did his very last shift on the morning that you murdered him"

The words stabbed into Ariadne, infusing her with terror. She was most definitely the victim again now. Paralysed and defenceless.

The woman finished securing her into the wheelchair and began pushing her out of the living room, all the while telling her story as if she were recounting a trip to the shops. She stopped at the padlocked door that led off the hall and paused before opening it.

"And do you know what? He got the job. I got the letter in the post a few days after you murdered him. You can imagine how pleasant that was for me to receive. Can you believe it? I couldn't!"

She took a single key from her pocket and unlocked the heavy padlock on the door. Once removed, she flipped back the latch and flung the door open. A magician, drawing back the curtain with a flourish.

In an instant, Ariadne realised why she had felt that there was something odd about the other room.

It wasn't because it had been too perfect, it was because something had been missing.

Photographs.

The widow had absolutely no photographs of her husband in the front room. No wedding picture, no portraits, nothing at all to remember or honour him with.

Which was, in short, the complete opposite of the room which Ariadne was now staring into from the wheelchair.

There were no windows here, and three of the walls were covered top to bottom with photos of the woman's husband. Some were in colour, some black and white. A few of the photos were framed and hung on the wall, but most of them were pinned crudely with thumbtacks. There was a faded quality to most of them, and some were curled at the edges. They overlapped each other, creating an explosion of colour all with one thing in common.

The man's face.

His face.

The remaining wall was covered with fewer photos than the others, and there seemed to be scraps of wallpaper hanging off too, which again was in stark opposition to the pristine room which sat only feet away. At the foot of this wall, in the centre, stood an altar adorned with a metal bowl. Thick, black candles burned around it. The spacing between them was identical on all sides and Ariadne got the impression that they'd been placed at specific points with the utmost care. There were only a handful of them but their bright flames somehow illuminated the entire room with an eerie, flickering glow.

Ariadne's eyes widened as she saw what looked like a dead baby on top of the altar, its head raised slightly above the rim of the bowl. There was a mat at the foot of the altar which was worn almost threadbare in the centre, presumably through overuse.

She wondered just what that use might be, and got the uncomfortable feeling that she would soon find out.

The woman began to wheel Ariadne over in the direction of the altar now. She tried to force herself to move, willing the feeling to come back to her limbs. Her mind flashed back to the times she'd been paralysed at night, times when sheer determination could cause a flicker of movement that would sometimes cause the feeling and strength to rush back to every part of her body. Like a dam breaking, where one small trickle would suddenly cause the whole barrier to collapse. By focusing hard enough she could sometimes do it.

Not this time though. This wasn't the same. Her body felt alien, useless.

In her mind's eye she suddenly saw the image of a car without an engine.

The woman wheeled her violently to the altar, slamming her unfeeling legs against it.

Now that Ariadne was closer, she saw that she had been mistaken about the scraps of wallpaper hanging off the wall. That's not what they were at all, they were newspaper clippings. Yellow and brittle like the old newspaper at her mother's house. Each one told the story of the woman's husband at various stages. Some from just after the accident, some from a few months later, a couple from the ten year anniversary. There were newer clippings too, dated only a couple of weeks ago, obituaries and remembrances.

Ariadne next looked at the photographs on this wall, noticing that they were much blurrier and more out of focus than the others.

As she stared, a realisation came to her that caused fear to burn through her veins like acid. Terror gripped her stomach, twisting and churning, and she felt her breath being snatched out of her throat.

She was in every single photograph.

Some of them had been taken outside her house, others showed her as she was leaving her office. There was even one of Anthony being led out of her house in handcuffs as she stood in the doorway, flanked by police officers. Her facial expression was vacant, as though her soul had been removed leaving nothing but the biological matter of her body. She saw her own eyes staring lifelessly toward her friend's terrified grimace, testament to his uncontrolled fear at being arrested. That picture had a green tinge as if taken through night-vision goggles.

She'd been watching.

Ariadne felt as though she was going to be physically sick. There was no defiance in her fear anymore, it wasn't galvanising her resolve, but weakening her. An exhaustion flowed through her, although she couldn't be sure if that was the tiring effects of the constant adrenalin, or from whatever she had been drugged with.

A primal, guttural noise came out of her mouth, a defeated moan, the last gasp of some prey in the jaws of a predator.

"Shhh", the old woman said, as soothingly as she had done earlier. A mother nursing her baby.

The image reminded Ariadne that she had seen a baby on the altar. Her eyes involuntarily flicked toward the bowl, and in that split second Ariadne found herself wondering what new horror was awaiting her gaze.

The fear and nausea gave way to a faint relief as she realised it wasn't a baby at all, but a doll.

It was very life-like, and looked like one of those toys that probably made a crying or giggling noise if squeezed, but at least it wasn't real. At least this woman hadn't subjected a living creature to this…*place*.

Until now.

Ariadne saw her own name scrawled on the doll's chest, seemingly in blood. The limbs were made of plastic, but the torso was fashioned from some kind of soft, white material. It looked like a cushion packed tight with stuffing. The perfect blank canvas on which this deranged woman could drip blood onto to create a pattern, or spell out a name. The doll had been battered, and there were cuts and what looked like charred, melted scars on its face and limbs.

The hair had been crudely chopped off and the doll was near-bald except for one patch, which looked like it didn't belong due to the length and colour of the hair. It was darker, and looked somehow familiar to Ariadne. It reminded her of the locks of hair her mother kept when she was a little girl...

"That's your hair, Ariadne", the old woman said, confirming her unspoken fear, "I hope you don't mind. I only took a bit of it, and it was a very long time ago"

She stroked Ariadne's face.

"You were a child then. An innocent. Except, as we both know, you weren't an innocent were you?"

The woman grinned. *His* grin.

In her panic, Ariadne began to wonder what purpose this room served, what need it fulfilled in this woman's life.

Was whatever she did here somehow causing the dreams?

Was she orchestrating this, creating the nightmares?

"You see", she continued, "I'd been waiting for you to come and see me for a long time after the accident. But when you didn't, and when Mark died and you *still* didn't come to see me.... Well, I had to use something else instead. Something I'd taken a long time ago from your mother's house but never thought I would need to actually use... Someone had to pay you see, and that someone had to have at least some part of you attached to it"

She leaned over and picked up the doll, holding it in front of Ariadne's face. The extent of the mutilation and scorching was severe, and she was surprised it had taken so much abuse and not fallen apart. One of the eyes was missing, and the other – which once must have been a piercing blue – had been scratched and scraped with some kind of tool. The lock of Ariadne's hair had been stapled to the top of its head in some places, pinned in others. Ariadne could almost sense the rage that had been unleashed on this doll, it pulsated through its small body, throbbing like a fresh wound.

"But you're here now, Ariadne. So we don't need this anymore, do we?"

She threw the doll back into the bowl on the altar, almost knocking over the candles in the process. She slowly and purposefully reached down beneath to some kind of chest that Ariadne hadn't noticed was even there. The dark wood had simply blended into the shadows. Ariadne watched as she slid the chest out and retrieved one of many plastic bottles. She flipped the top off one of them and squeezed it into the bowl, spraying a strong-smelling liquid all over the doll.

The woman took one of the candles and dripped wax around the bowl, chanting quietly under her breath. She replaced the candle and carried out the same ritual with the second one, dripping the wax anti-clockwise this time. Then she took the first candle again, and slowly held it above the doll, reciting some unintelligible mantra as she lowered it down into the bowl. Ariadne saw the flame of the candle flickering as the doll's head ignited, sending a thin plume of black smoke snaking into the air.

As the flames quickly caught and began consuming the effigy, the woman stepped back.

"There!", she said, satisfied with her work.

The flames licked and flickered, and the sick sulphurous stench of burning hair and plastic filled the room. Thick black smoke now erupted from the bowl in waves, threatening to engulf both Ariadne and her captor.

"Don't worry, Ariadne, I know what you're thinking…"

She walked to the wall and carefully lifted one of the photographs. She flicked a switch and Ariadne heard the whir of a fan.

"See? We won't suffocate, it's all taken care of!"

Registering something in Ariadne's face, the woman smiled.

"You didn't think you'd get off that easily did you?

That we'd both asphyxiate and die quietly and that this would all be over?"

She stared at Ariadne, as though waiting for her at any moment to begin speaking. She lowered her head and looked into Ariadne's eyes from below her thick brow. Her face burst in a joyous, cruel grin.

"Oh, you did! Well, too bad Ariadne Perasmenos. Too. Bad"

She stepped behind the wheelchair and leaned down, unbuckling the restraints.

"I don't think we need these anymore really, do we?"

Her face was so close to Ariadne that in any other context she would've been able to feel her breath on her ear.

"I know all about you, *Ari*. Would you like to know more about me? No, don't answer! It's ok! I'll tell you about me. I used to work for a pharmacist. I did. I've studied all types of medicines and potions. Not just legal ones either, but illegal ones. Concoctions used all over the world in different societies and tribes. And do you know what I've found? Medicines can do anything you want them to. Within reason of course, I mean, they can't cure your husband who was run over and left for dead years ago by a little bitch, but I suppose you already knew *that*"

Her voice lowered now, and she adopted an almost conspiratorial tone as though letting Ariadne in on a great secret.

"Did you know, Ariadne Perasmenos, that there are some medicines that actually simulate death? Did you know that? So somebody can appear quite dead, no heartbeat or anything - the whole shebang - but then a short time later they wake up again. Can you imagine that, Ariadne? Falling asleep, and waking up later, trapped in a coffin?"

She spun the wheelchair around so Ariadne was facing her.

"What am I saying? You won't have to"

The dread slammed into Ariadne harder than any

car possibly could – real or imagined. She suddenly felt the urge to be sick again and experienced the strange sensation of wanting to vomit but not being able to use her muscles to do so. The panic she'd been feeling coupled with this new sensation made her feel faint. She fought to move her muscles – any muscle – but it was futile. Once again, Ariadne found herself paralysed, only this time she knew she wouldn't simply wake up from it.

The woman must have read something in her eyes.

"Oh, are you feeling faint? Here, let me turn you back around to the bowl"

She violently spun the chair back around so Ariadne faced the altar.

As the black smoke swirled and was sucked into the vent, looking to Ariadne like some strange reverse tornado, the doll's face came into view. It was twisted into a horrific rictus. Nearly half of it had melted into a thick liquid which oozed down into the bowl, but the single eye still remained. The blue no longer the colour of a calming sea now, but a raging whirlpool, a vortex from which there would be no escape. The doll hissed and popped as it burnt, sending tiny explosions of molten plastic erupting into the air, getting ever-closer to Ariadne's paralysed legs.

The woman walked over and stood defiantly in front of the altar now, inadvertently protecting Ariadne from the heat. Like a dog with a too-short leash, she ferociously thrust her face towards Ariadne, stopping short of making contact. Ariadne's brain sent a message to her muscles to flinch, to recoil from the threat, but the attempted communication was futile.

The woman's voice came out as a mocking whisper.

"Did you really think it was over, Ariadne P? Did you actually believe that all you had to do was apologise-*grovel* - and that would be it? Do you know what I've been through? Do you have *any idea*?!"

In the midst of her fear Ariadne felt a feeling which seemed alien and out of place in this terrifying lair. It was a small but definite sense of optimism. Confused, she wondered whether the drug she had been given had some hallucinogenic properties, causing some kind of euphoria. A milder version of laughing gas? Some kind of analgesic effect? Then she realised the source of her optimism – she could feel the woman's breath on her face.

Which meant the drug was starting to wear off, didn't it?

In the absence of any other rays of hope to clutch onto in this horrific pit, she held onto that one for dear life, however tenuous it may have been.

The need to scream for help rose up in her again. She wanted to shout as loudly as she could, to cry out to someone, anyone. She thought of the last time she saw Anthony – the last time she'd *ever* see him? - asleep on her mum's sofa with Harry curled up by his side. She wished she could call out to him. She knew it was nonsense, but somewhere in her panicked mind she felt that if she could scream loudly enough, he'd hear her somehow. He was her protector, wasn't he?

The woman was still staring at her, standing over Ariadne as if to ensure she wouldn't suddenly try to escape. Her very presence mocked Ariadne, who couldn't have moved if her life depended on it.

Which, she thought with a rising panic, it probably did.

She heard a loud pop – much louder than the others - and the woman's face suddenly turned into a grimace. She gave a shriek of pain like a wounded animal, and her legs buckled slightly. Ariadne knew what must have happened, and for a moment she could smell a new type of odour in the air. Burnt skin. She watched as the woman spun around, her flailing arms inadvertently knocking over the bowl containing the melted travesty that was the doll, and then pushing over the altar itself. The molten plastic spread like lava over the carpet, igniting the fibres and adhering to them like napalm.

The woman screamed again, not in pain this time but in frustration. She looked at Ariadne with terror in her cruel eyes.

"You did this! You did all of this!", she screamed. She looked almost comical, flailing around and trying in vain to stamp out the flames which were spreading uncontrollably across the carpet.

Ariadne fought harder to move her arms. Surely the fact that she'd felt the woman's breath must mean that the drug didn't have as much of a hold on her? Maybe she had sweated most of it out, or maybe the woman hadn't used enough. She didn't know or care at this point, but if she could just move *something*, then surely the rest of her body would follow? Surely the dam would break, if only through sheer force of will? This had happened to her over and over again this past few weeks - inadvertently training her for this very moment.

She strained against the invisible bonds holding her down to the chair. She thought of stories she'd heard of people exhibiting superhuman strength to save their loved ones from some horrific fate, parents who'd lifted cars that were crushing their beloved child. Whether true or not, they gave her more determination to keep fighting. The fear began infusing her with a new strength again now too. She had come here to end this, and that's what she intended to do.

A primal survival instinct overtook her and she felt herself preparing for a war. She was absolutely in the arena now, and she would fight this battle to the death.

She felt a sudden twitch in her finger, causing her to momentarily stop struggling to move, as if the woman frantically trying to stomp out the flames on the carpet would have noticed such a slight movement. Ariadne couldn't be sure whether the feeling was the product of her imagination or whether it'd actually happened, but either way, it spurred her on even further.

She needed to move before the woman turned her

attention back to her, otherwise this would be over, but not in any way that Ariadne would want.

Then, out of nowhere, something happened that stopped them both.

The doorbell rang.

The unmistakable noise cut through the whir of the fan and the pained shrieks of the woman.

Ariadne's captor froze and looked at her hostage. She held a finger to her lips and gave a sick grin.

She leaned over to Ariadne, apparently forgetting about the fire burning just behind her.

"Who did you tell?"

In spite of the paralysis, Ariadne was sure she felt the muscles in her neck move this time when she tried to flinch. She could smell the woman's breath now too, although couldn't quite remember if she'd been able to previously.

Time seemed to stop as neither of the women moved – although for Ariadne this was through no choice of her own. There was no sound now except for the flames crackling through the carpet and the low humming of the fan. Ariadne's eyes were fixed on the woman, but internally she fought to get free. She'd felt another finger move – she was sure of it this time. She would keep straining until she could move, and when she could she had no doubt who would win this fight.

After thirty seconds, which felt to Ariadne more like thirty minutes, the woman slowly opened the door and leaned her head out into the corridor. Ariadne struggled harder now, as if any of her exertions would be seen anyway, and tried to jerk her body from side to side in the hope that something would move.

She began to realise it was futile. Her finger hadn't moved any more than her neck had. She was trapped here. A prisoner in her own body, fighting merely to move her own muscles.

She felt momentarily weakened, but then forced the

negative thoughts out of her mind as a new defiance empowered her. She thought of Anthony's hand on her cheek, and imagined him convincing her to fight.

The woman leaned back into the room.

"They've gone", she said, before seeming to realise all over again that there were flames licking across the carpet. The fire was getting closer to the upturned altar and Ariadne could smell the stench of the carpet fibres as they burned.

"Ari!", a muffled voice called out, seemingly from the back of the house.

Ariadne's heart leapt as she recognised the speaker – it was Anthony. Her protector was here.

The woman turned to Ariadne, unmistakable rage in her eyes.

"It looks like we might have to move my plan forward a bit, doesn't it now?"

She hurried out of the room, and Ariadne heard what sounded like cupboards being opened and closed. Each bang of the cupboard door shot through her like the report of a shotgun.

"Ari!", the voice called out again, "Is that you?!"

Anthony was here, he was right *here*. She just had to call out to him and let him know that she was here too.

She stopped trying to move her limbs now, and focused all her attention on her throat. She wanted to scream, she *needed* to, but no sound came out.

At the realisation that her neck muscles hurt – she was *feeling* again - she strained harder with every fibre of her being. Her mind allowed the same stray thought to float back into consciousness - she'd got control of herself through paralysis in her dreams before, surely she could do it now.

After what felt like an eternity, she heard a slight whisper come out of her throat. A hoarse nothingness, audible only because she'd been listening out for something. In spite of it not being the roar that she'd hoped, it encouraged her, and she started again trying to move her limbs. She seemed to have some feeling in her toes now too, and could feel the unmistakable heat of the flames.

"Ari! I've called the police! It's ok!"

Anthony's voice. Further encouragement. She was going to beat the woman to it. She was going to shout and she was going to move before that bitch ever had the chance to-

The woman entered the room.

"It's not ok, Ari!", she said mockingly.

She held a surgical tray in her hand and Ariadne could see a syringe and two small vials placed on what looked like a small piece of white cloth.

The woman came over and roughly grabbed Ariadne's arm, holding the dead weight up in the air. Ariadne wasn't sure if she could feel the woman's grip, or if her mind was just telling her that she could.

"This won't hurt Ariadne Perasmenos. Well, not until you wake up. Underground"

A loud crash erupted from the back of the house, the sound of wood splintering and glass smashing against something solid. Then, two more smashes, shorter and quieter than the first one.

The woman threw down Ariadne's dead arm – causing her to feel a slight tug in her neck which was pleasing in this context - and pricked the first vial with the syringe. With a deftness usually reserved for medical professionals, she flicked both items upside down with one hand and pulled back on the plunger rod. Ariadne watched as the barrel filled with the dark liquid, the panic causing her to stop trying to move. As the woman half-filled the syringe and grinned, Ariadne was shocked back into the present, and began fighting to get free. She felt her foot jerk now, so much so that she froze again in order to see whether the woman had noticed.

She hadn't, her eyes were firmly on the syringe. She threw the vial of dark liquid down onto the carpet, and began filling the syringe from the other vial.

Ariadne could hear Anthony calling her name, and the tornado raged within her. A hybrid of determination and panic and fear spun relentlessly now. The feeling had definitely returned to her legs, not just her feet, so she focused on them more than her arms. If she could just get one of them free, she would have a chance of pushing herself up and getting out of this room.

The black smoke was becoming thicker and more suffocating now as the extractor fan strained to do its job. It looked to Ariadne like a fan used to remove odours and light smoke from a kitchen, not thick, toxic smoke from a house fire.

The woman finished filling the syringe and flicked the needle.

"All done", she said gleefully, as she turned back to Ariadne.

She held the syringe in between her teeth, and wrapped a tourniquet around Ariadne's upper arm, pulling it sharply and drawing blood. She angrily slapped Ariadne's forearm, hoping to find a suitable vein to inject. With her other hand she retrieved the syringe.

"You deserve this", she said, a sadistic glee in her eyes.

"This is for my Mark"

In a second Ariadne's leg shot forward, as if released by a slingshot. Shocking them both, Ariadne's foot connected with the woman's knee with a sickening crack. The woman's leg crunched back at an impossible angle, and she fell to the floor, grabbing her destroyed knee with both hands and screaming. She dropped the syringe, which broke beside her.

The adrenalin flooded Ariadne now, and as suddenly as her leg had shot forward, she found the hold on her vocal cords had dissipated too. Her face and tongue were still paralysed, and she couldn't formulate words, but a guttural noise now left her mouth. The drugs were wearing off.

"Ari! I'm coming Ari!", Anthony shouted.

Ariadne felt a flash of optimism as she realised his voice sounded louder now. He must be closer, somewhere in the house.

She continued frantically kicking her leg out while trying at the same time to move her other limbs. She'd got a good strike in and wanted to capitalise on it. The sooner the woman got up, the sooner Ariadne would have to fight again.

She looked at the old woman, who was holding her bleeding, broken knee and howling from the floor. She didn't look like she'd be getting up soon, but Ariadne didn't want to take the risk.

In between screams, the woman stared at her destroyed leg with a look of hideous disbelief on her face.

She looked up at Ariadne and screamed at her. Like a wounded animal, not using any words but seemingly trying to communicate something. Her face was a mask of pure hatred, and she pushed down on her arms in an attempt to get herself up again. After trying twice, she fell back down and grabbed at her leg.

Seemingly bolstered by a renewed rage, she scrabbled around trying to find the broken syringe, every so often looking back up at Ariadne as if checking she hadn't escaped. Her stare was chilling, as if all of her anger and rage from the past two decades had built up and was somehow being concentrated into a laser. It was a look that told Ariadne she would soon be in more pain than she could ever imagine. Than she could ever *dream*.

The woman smiled as her hand clasped around the syringe.

She crawled over to Ariadne, careful to avoid both striking range and putting any pressure on her broken joint. She reached Ariadne and raised herself on her uninjured knee, brandishing the syringe above her head like a dagger.

"This is the next best thing, Ariadne Perasmenos. You killed him, now I'll kill you"

She lurched forward, dropping and focusing her

entire bodyweight behind the syringe which was poised to stab the centre of Ariadne's chest.

Ariadne kicked out with both feet this time. The speed and ferocity of the attack again surprised them both. It was as if all the pressure that had built up over the past few weeks suddenly exploded with full force. Ariadne's legs hit the woman directly in the stomach and she crumpled into herself, dropping the syringe and clutching her midsection as if afraid her guts would spill out.

Anthony appeared in the doorway now, his eyes widening at the scene in the small room. Seeing his friend in the wheelchair, he rushed in and knocked into the woman. She fell awkwardly onto the chest, screaming as her leg now snapped completely. She lay on the upturned chest, which had spilled the bottles all over the floor. Her lower leg was at a right angle and almost entirely unconnected to her now.

Anthony felt a slight nausea rise in him as he took in the full horror of the scene. He grabbed Ariadne and pulled her towards him. Even though she had movement – strong movement – back in her legs, she was still unsteady, and fell onto him clumsily. Realising but not understanding why his friend wasn't fully able to move, he swooped her up into a fireman's lift and began carrying her out of this room of horrors.

He turned in the doorway and stared, momentarily frozen by the sight of the woman, her near-amputated leg, the upturned altar and the burning doll. He scanned the walls, and for a surreal second thought he'd seen his own face in some of the photographs.

The woman looked up at them from the floor, breathing heavily, one trembling hand still clutching her stomach. The fire had ignited the bottom of her dress. She looked down at the flames, then back up at Ariadne through the heat haze that vacillated between them. It gave everything an even more surreal, nightmarish sense.

She stared at Ariadne with those hateful eyes, even as the flames reached her legs and began eating through her flesh.

"I will see you again", she spat, barely able to conceal either the searing pain tearing through her body, or her hatred for Ariadne that was doing the same.

A sick smile crept across her face as she grabbed the syringe which lay next to her, without breaking eye contact. She ferociously plunged the broken syringe into her neck behind her windpipe and wrenched her hand forward, tearing her own throat open. The blood pulsed in bursts and Ariadne could see the woman's neck and shoulder muscles tense. She seemed to be fighting to keep her features still while trying desperately to keep her stare focused on Ariadne. A nauseating gurgling sound came from her throat, and then another sound almost like the suck of a nearly-blocked sink.

In a matter of seconds – which both Ariadne and Anthony would replay for the rest of their lives – the noise dissipated and the woman slumped back onto the chest.

Her eyes never left Ariadne.

The flames took an even greater hold of the lifeless woman now, and the stench of burning plastic and flesh quickly became overpowering. Somewhere amidst his shock, Anthony was able to regain focus and spur himself back into action. He carried Ariadne down the corridor and into the pristine front room and lay her on the oversized sofa.

"I'm going to get her", he said.

Ariadne fought in vain to shake her head, and a harsh, incomprehensible noise came out of her mouth. She used her finger to hook onto Anthony's clothing, her eyes willing him not to go.

"What is it Ari?"

She kicked out with her legs, the only parts of her that still seemed to be working properly.

"There's evidence of what she did in there Ari, I need to go ba-"

There was an explosion from the room which shook the house and pushed Anthony forward violently. He fell onto the sofa, almost head-butting Ariadne.

Another sound came out of her mouth now but Anthony couldn't make it out.

"What did you say?", he asked, an unmistakable quiver in his voice.

He leaned down slightly, so his ear was barely an inch away from her mouth.

"Bottles. Explode"

He didn't fully understand the first word but definitely understood the second. He leapt up and grabbed Ariadne, hauling her up from the sofa and once again carrying her – this time out of the front of the house. He carried her through the door which, an eternity ago, she had stepped through apologetically with the old woman whose life she felt she had ruined.

He began running away from the property, focusing on nothing else but getting back to Ariadne's parents' house. He jolted her up and down as he ran, but she didn't care.

As they raced down the driveway, she sensed that the gnomes were imps again now. Their cold eyes drilled into her, just like the old woman's had as she'd died. She knew she'd never forget that look.

They cleared the drive and Anthony kept going. The images he'd witnessed spurred him on to just keep running. He wanted to outrun what he'd seen. His friend in that chair. The old woman and her damaged leg. The doll melting into the carpet. The syringe tearing through the woman's throat. Not to mention the stench of the room, and the sounds….those gurgling sounds…

He ran faster, harder. The horrors were behind them now, he just needed to keep running.

It wasn't until they were halfway down the road that there was another explosion, this one seeming to shake the very ground beneath them.

Anthony didn't look back, just kept running. He stared into the distance ahead, not wanting to remember anything behind. He knew that nothing would stop him until they got to Ariadne's parents' house. To safety.

Ariadne closed her eyes and breathed the cool air of freedom into her lungs. She allowed her mind to go to a place she didn't usually like to go, and actively concentrated on the shadow man, trying to work out whether he was grinning or not now. Was he pleased? Angry? Somehow even at peace?

She tried to block out all other thoughts and focus only on him.

On his grin.

But she couldn't.

In fact, she couldn't sense him now at all.

Thirty Four

After nine days of seemingly endless police interviews and hospital appointments, Ariadne and Anthony finally got a chance to sit down and get some rest – albeit in Doctor Illari's waiting room.

Ariadne hadn't had any more dreams or disturbances since the fire. Not about the shadow man, although she'd had plenty of nightmares about being buried alive. Not to mention the woman's hateful, piercing eyes as she lay bleeding and burning in that room. Those dreams had felt different though. He seemed to be silent now.

Not just silent. Gone.

She sat looking at the picture of the pebble and the water, remembering how a lifetime ago she'd been here in this same position wondering what new horror the night would bring. She looked from the picture to Anthony, her protector. Her heart skipped, as it often did now when she looked at him. He'd been incredible, from staying with her that unfortunate first night, to finding her at the old woman's house and bursting in to get her.

She'd spent a long time wondering why he'd broken in at all, until he'd explained that the thick black smoke coming from the back of the house let him know that something was happening in there that shouldn't be. She was also impressed with his apparently excellent orienteering skills, although he insisted that the only reason he knew which house she was in was due to Alex's instructions. He saw the Church which towered above the surrounding properties, and just walked towards it until he saw a detached house with a double garage opposite.

Good old Dad, she thought, wondering whether he even remembered their visit at all now.

Anthony turned towards Ariadne, and caught her staring at him.

"Stop doing that!", he said.

"What?"

"Staring at me like I'm in a zoo!"

"I'm not!"

"You are! You've been doing it for days!"

"I'm just happy that's all. Things are good, aren't they?"

"Yes", he said, taking her hand and kissing it, "they are. Really good"

They held eye contact and Ariadne took his other hand and gave it a squeeze.

"Although…", she said.

"What?"

"I do think you should've waited until I was well before you seduced me…"

"Seduce *you*?! You're the one that kept inviting me round and asking me to stay! You even took me home to meet your parents – the whole thing was a ruse"

"I was vulnerable, Anthony", she said with a coquettish look. "It was you that took advantage of my helplessness"

"And that's another thing, I think you should start calling me Jackson again. My name sounds really weird when you say it"

"That's because it's a weird name"

"Right, because the world is just teeming with women called Ariadne…"

She gave him a playful slap.

At that moment, Doctor Illari appeared.

"Miss Perasmenos! Mr Jackson! Please, do come through"

Ariadne found herself enjoying the few steps down the corridor to his office this time. It felt more like a victory lap now, rather than the uncertain and fearful walk it'd been previously.

Doctor Illari sat them down, and then took his own seat.

"Well, Miss Perasmenos, I am very pleased to see

you looking so well. No more shadow men? No more episodes of microsleep?"

"Nope. Nothing. I can't sleep on my front because of the discomfort, but that seems to be passing. Otherwise, all fine"

"I am glad. And I understand you've been fine since … the incidents of last week?"

"That's right", Ariadne said with a cautious confidence, "so far things have been fine. So far…"

"That's very good. Although I feel that we probably have differing views on the reason for that"

"What do you mean?"

"Well, as a man of science, I might well say that this can all be explained rationally, whereas I imagine you might well feel differently. Based upon our previous conversations, that is, and no doubt encouraged by Derek"

"How could it be explained rationally? I mean, the shadow man might have just been a dream, but the cuts and bruises? And the doll that the old woman was using…?"

"I just mean it's a matter of interpretation, Miss Perasmenos. The dreams and paralysis you experienced for instance are quite common. So common in fact that whole mythologies have been built up around them. In Fiji sleep paralysis is even given a name which when translated means 'eaten by a demon'. People throughout history have woken up, unable to move and with horrific things seemingly happening to them, and they have named the phenomenon accordingly"

Ariadne thought of the old lady in the hospital, who had said something similar.

"But, there were injuries, Doctor. I wasn't just paralysed"

"As I told you in our first meeting, the power of the mind can be incredible. We can *think* injuries onto ourselves. Wounds and scratches can be psychosomatic, just as I said after your stay here at the clinic. I don't mean to denigrate anything you've been through Miss Perasmenos, on the contrary I think it has all been terrible and very traumatic for you. But I do feel that it can be explained by scientific and psychological means, rather than supernatural ones"

Ariadne frowned.

"You still think it was my voice on that recording then?", she asked.

He paused before answering, chewing his bottom lip and weighing his words carefully.

"Not necessarily Miss Perasmenos. I'm just saying, I don't know where that came from, but that it could be explained through means other than supernatural ones"

It was Anthony's turn to ask a question.

"What about the old woman though Doctor? Surely she must have been doing *something*? Why else would it all have stopped when she…"

He didn't finish the sentence. Neither he nor Ariadne liked referring to the old woman's death - which was difficult given the media attention that the explosion had attracted.

Ariadne thought of the doll on the altar, how desecrated and mutilated it had been.

"From what I understand, there was a funeral for this man, this chef, which was reported quite widely in the media. Seeing the picture of the man may have subconsciously triggered something in Ariadne, so causing her to begin dreaming. The fact that at the same time a bereaved and, let's be clear, unhinged woman was lighting candles and inflicting injuries on a doll may well be coincidental. Yes, she was trying to do *something*, but that doesn't mean that she was. And in terms of why it all stopped, the Americans have a phrase called 'closure'. It's possible that the events that transpired and the death of this woman brought closure to Ariadne. Maybe being forced to confront the past in a very real way in the present was enough to allow Ariadne to move forward. In fact, if the dreams were caused by unrepressed guilt, then it sounds as though the whole episode at the house would've stopped any guilt at all. How can you feel guilt at someone who tried to kill you?"

"But I didn't feel guilty about the woman, I felt guilty about her husband. Well, at first at least. And I still do feel guilty, Doctor. I'll be struggling with that for the rest of my life. I still did what I did. The fact that the old woman... The fact that this all happened doesn't make me any less responsible"

The doctor nodded.

"But surely, Miss Perasmenos, the alternative is even harder to believe? That this woman was somehow conjuring a spirit which attacked you?"

"At this point, to be honest, I think both things feel as unbelievable as each other. Also, who is the old hag from my dream?"

The doctor smiled. A teacher who approved of his student's insightful question.

"Ah, yes, Miss Perasmenos, I have thought about that myself. Are you sure the old woman at the house wasn't the same woman you saw in your dream?"

"Definitely. The woman that attacked me in the dream was shorter. Her face was a completely different shape too, her cheekbones were really high up and she was...kind of...*broader*"

Ariadne stared into the distance as she remembered the dream, her eyes glazing slightly. She suddenly snapped herself out of it and was back in the present.

"No. It wasn't her. I'm sure of it"

He nodded.

"Hmm. Then, could it be possible that she was someone you saw in the newspaper or on the news when you heard about the man's funeral? The players in our dreams are comprised of the people we've seen throughout our lives. They are all *real* people we have encountered, we don't generally make them up. They may be someone that you've seen in the street or even just somebody you saw once on television as a child, but the person you saw is a real person. Given the nature of the dreams, it would be strange if this woman wasn't significant in these events in some way"

"I don't know. I don't even remember hearing about the funeral let alone seeing any of it. It's possible that I saw a story about it I suppose, but I don't remember it. I'm sorry to say, and with all due respect, I'm not sure if I agree with your theory Doctor"

"That's perfectly fine, Miss Perasmenos. The important thing is that you are alright, and that the dreams have stopped and that you're sleeping better. In addition, I believe that you and Mr Jackson have become much closer as a result of this"

"How do you know that?", Anthony asked.

The doctor turned to Anthony.

"Mr Jackson, I may be an old man, but I'm also a very perceptive one. Let's just say you are both looking at each other very differently now. And in a good way"

He smiled and stood, prompting both Ariadne and Anthony to get up too.

Doctor Illari shook Anthony's hand.

"Look after her", he said.

"Always"

Doctor Illari turned to Ariadne.

"Miss Perasmenos, I am sure that this is over and that you have nothing to worry about. But, just so you know, I am always here if you'd like to discuss anything or if you feel concerned about any dreams you are having"

"Thank you, Doctor", she said. She embraced him, "Thanks you for everything"

"You're quite welcome. You'll be fine Miss Perasmenos, I'm sure of it"

And, for the first time in what felt like an eternity, she was sure of it too.

Epilogue

The woman stood at the grave.

Tears rolled from her eyes, down her pronounced, high cheekbones. She angrily brushed them away.

She held a single white rose in one hand, a handkerchief in the other.

She bent down and carefully placed the rose onto the grave, burying it slightly in the stones so the wind couldn't take it.

"My son…", she said in a whisper that was stolen by the wind as soon as the words left her lips.

She thought back to the funeral – mere weeks ago - and how she'd tried in vain to keep her composure. She knew the cameras would be trained on her – the scavengers out in full force looking for more trash for their newspapers.

Her son had been destined to become one of the top chefs in the world, just like his father. The media wanted to make a story of it even if twenty years had passed.

At least father and son were together now.

She stared at the gravestone. After last week's events, she was the only one left.

A single thought reverberated through her mind.

This isn't over…

If you enjoyed this book, why not leave a review?

And check out Angelo Marcos' other books at **www.angelomarcos.com**

Praise for 'The Artist'

"a well paced, well-written and exciting novel, with an incredible twist at the end that few could possibly anticipate"
- DustJacketGang.com

"a real page turner, with twists that will stun you. Thoroughly enjoyed this one!"
- Iconicgifts.com

"...similar to Shutter Island in that it causes the reader to reconsider a number of events in the book...a tense psychological thriller"
- Parikiaki.com

Copyright information

SLEEP NO MORE

Copyright © 2013 Angelo Marcos (pen name of Angelo Makri)

The right of Angelo Marcos (pen name of Angelo Makri) to be identified as author of this Work has been asserted by him in accordance with the Copyright, Designs and Patents Act 1988.

All rights reserved worldwide, including the right to reproduce this work, in whole or in part, in any form.

This is a work of fiction.

Printed in Great Britain
by Amazon.co.uk, Ltd.,
Marston Gate.